CAPTIVATED HEARTS

YAHRAH ST.JOHN

OLIVER HEBER BOOKS

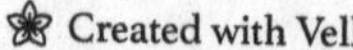

1

"We're getting a new station owner?" Jada Hart asked as she sat in the Monday morning meeting at San Francisco's WLB-TV station. She'd come into the office excited to discuss options for her *On the Town with Jada Hart* segment, a showcase for the latest events around the city. But a new owner? What did that mean for her?

Jada had left her family in Dallas, much to her father Duke Hart's chagrin, and come to San Francisco for her dream job: to be on television. Even though she had a journalism degree from the University of Texas at Austin, the station's former owner had relegated her to doing fluff pieces. She didn't let that bring her down though. She'd toiled away at WLB-TV for five years hoping for a break to sit in the morning anchor chair.

"Yes, we are," station manager Andrew Paxon replied in response to Jada's question about a new owner. "And he'll be here soon to meet the entire team."

Just great, Jada thought. Inevitably, a new owner would want to make changes and put his or her own mark on the station. Once the new owner saw her portfolio, would he or she realize she was capable of more? Everyone in upper management thought Jada was nothing more than a pretty face, so she'd never had even a remote shot at the anchor desk.

Did she play up her looks to get ahead? Yes indeed. She'd learned a long time ago to use her best assets. She had flawless skin, a curvy size-six figure, and long, dark hair thanks to the good genes she inherited from her mother, Abigail Hart. Thinking about Mama made Jada homesick. All she wanted to do right now was get on the phone and call her. And if she wasn't free, then she wanted to talk to her big sister Bree Hart-Wells. A couple of years older, Bree always had a level head and would know what to do in a situation like this.

"I thought WLB-TV was doing much better in the ratings," said Jay Blair, one of the anchors of the morning news program. Jada desperately wished to co-chair it with him.

"Not by much," Andrew commented. "I guess the Barnetts decided to get out while they could. I heard the new owner made them an offer they couldn't refuse."

"And who would be dumb enough to place a bet on a sinking ship?" Jada asked. "I mean, let's be real, folks, there was some real ineptitude going on with upper management. Who's to say the new leadership will be any different?"

Her harsh commentary garnered several stares from her coworkers, including a lethal one from a pair of dark-as-midnight eyes that were glaring from the doorway. They belonged to a man, who, by definition, would be labeled sexy chocolate. He wore a tailored suit that, simply put, fit him like a glove. He topped it off with a lavender and gray silk tie. He wore his hair cut close, had bushy brows, and his goatee was shaped up precisely around thick juicy lips. Jada was sure there had to be an incredible body underneath his suit —one that would make a woman want to take a first and second look. He was devastatingly handsome, but there was also something very intimidating about him if his stance was anything to go by.

"I guess that makes me the man dumb enough to bet on this sinking ship," he replied with a frown.

Jada gulped. *Damn!* She'd just insulted the new owner of WLB-TV.

DAMIAN MCKNIGHT STARED at the beautiful creature with the opinionated mouth. She was just as gorgeous as the promo photographs had indicated—hell, more so in person. She had deep-brown expressive eyes and a wide, inviting mouth. Then there were the silky strands of black hair that fell straight down her back and her smooth hazelnut skin that glowed from being sun-kissed. She was just the type of woman he needed to avoid—a woman who was aware of her sex appeal and her effect on men; she probably discarded them with equal ease. She spelled trouble with a capital "T".

"Mr. McKnight." The station manager fumbled over to greet him. "I'm sorry you had to hear that." Andrew turned to openly glare at Jada. "But we're excited to have you here with us. Please," he said, motioning him over to the table, "allow me to introduce you to the team."

Damian walked toward the table, but he was unable to take his eyes off the woman with the sassy mouth whose cheeks now flamed red at having been so openly outed. He shook hands with producers, directors, and television personalities until finally he came to *her*. Surprisingly, however, she stood up and faced him head-on as if she wasn't afraid despite having made a potentially career-ending bluster.

He was unprepared for what he saw when she stood up from her chair. She was nearly as tall as he was at six foot one due to her high heels and alluring legs that just went on and on. At first glance, she appeared slender, but now that he was up close and personal, she was much curvier than he'd thought. Her pert breasts stuck out in the satin button-down shirt she wore with a pencil skirt. On most women the outfit would be professional and demure, but on her it was a come-on if ever he saw one. It had him imagining all kinds of wicked things.

"Jada Hart." She stuck out her hand.

He glanced down at the petite fingers on offer and then his eyes traveled up to her face and she raised her brow, daring him not to accept. In the end, he was always professional. He grasped her delicate hand in his and liked it when she gripped back with confidence. He hated a wimpy handshake. "Damian McKnight."

"Mr. McKnight, it's a pleasure to meet you." She didn't apologize for her earlier gaffe and instead sat back down in her chair.

Damian continued the introductions until he made his way back to the head of the table. "I'm sure you're all wondering what my plans are," he began, "so I'll dive right in. My first objective is the morning news program. Over the next few weeks, I want to see everyone in their natural habitat so I can assess and see for myself what is or is *not* working." His words were meant to be a warning. For now they could relax, but they shouldn't rest on their laurels because he would be watching.

"And if it's not working?" Jada asked boldly. Damian wanted to wipe the smile from that impertinent little mouth of hers. She didn't know when to let well enough alone.

"Then you're out." His eyes didn't leave Jada's, and she didn't look away either. They were having a battle of wills in a stare down. But he always won. Losing was never an option because he wouldn't allow it.

"Well then." Andrew coughed. "Why don't we get back to work and talk about ideas for this week's segments. Isn't that right, Jada?" He came behind her chair and patted her shoulder.

Jada shrugged her acquiescence, and she and the new boss lost eye contact. Damian had won that round. He moved to the back of the room to rest against the settee and listen as the groups bounced ideas back and forth. Some were good, others not so much. He paid attention to who was on the pulse of current news and others who might be coasting. He made a mental note to keep an eye on them.

After the meeting, everyone began to shuffle out of the room as if Damian might change his mind and fire them all. Jada Hart was included in the fray, but he wasn't done with her yet. It was time he let her know who was in charge.

"Ms. Hart, a word please."

She turned at the doorway and glanced at a co-worker before slowly easing her way back into the conference room. "Yes?"

"Close the door."

She didn't react immediately. Damian thought she was going to openly defy him, but she did as he asked and closed the door. As she did, Damian got a view of her backside in that skirt, which made a certain member of his anatomy tighten. He willed it down.

Jada walked back toward him.

"Sit."

"If it's all the same to you, I'd rather stand."

Damian felt a frown forming. He didn't like being refused but wasn't going to make a big deal of it. "Suit yourself." He sat down in one of the executive chairs and leaned back to regard her. "You've been at WLB-TV five years, correct?"

She seemed surprised that he knew who she was, and he watched as she stood up straighter. "That's correct."

"I assume you want to go further at this station." Damian rubbed his goatee.

"If you know so much about me, then you know that's true," she responded curtly.

He leaned forward in his chair. She was feisty *and* stubborn. She had to know she was in a precarious position and that antagonizing him wasn't in her best interest, yet she was egging him on. "Then you know that getting on my good side would be to your advantage. So, let me make a suggestion to you."

She folded her arms across her chest, causing her breasts to push upward in her button-down shirt and give him a view of her cleavage. "And what might that be?"

He rose to his full six-foot-one height. "Don't *ever* speak out of turn again when you don't know the facts. I have big plans for WLB-TV, and if you want to be a part of them, I suggest you learn when and *when not* to give your unsolicited opinion."

Jada Hart shot daggers at him with her eyes. Damian was certain that if those daggers were real, they would have mortally wounded him. "Thank you for the advice, Mr. McKnight. Am I free to go now?"

She was purposely being overly solicitous, but at

least she knew when to keep her mouth shut—otherwise, he might have to shut it for her.

Damian nodded yes in response to her question, and with a quick flip of her hair, Jada walked out the door.

Damian sighed. Despite the bravado he'd shown, his stomach was tight with tension—a tension he recognized as sexual desire. To be brutally honest with himself, he'd felt an urgent need to lift that tight skirt of hers and bury himself deep inside her. That scared him. He'd never crossed the line with an employee, let alone wanted to lose control. Jada Hart was a dangerous woman.

He would need to keep a wide berth from her.

"Is everything OK?" Kyler Barnes, one of the news reporters asked when Jada walked back toward her cubicle.

Jada glanced around and felt as if everyone in the newsroom's eyes were on her. They'd all just basically seen her get called into the principal's office and get a talking-to for her insolence. But how was she supposed to have known that her world was about to change that morning? That Damian McKnight would drift into her life like some sort of cyclone and shift her off her axis?

He'd openly stared at her throughout much of the meeting, making her extremely aware of herself. She'd smoothed her hair, worrying if a strand was out of place. She'd licked her lips that had felt dry all of a sudden. Then she'd shifted uncomfortably in her chair as she'd begun to feel an ache between her thighs. But surely, she couldn't be attracted to him, could she?

Not after he'd just given her a dressing down.

He was arrogant, and she had disliked him instantly. So why was her body reacting to him? Her nipples were puckering in her bra as if they recognized Damian as someone who knew exactly what to do with them—like put them in his mouth and suck on them hard.

Jesus! This is ridiculous. She'd just met the man and already she was fantasizing about having sex with him? She was no prude. Jada liked sex and had no problem finding a man to share her bed with, but none of them had gotten under her skin quite like Damian had done just minutes ago.

"Did you hear me?" Kyler asked as he grabbed Jada's arm and pulled her away from the curious stares of their coworkers. She walked them to a room they used for breakout sessions and closed the door.

"Yes, I heard you." Jada turned her back on the glass window so no one could see her. "And everything is fine."

"It didn't look that way when you came out."

Jada shrugged. "Mr. McKnight let me know who's in charge and that I should mind my p's and q's."

"Figures. Men like Damian McKnight can't take an assertive woman." Kyler laughed and her beautiful, slightly tousled blond locks moved from side to side. Jada envied how effortless Kyler could look without doing much. Although she was only five foot six, Kyler had the kind of body that designers killed for. She easily fit into the sample sizes that were sometimes sent to the studio. And with Kyler's all-American, clean-faced look, she was easily Jada's competition—

but that hadn't stopped the two of them from becoming friends.

Kyler was from a small town in the cornfields of Ohio. She was so homegrown, Jada couldn't help but love her honesty. She even appreciated her naiveté and loved going out on the town with her, if only to see how Kyler reacted. After five years on the San Francisco market, Jada had become somewhat jaded.

"Am I starting to rub off on you? That sounds like something I'd say, not you."

"I'm starting to learn," Kyler said with a sly grin, "that this town and industry aren't as easy as I thought they were going to be."

"I hear you. Sometimes I think about going home to Dallas."

"What stops you?"

"My father didn't raise a quitter. Failure is not an option."

"You're not a failure, Jada. You're amazing. And sooner or later, the powers that be are going to see that."

Jada glanced through the glass doors of the breakout room and saw Damian McKnight walking through the newsroom. As if sensing her watching him, he turned and caught her staring. Immediately, Jada spun around to face Kyler. "I don't know. I didn't do myself any favors by getting on the new boss's bad side."

"You can turn this around. Use that brilliant charm of yours. You're vivacious and a natural flirt. He'll come around."

"You're right. He's a man, isn't he? How can he resist me?"

∾

JADA SOON FOUND out that Damian McKnight could resist her just fine. What usually worked on the opposite sex didn't work on him. Over the next few days, he sat down with each member of the staff individually to get to know them. Jada suspected he was doing this to find out their strengths and weaknesses as well as what they thought of their colleagues. But as each day drew to an end, she grew increasingly impatient. Damian had yet to call her into his office.

A couple of nights ago on a dateless evening at home, Jada had researched the man. There was very little online about his personal life. Clearly, he didn't want the press digging into his past, but what Jada did find was quite surprising. Damian McKnight didn't come from money. He was a self-made millionaire who'd grown up on the streets of Los Angeles. Jada surmised that's what probably gave him his edge. He was streetwise until an elderly couple had taken him in at fifteen. They'd nurtured him until he'd gone to college and business school, graduating magna cum laude.

His story was impressive, and Jada couldn't help but admire that he'd pulled himself up by his bootstraps. He'd been lucky when his first venture to turn around a struggling radio station had turned into a goldmine. From there, his interest had branched out from radio into television. It didn't surprise her that he could see a gem in WLB-TV, but that didn't mean he had to snub her. Was he purposely baiting her so that she would confront him and demand an explanation?

By the end of the week, even Kyler commented on the fact that Jada had yet to have a sit-down with him. "You really must have rubbed him the wrong way," Kyler said as they stood in the breakroom on Friday morning. They were both desperate for their morning cup of joe and were in front of the Keurig machine, each waiting for their coffee to brew.

Jada shrugged. "I would have thought after he'd given me the 'talk'"—she made quotation marks with her hands—"that his almighty greatness would deign to speak with me." Kyler made a face and shook her head, but Jada was on a roll and not about to stop. "But apparently, I'm at the bottom of the barrel in his book and I'll just have to accept my fate."

"Or perhaps you could learn some patience, Ms. Hart," a masculine voice said from behind her.

Color drained from Jada's face. Her eyes grew large as she glared at Kyler for allowing her to walk into a minefield. She inhaled sharply and turned around to face her nemesis. "Mr. McKnight."

Damian wore a navy-blue suit that Jada recognized as designer. Aside from the top-quality material, the single-breasted jacket was superbly tailored. The man looked well-built, and not a wrinkle could be seen on the sleeves across his interminably large shoulders. "Would you care to join me in my office, or would you like to continue to talk about me behind my back? I warn you that you get three strikes, then you're out."

Jada grimaced and turned to Kyler. "If you'll excuse me." She plastered on a smile and walked toward him. "Lead the way."

"No. After you. I insist."

Jada didn't respond and instead forced herself to put one foot in front of the other and move toward the stairs that led to the second-floor executive offices. Damian remained silent behind her, so she truly had no idea what was in store for her.

When they made it to his office, she walked in and took a seat across from the large glass desk that held nothing but his Surface laptop. Apparently, McKnight didn't like clutter. She heard the click of the door, indicating the need for privacy. Did this mean he was about to fire her? His three strikes and you're out comment hadn't been lost on Jada.

Several seconds later, Damian sat across from her. Without looking up, he opened his laptop and clicked several times before training those infinitely dark eyes on her. "Why stay at WLB-TV?"

"Wow! You go right to the point, don't you?"

"I see no reason for beating around the bush."

"I do not accept defeat. What I do have is my will and determination to succeed."

"Ah." He greeted her with a smile, which was quite rewarding because it lit up his entire face and showed off his brilliant white teeth. *He should smile more often instead of glower.* "So, you're hoping that your pretty face will propel you to stardom?"

Jada frowned. "What does my face have to do with anything? I have a degree in journalism from the University of Texas at Austin. Was top of my class and graduated summa cum laude."

"And yet you're doing the entertainment beat."

"I've tried to obtain more substantial pieces, but the prior ownership had a vision of who they wanted in the anchor spot."

"Which yet again begs the question, *why stay?* There're any number of beautiful leading anchors at this station." When she began to balk, Damian held up his hand and continued. "They all have the same, or similar, credentials as yours, Jada. What makes you think you're ever going to get in the anchor chair?"

"I thought in time I could prove I'm capable of more. I don't give up, Mr. McKnight. My daddy taught me that quitters never win, and I've held true to that all my life. I won't stop trying to reach the top of the ladder. So, let me ask you, are you going to help me get there or are you going to hold me back?"

Damian's brow rose. "That depends entirely on you, Ms. Hart. Do you have any stories that you would like to pitch?"

"P-pitch?"

"Yes, or did you think I called you in to talk about the weather?"

Jada couldn't resist a chuckle. She could do without his sarcasm, but not without the opportunity to get her ideas in front of someone who would finally listen. "Definitely not the weather." She returned and leaned over the desk until she was mere inches from his face. "Let's talk hard-hitting news."

AN HOUR LATER, Damian was in his car and driving to the McKnight Media offices. He'd left the station twenty minutes ago after meeting with Jada. She'd gotten to him. It hadn't been because of her great ideas for an exposé on school lunches or the opioid epidemic. It was because being around her made his system go haywire. He knew that if he had stayed in her company with that provocative perfume she wore, he might just lose his cool.

He'd stayed away from Jada all week because she was the type of woman who made men ogle. For some inexplicable reason, she had become a forbidden fantasy to him. Damian supposed it was because he'd been celibate lately, choosing to work twelve-hour days. Not that it meant he went without entirely. Every now and then, he attended social events that were conducive to meeting women, and he usually found one who was willing to spend a night or two with him for a brief sexual liaison and nothing more. He had no time for emotional entanglements.

Yet, Jada fascinated him. Throughout the week, he'd found himself watching her. She was an incurable flirt—the way she sat on the edge of men's desk showing off those long legs or gave them that winning smile. She practically had every man in the station eating out of her palm, but somehow she hadn't translated that into a seat at the table of the morning news program she coveted. She intrigued him.

Rebranding and repositioning the station were going to take time and patience. He shouldn't get embroiled in an affair, especially with a subordinate.

But it didn't mean he didn't want to try.

2

———

Later that evening, Jada hung up the phone and sighed. It was a Friday night, and she was dateless. She could call Kyler and try to hit a nightclub, but she wasn't in the mood. She'd unsuccessfully tried to reach her sister Bree to get some advice on what to do about Damian, her career, the station, all of it. She was at a crossroads.

Jada suspected her newlywed five-months-pregnant sister was probably cuddled with her husband, Grayson, and if not, watching a movie with him and his autistic brother, Cameron, who lived with them. Jada was so proud of how accepting Bree had been of Cameron and vice versa. Grayson's brother thought the sun and moon hung on Bree. Jada felt the same too. There was nothing her big sister, a renowned geologist, couldn't conquer when she set her mind to it, and now she was a wife and a soon-to-be mother.

If you'd asked her many years ago, Jada would have said that being a wife and mother was her greatest wish. She'd never thought she'd be a career woman like Bree or even like her oldest sister, London, who'd started off studying marketing at Tulane University only to chuck it and become a chef and open her own restaurant, Shay's, in New Orleans.

But Jada's hopes and dreams had been dashed shortly before her wedding when she'd discovered her fiancé, Joshua Allen, having sex with another woman. It had humiliated her. And when she'd confronted Joshua, he'd merely stated that he'd grown weary of their sex life. He'd said he needed a *real* woman who knew how to satisfy him in the bedroom.

Jada and Joshua had been together since they were sixteen. Their families knew each other. Even though they'd gotten engaged young, Duke hadn't balked because Joshua came from a good family. Jada had thought they'd get married and she'd have lots of babies. But Joshua had other plans. He'd told her that all she was good for was as arm candy and that he had no intention of getting hitched to a cold fish like her.

Jada had prided herself on being the perfect Southern belle like her mama had taught her by going to cotillion and saving herself for the right man. And still, she'd been duped. Immediately, Jada had gone back to college and thrown herself into her studies, eventually emerging as one of her university's top students.

She would show Joshua and even her father, Duke, that she was capable of looking after herself. She didn't need a man to define her. Moving away from Dallas and the Hart ranch was Jada's way of making her way in the world. However, her salary didn't completely cover her expenses. San Francisco was pricy, and although she tried to pare back, she could only do so much. She was used to a certain lifestyle. Jada had been subsidizing her expenses with earnings from her shares in Hart Enterprises. After growing up on the ranch, where her every need was taken care of, she wanted the same in her new city.

She'd purchased a two-bedroom condo in Pacific Heights that had a concierge, fitness center, game room, and rooftop terrace. Meanwhile, her condo had floor-to-ceiling windows and provided panoramic views of the city and the bay. Her kitchen was state of the art with modern fixtures and stainless steel appliances. Her master bath was an oasis with a porcelain-tiled shower and soaking tub. It was expensive, but it suited Jada's needs and included a reserved parking space for her Jaguar.

With her new career and condo in the bag, Jada was poised for her new beginning—but one thing eluded her.

Sexual experience.

Jada hadn't forgotten Joshua's long-ago words when he told her she was a cold fish. Since then, she'd dated all types of men to figure out who or what type she liked best. Sometimes, she was pleasantly surprised at the end of the night. Other times, she could have had a V-8.

Jada didn't consider herself a hussy. She was a beautiful woman with a healthy appetite, and when the *right* man came along, she'd be ready for him. The cold fish would be a thing of the past.

BY MONDAY MORNING, Jada's outlook had improved. She was ready to face the workweek. Her outfit was perfect for her second week with Damian McKnight at the helm of WLB-TV. Although he'd said he wasn't making sweeping changes, Jada knew he would be watching her and she had to put her best foot forward.

Today, she wore a classic, fitted sheath dress that featured her signature bold, bright colors. The burnt orange highlighted her fair complexion, and the cutout at the top of the bodice stopped just above her cleavage. The side slit showed her leg, but nothing indecent. She accentuated her look with three-inch strappy sandals that matched the color of the dress perfectly.

Her hair was simple in a sophisticated updo with chandelier earrings and minimal makeup—just some mascara, blush, and a sweep of lip gloss. She stood back and stared at her reflection in the pedestal mirror in her bedroom.

She looked damn good.

Later, in the office, she was feeling great about her appearance and confident as she went over a few last-minute notes with the producer before her weekly segment. But suddenly, her antennae went on red alert. Her sixth sense felt danger was near. She turned around to find Damian staring at her with a frown.

What did I do now?

Since arriving this morning, she'd kept her nose down and out of his way. On her drive to work, Jada had decided to ignore him and do the best job she could. If he wanted to sack her, he could have done so after she'd put her foot in her mouth last week. Jada took that to mean he saw potential and wasn't going to throw the baby out with the bathwater.

She noticed Damian motion Martin, a producer, over to him in the shadows and whisper something in his ear. Jada wished she were a fly on the wall to hear what he was saying.

Seconds later, Martin returned to the set. He seemed uncomfortable as he shifted from foot to foot.

"What is it, Martin?" asked Jada as she glanced into his bespectacled face.

"Mr. McKnight requested that you lose the chignon. Said it makes you look matronly on camera when you're usually more approachable."

Jada was opening her mouth to respond when Damian himself joined them on the set. "That's only part of what I said. If you're going to relay a message, please be accurate."

"And would you care to expound?" Jada lifted a brow. *What is his problem?* She thought he was going to be observant before jumping into the fray, but maybe that didn't apply to her.

"You never wear your hair up," Damian said. "It's always down."

How in the hell does he know how I usually wear my hair? Then it hit her—he'd been watching her, and probably all of the staff, to find cracks or fissures in their demeanor. Jada's heart began pounding. "I was trying a new look."

"Don't."

Jada saw Martin blanch beside her. Meanwhile, she felt defiant. "What if I don't want to?"

Yes, she was challenging him. He had no right to tell her how to wear her hair.

"I would think you would get the adage, 'If it's not broke, don't fix it,'" Damian responded. "But since you don't, let me be clear: *I* don't like it. Take it down. Now."

Jada fixed her eyes on Damian's. Once again, a battle of wills was taking place between them. She wanted to disobey him, but there was a brightness to his dark gaze that told Jada if she tried it, it might be the last time she was on this set. She didn't want to go back to Dallas with her tail between her legs.

Slowly, her hands reached behind her to the chignon she'd spent a painstaking amount of time on this morning, and she began to pull the pins from her hair. One by one, she dropped them in her lap until, eventually, her entire mane fell to her shoulders. As she shook her hair out, she stared at him defiantly. "Happy?"

~

DAMIAN WASN'T HAPPY. He wanted to run his fingers through those luxurious strands, not just look at them. He sucked in a deep breath. He should never have come over here. He'd been busy with the station manager and several program executives when Jada walked in. It had been impossible not to notice her in that striking orange dress.

She looked vibrant and as delicious as a juicy orange. He loved the way her dress skimmed her luscious curves and round backside. But her hair . . . since when did she wear it up? When it was down, she looked youthful. So why was she downplaying her vitality? Had she guessed he'd had carnal thoughts about her? Is that why she was trying to be something she wasn't?

After he'd requested she take her hair down, she'd responded like a child acting out when told what to do. She could stew for all he cared. He had a job to do: turn this struggling station around. He spun on his heel and left the stage even though he could feel her eyes on the back of his skull.

His team at McKnight Media thought he was insane to take on the station, but Damian saw potential. WLB-TV was a diamond that needed some polishing.

With the right management and news programming, it could be a moneymaker. Jada Hart fit into that picture. He'd seen star potential in her video clips, but he felt she was underutilized. She needed to be given meatier subject matter so he could see if she could run with it. She had a degree from the University of Texas, so surely she had more underneath her beautiful surface.

"Mr. McKnight." Andrew came toward him. "If now is a good time, can we talk about advertising numbers?"

"Absolutely," Damian said, walking toward him. "Let's do." Damian knew that Jada Hart was watching him as he disappeared.

~

"The entire station is buzzing about what happened to you today," Kyler said over lunch with Jada. It was a crisp fall afternoon in San Francisco, and they were dining outside. The high for the day was seventy degrees, so they had to take advantage of it while they could before the smog rolled in.

Different food trucks came and parked outside the building each week, so they could try new offerings weekly. Today's menu was from a Greek eatery that locals had given rave reviews. Jada opted for the chicken souvlaki with a side Greek salad while Kyler selected the same, but with French fries. If Jada ate like Kyler, she would blow up like a balloon.

"It was nothing," Jada said as she placed a forkful of salad in her mouth and chewed. It had to be, because if Jada allowed herself to think it was more, then what would it mean?

"The new owner, Damian McKnight, has set his

eyes on you," Kyler said. "I can't tell if it's in a good or bad way, but you're certainly in his crosshairs."

"Why would I be?" Jada put down her fork. "I made an out-of-turn comment once, and he promptly put me in my place. Why is everyone making a big deal out of it?"

"Because he didn't singlehandedly come over and tell anyone else to put their hair down. He told you." Her blue eyes focused on Jada's brown ones.

"And I did what he asked. End of story." Jada picked up her fork and continued eating.

"True." Kyler sipped on her Perrier. "But I just wonder what he has in store for you—hell, for all of us. If your slightest hairstyle change has him out of whack, what's next?"

Jada shrugged. "If you ask me, he's a bully throwing his weight around when he knows we all have no choice but to do as we're told if we want to keep our jobs."

"I'm with you. I can't afford to lose my job either. Otherwise, I'd be heading back to the great state of Ohio."

Jada leaned in and whispered, "You wouldn't leave me in this pit of vipers, would you?"

Kyler smiled. "Only as a last resort, but let's think positively. Damian McKnight may be just the breath of fresh air WLB-TV needs to put us on the map."

∼

DAMIAN STARED BACK at the station's abysmal quarter advertising figures. He'd never seen anything so improperly managed his entire life—except maybe when he took over that radio station from a reality star who'd been using it as a platform for his entire family to make a name for themselves. Damian had done the impossible and put that radio station in the black after it had operated for years in the red. He could do the same thing here.

From his office, he glimpsed orange shoot past him, and instantly, he was on alert. Jada was back in the building after completing an assignment. He'd successfully put his rampant erotic images of her on the backburner for much of the day, but that didn't stop his mind or other body parts from wanting her.

Damian had learned a long time ago that he had to stay focused. When he'd been shuttled from foster home to foster home, he had seen that another future was possible. It had started when he was nine years old. He'd been with a foster family in which both parents were educators. They'd instilled in him how important having a higher education was to achieving his goals. Damian had decided right then and there that he would go to college, somehow, someway.

He'd hoped to get adopted, but when the once childless couple miraculously became pregnant, he was placed back into the system. He'd run away from the next foster home because the father was a drunk and beat the children. Damian had been older and refused to be pushed around, so the father had told him to hit the road. He'd been a sophomore in high school and struggling with honors classes, but despite living on the streets for a few weeks, he'd shown up to class each and every day. He had stayed at the odd shelter until one day an elderly woman, Mrs. Lockett, had seen him sifting through the trash for some leftovers at the local neighborhood diner.

Much to the dismay of Mrs. Lockett's husband, she took Damian in and offered him a place to sleep for the night and breakfast the next morning. Damian didn't know what to expect and asked what he was required to do for the handout, but she looked at him strangely and said he owed her nothing. When she dropped him off at high school that morning, Damian thought he'd never see her again. So, he couldn't have been more surprised when after school, he found Mrs. Lockett waiting for him, standing by her Honda CR-V.

Damian smiled at the memory and the way his heart turned over just thinking about the kind elderly couple who'd taken him in. Mrs. Lockett had seen something worthwhile in him that made her take a chance on a street kid and give him a home, a future. Unfortunately, in Damian's freshman year of college, Mr. and Mrs. Lockett died in a car crash when a drunk driver hit them. Afterward, Damian learned that the Locketts had ensured his entire college education was paid for in the will.

"Mr. McKnight, I was heading out for the evening. Is there anything else you need?" Andrew asked.

"No, I'm fine. Have a good night." Damian must have been staring at the facts and figures for a few hours because it was indeed after six p.m. But his night at the office was just getting started. It's not like he had anyone to go home to. And that was just fine with him.

"It's so good to hear your voice," Jada said when she finally reached Bree later that Monday evening. She'd just kicked her heels off and was padding through her living room with the phone in one hand and chopsticks cradling a takeout-sushi roll in the other. Jada was not a cook. She could barely boil an egg, and even then she had problems. Most nights, she ate out or grabbed something on the go.

"It's good to hear your voice too," Bree said from the other end of the line. "I'm sorry I missed your call the other day. Grayson, Cameron, and I were playing chess."

"You ignored me for a board game?"

"I didn't ignore you. You know if you need me, you need only call the house phone and Sonya will come and get me."

Jada sighed. "I know. I know." Sonya was Grayson and Bree's live-in housekeeper and Cameron's everything. She'd been with him since he was a toddler and hadn't left his side since, not even when his and Grayson's mother, Julia, passed away.

"So, what was so urgent?"

"The new owner of WLB-TV."

"I would think new ownership is a good thing. They could shake things up, and you'd finally get your chance to be front and center."

"That might've happened if the owner didn't hate me on the spot."

Bree chuckled. "I doubt that's true. There's never been a man or woman alive you couldn't charm when you set your mind to it."

"Not this man."

"So, it's an individual? Not a corporation?"

"It's more like the man behind the corporation," Jada said. "And he wants no part of Jada Hart."

"C'mon, you're exaggerating. When did this happen?"

"Last Monday."

"And you're already throwing in the towel? That's not the Jada I know. You never give up. I remember when you were eleven years old and Daddy told you

you couldn't ride a big horse and still needed a pony. You were determined to show him you were a capable horsewoman. And you did. You wouldn't have won those jumping competitions if you were a quitter."

"Yeah, well that was a lifetime ago." Jada smiled to herself as she recalled how furious Duke had been when she'd steadfastly refused to get off her first palomino. *It's too big for you,* he'd said. *What if you fall and break your neck? Your mother would never forgive me.* But Jada had been relentless. And slowly but surely, she made Duke see she could handle the large animal, and eventually, her daddy respected her decision.

"That doesn't matter," Bree said, interrupting her thoughts. "You have what it takes."

Bree was right. Damian McKnight was no different.If her usual charm and vivacious personality didn't do it, she'd have to show him that she was made of strong stock. "Thanks, Bree. Talking to you was exactly what I needed."

"Hey, I'm always here for you when you need a pep talk."

"Enough about me." Jada fell backward against the sofa cushions. "How are you? How's the pregnancy going?"

"Not bad."

Jada sat upright. "That doesn't sound good."

"I have a little high blood pressure is all, and the doctor wants me to take it easy."

"Bed rest?"

"No, thank heavens," Bree said with relief, "but I am cutting back my hours. There's nothing more important than delivering a healthy baby girl."

"That's right. You have to take care of my niece and keep her safely tucked in your oven."

Bree chuckled. "That's why I love you, Jada. You always know exactly what to say to lighten the mood."

After hanging up, Jada felt better about her situation at work. Yes, she'd made a horrible first impression on Damian McKnight, but surely she could turn the tide, right? Get him to see that she was a great contribution to the team and that she had the chops to do more than just fluff pieces?

Jada leaned back on the couch. Tomorrow, she would put her best foot forward.

THE REMAINDER of the week didn't improve for Jada where Damian was concerned. He seemed determined not only to find fault with her but with several staff members. By Friday, he had already fired a producer, cameraman, and director. Everyone was on edge about their jobs, including Jada.

She was not Damian's favorite person. From the start, she'd offended and antagonized him, but she'd been making a concentrated effort to redeem herself this week. She put forth her best ideas in the production meetings, all of which Damian had been staunchly against. It was as if whatever story she championed earned his automatic veto. It was driving her crazy. How could she do her job if he was always in her crosshairs?

She couldn't wait for today to be over and the weekend to arrive. Fridays were casual at the station. Everyone wore jeans or khaki pants, and an air of lightness marked the workplace. Usually, that is, until Damian's arrival last week had everyone worried about their jobs.

Jada arrived in her normal Friday ensemble of

skinny jeans, crop top with a flyaway sweater, and Louis Vuitton Pochette Metis leather handbag. Because it had been raining outside and she didn't have her umbrella, she'd run inside the station forgetting her garment bag in the trunk of her car. She was glancing out at the deluge when she felt a familiar unease come over her. She turned to find Damian with his arms crossed over his chest. He was staring at her.

He was dressed in dark jeans and a black T-shirt that revealed muscled arms. Someone knew his way around a gym. Jada hazarded him a glance before looking back out the window.

"I hope you're not going on air dressed like that," Damian said.

She turned back and glared at him. "That's exactly what I was going to do. I was going to show my belly button to all of San Francisco because that's exactly what they want to see with their morning coffee and bowl of cereal."

"Aren't you feisty this morning?"

"And don't you have anything better to do than sneak around in the shadows watching people, waiting for them to mess up so you can pounce and fire them?"

His eyes narrowed. "Is that what you think?"

"It's what we all think, Mr. McKnight. I'm just the only one brave enough to tell you."

His piercing black eyes were furious with rage. He took a few extra steps toward Jada until his face was within inches of hers. If Jada didn't know any better, she'd swear he wanted to turn her over on his knee and spank her.

"You think being so outspoken is brave?" he hissed. "I would say it's rather shortsighted considering where you stand."

"And where's that?"

"On loose footing."

Her eyes narrowed, but she instinctively took several steps backward. Her back hit the lobby wall. "Are you firing me?"

Damian stepped closer, invading her personal space. "Not yet. But don't push me, Jada. You might not like what happens."

"Oh, I think someone *should* push you," Jada said tartly, jabbing her finger in his chest. "Maybe then you'd see you have everyone around here scrambling around like frightened rabbits because they're afraid of losing their jobs."

"And you're not afraid?"

"Of you?" Jada scoffed, but inside her stomach was somersaulting. Why the hell couldn't she just shut up and walk away? But she couldn't seem to stop having diarrhea of the mouth whenever she was around him. "Should I be?"

He closed in further until he had her caged in between the hard wall of his chest and the wall of the building. Jada didn't like it one bit. She lowered her gaze. "Didn't your mother ever teach you not to mess with scorpions because you might get stung?"

"If she did, I never listened," Jada said as she glanced up at him under lowered lashes. He could not intimidate her like he did everyone else. She'd grown up around Duke and a hell of a lot of cowboys, which made her immune from being afraid of the likes of Damian. But she did recognize he held her future at WLB-TV in his hands, so she had to tread carefully.

"That's a shame," Damian said, "because you should be afraid." With that comment, he grasped the keys from her trembling hands and ran out into the downpour.

Jada was shocked as she looked through the window to see him push the button to open her trunk, retrieve her garment bag before closing it, and run back inside the studio. He handed her the bag, and all she could do was stare at him open-mouthed.

He was dripping wet all because of her, because he'd gone out on a limb to help her. Damian McKnight was a mystery, and Jada doubted she would ever understand him. But she did like what she saw. Damp jeans and a soaked T-shirt clung to every inch of his well-defined chest. She could even see his nipples puckering from the chill of the air conditioning. Tiny beads of water clung to that handsome face of his, coating his bushy eyebrows and chiseled jaw.

Suddenly, Jada's mouth felt parched. She licked her lips to wet them. Damian caught the action, and his gaze landed directly on her mouth. Heat rays shot from his eyes, and Jada found she couldn't speak. She could hardly breathe.

The spell was broken when one of the crewmembers came running through the entrance doors. "It's nasty out there," the man said to no one in particular because Jada and Damian were still staring at each other.

"Yeah, it is," Damian said. He looked away first, breaking their trance.

Jada was glad he did because she hadn't been able to. What was it about this man that made her act completely out of character? With every other man, she was all charm and grace. Jada had perfected the art of batting her eyelashes to get her way, but it didn't work on Damian. Instead, she was all fire. It didn't make any sense.

Once the crewmember left and it was just the two

of them, Jada managed, "Th-thank you." She held up the bag. "You didn't have to do that."

Damian turned back around to face her. "Didn't I? Somehow, I didn't see you going out in the rain."

"I don't mind getting wet," Jada huffed, and as soon as she said the words, she wished she could take them back. Taken out of context, they could mean something entirely different. Her cheeks flamed.

Damian smirked. He knew that her thoughts had gone down a different road, an intimate road.

"I have to go, or I'll be late."

"And I need to get out of these wet clothes," Damian said. "Care to help me?"

Jada flushed and immediately rushed out of the lobby without answering.

∾

CARE TO HELP ME? Damian still couldn't believe he'd solicited Jada's assistance in relieving him of his clothing. *What the hell has come over me?* He could be accused of sexual harassment for such a blatant comment. But dammit, that's what happened whenever he was around that woman: He couldn't control himself.

She infuriated and surprised him in equal measure.

She had a way of speaking whatever came to her mind regardless of the consequences. She was direct and outspoken, and he kind of liked it. Damian knew he shouldn't. He shouldn't appreciate her insubordination, but he did.

He enjoyed sparring with her. She challenged him. She didn't back down from a fight. Oh no, not Jada

Hart. She gave as good as she got. It turned him on. A lot.

He didn't have to go out in the rain, but when he'd stood by the sidelines watching her look forlornly at her car, he'd known he would step in. And he'd done it after she told him off and pretty much called him a tyrant who had his entire staff on pins and needles.

But that was his style—always had been and always would be.

He couldn't come in there and behave like he didn't know what he was doing. He had to make decisions and be authoritative, and sometimes that meant lackluster individuals who weren't adding to the bottom line lost their jobs. WLB-TV would be a success by the sheer force of his will because Damian never lost. Just like he hadn't lost a conversation yet in his verbal repartee with Jada Hart.

~

HOURS LATER, after her broadcast, Jada sat in her chair in the newsroom. She still didn't know what to make of the exchange she and Damian had engaged in. At first, their conversation had been highly combative as it always was with him, but then something changed and the air between them had crackled with sexual tension!

Damian was a good-looking man, there was no denying that. With those broad shoulders, slim hips, and what Jada's overactive imagination suspected was a washboard stomach, she was tied up in knots. *But why him?* She found Damian to be conceited and arrogant, and she'd love nothing better than to tell him so, but she wouldn't get the chance—not if she cared about her career.

WLB-TV was just a stepping stone, and if she had to go through Damian McKnight to get to the next rung of the ladder, then so be it.

Whatever tension that had developed between them in those few minutes this morning had to be nothing more than a one-off, an anomaly at best. Jada liked her men attractive, charming, and jovial, and she could certainly do without Damian's perpetual frown and creased forehead staring at her.

"So, are you excited for tonight?" Kyler said when she stopped at Jada's desk and interrupted her musings.

"Excited about what?"

"The media awards dinner. Did you forget the entire team was invited to go?"

Of course she had, considering all the drama in the newsroom. "Yeah, I guess I did. I'm going to pass."

"Since when does Jada Hart pass on an event? You're the life of every party."

"Perhaps I don't wish to be the main attraction."

"And miss an opportunity to cozy up to boss man? I thought you needed all the help you can get?"

"McKnight is coming?" Adrenaline surged through her at the prospect of seeing him again.

Kyler nodded. "The entire team is going, and if you bail it will look awfully suspicious and be very unlike you. You don't avoid—you attack things head-on. That's what I love about you. You're direct."

"I dunno."

"Yes, you do. You're going to take that gorgeous tush of yours home, shower, shave, and shine. And you're going to be at the media dinner and show McKnight that he hasn't broken you."

"Is this some sort of pep talk?"

"It is indeed."

Jada smiled. "Alright, I'll do it, but only because you're going to be there. And you promise to back me up, right?"

"Of course."

Jada certainly hoped so, because something told her that tonight was going to be very interesting.

3

—————

Jada spent an extraordinary amount of time selecting her dress for the evening. It had to be classic and elegant, yet true to herself. That was hard to do with a closet that held nothing but bold and daring outfits. She settled on a demure dress she'd worn once to a Hart Enterprises function.

It was a strapless gown of deep violet with a square bodice that cinched in at the hip to show off her figure before flowing out like a mermaid to her ankles. She added four-inch sandals and chandelier earrings to top off her ensemble. She looked stylish, and Jada knew she wouldn't offend anyone at the dinner, least of all Damian.

With her clutch in hand, Jada headed out of her condo to the car waiting for her outside. She had opted not to drive so she could enjoy some bourbon and wine with her meal. The drive to the hotel was uneventful and gave her time to prepare herself for the evening. She knew being cordial to Damian would require a lot of effort, but she was determined to find a happy medium when dealing with the man. She had to stop going from angry one minute to feeling her blood heat up because he'd stepped several inches too close to her.

When the car pulled up to the curb, Jada made arrangements for her pickup and exited the vehicle. The foyer in front of the grand ballroom was already filled with various men and women from the networks. Jada was happy to find that Damian hadn't arrived and that a small group from the news station had formed around the open bar. "Can anyone join in on this?" Jada asked, placing a hand on the station manager's shoulder.

"Of course, c'mon in," Andrew said. He was closest to the bar. "What can I get you?"

"A bourbon, please."

Jada turned to Kyler, who was standing inches away. "Thanks for talking me into coming. This is much more fun than staying home on a Friday night with a bowl of microwave popcorn."

Kyler returned a toothy smile. She looked magnificent in a blue sheath gown; it showed off her blue eyes while her blond hair had been styled in elegant waves down her slender back. She looked "very Marilyn Monroe." "Yes, it is. And I hope it stays that way because McKnight is coming toward us."

Jada's heart lurched, but she didn't dare turn around. Instead, she acted as if she were knee deep in conversation, until the group parted, making room for his arrival. When talk ceased, Jada was forced to turn around and acknowledge him.

"Good evening." Damian nodded in their direction.

A chorus of "Good evenings" were sung before the silence reensued. Jada used the opportunity to catch a glance. Damian wore a tailored black suit with a gray vest that hugged his lean abdomen, white silk shirt, and matching gray tie. He looked handsome, virile, and male despite his hooded gaze.

Why is everyone quiet? Jada pondered. *For Christ's sake, these people are acting as if he's a god instead of a man.* He was human like the rest of them, and if someone wasn't going to speak up, she was. "It will be interesting to see who wins best talk show," Jada said conversationally.

"Yeah," another member concurred. "Too bad we weren't nominated."

"I think we do a pretty bang-up job on the evening news program. You would have thought it would have merited us a nomination at the very least," Kyler said.

"Sometimes, I wonder if these things are rigged," another coworker said. "Year after year, we see the same folks nominated."

"Did you ever think to consider it's because they deliver exceptional news?" Damian offered.

A hush echoed throughout the group.

"It takes time, diligence, and focus to be the best, which WLB-TV lacks; but I think in time we'll get there," Damian added.

Does he not realize that he just insulted the entire group and all their hard work with one quick lash of his tongue? Jada tossed back her entire glass of bourbon. It was going to be a long night.

~

DAMIAN STEPPED AWAY to take a phone call. When he was done, instead of rejoining the group he stood back to view the office dynamics. There was Jay Blair, an anchor and the jokester of the bunch, then there was Kyler Barnes, who was beautiful to look at but vanilla. Then there was Jada. Her cheeks had blazed a fiery red after his remark. She'd been dying to give it back to him, but she'd held her tongue.

Maybe she's finally learning that you get more bees with honey? he mused. Damian rather liked his vantage point. It allowed him to observe Jada without fear of being seen. She had an understated elegance tonight that he most definitely appreciated. Her dress clung to her hips and behind, and the gown showed just a hint of cleavage. Her long sable hair was straight. She looked cool. Sophisticated. Untouchable.

He didn't like this version of Jada. She was all poise and confidence, and he wanted to ruffle her up. He strode from his corner. She was at the bar, and he sidled up beside her.

"Another bourbon?" he asked.

"Yes, do you have a problem with that?"

There it was. The fire. Damian saw it ignite in her eyes. There was the Jada he knew who liked to challenge him. "Of course not, so long as you're not driving." Then he told the bartender, "I'll have a bourbon as well." The bartender nodded and began pouring two glasses.

"I'm not."

She didn't offer any more information. When the bartender slid both drinks their way, Damian quickly grabbed them and he handed a glass to Jada. He noticed that she carefully avoided touching his fingers and looking at him directly as she accepted the bourbon. He smiled inwardly.

She felt it too.

Earlier, when they'd been at the studio and he'd been so close to her, he'd smelled the sweet scent of her perfume, felt her heat. She'd felt the connection and like him she was ignoring it, but something in him wouldn't allow it. "Did you come alone tonight?" he asked, sipping his drink.

"Yes. I doubt it would be much fun for a date during a work function."

"And would there have been a date?" He knew he'd overstepped, but he had to know if there was someone in her life.

She stared at him pointedly. "Are you asking me if I'm seeing someone?"

He shrugged and lied. "It makes no difference to me one way or the other." The file he'd received on Jada had only revealed her schooling and work history and a short profile of her parents, because they were the well-known Harts of Hart Enterprises, not if there was a man in her life.

"Good. Then I choose not to answer." She gave him a sweet smile and then walked off to join the others in the group.

Damn minx!

His attempt to act disinterested had backfired, and now she was gone. Well, she wouldn't get very far.

He'd see to that.

Why does Damian *want to know if I'm seeing someone? What right does he have to ask me such a personal question?*

The hair on Jada's neck prickled. She glanced around to find Damian's enigmatic gaze on her even though he was now speaking with several local leaders in the media industry across the room. He looked every bit the formidable man that he was. So, why did that bother her? He wasn't the first attractive man she'd come across, and he certainly wouldn't be the last, but an aura emanated from him tonight that radiated power. It spoke to her every female instinct.

There was something more between them, just beneath the surface, that if she allowed it out, could overwhelm her.

"Ready to go in?" Kyler interrupted her thoughts.

She'd been scatterbrained this last week since Damian's arrival, and she needed to get it together. "Yes, of course." She finished her remaining bourbon and placed her glass on a nearby table.

The double doors of the grand ballroom opened, allowing local news-media industry professionals into the room. It would be a night of celebration for some and loss for others. One day, Jada hoped to be one of the winners, but until then she would bide her time.

Kyler found their table, and Jada was just about to sit down when she felt her chair being slid underneath her and a distinct woodsy scent.

Damian.

Jada glanced behind her and found he'd supplanted Kyler and was now sitting beside her. Kyler shrugged and made her way to the other side of the table. Jada tried to keep from frowning even though she was seething inwardly. Why couldn't she get away from him? Must she make nice with him on her own time?

Apparently, the answer was yes.

"Wine?" Damian asked.

Jada turned and realized a server was holding two bottles. "Red or white, mademoiselle?"

"White, please." He leaned over and poured her a glass. "Thank you."

"My pleasure," the waiter said and continued serving the table.

"The menu looks intriguing," Damian said from her side.

Jada rolled her eyes. *Is he really going to just utter pleasantries?* She glanced around the table, desperate to join a conversation, but she was too far away from Kyler. She was going to have to talk to Damian. "Yes, it does."

Damian leaned toward her and whispered, "If you would just learn to relax around me, we could find some common ground."

Stunned, Jada stared at him. He couldn't know he made her uneasy, could he? She didn't have nerves around men. Usually, they were eating out of her hands, but Damian was not one of them. Was *that* what made him different?

"I *am* relaxed," she hissed.

He laughed and leaned back in his chair to regard her. "Sure you are. Sure you are."

The emcee for the evening chose that moment to walk on stage and thank them all for coming. He high-lighted some high moments in news reporting that year and received many cheers.

"I think WLB-TV has what it takes to become an exceptional station," Damian whispered in Jada's ear, once again causing her stomach to flip. "We can't be afraid of tackling hard-hitting stories."

Jada turned to him. "We're not afraid. Prior management wanted us to keep our stories with a focus on the community."

"We can still do that and deliver hard-hitting news."

"How would we go about it?"

"I have a few ideas. Would you care to hear them, or would you like to continue bickering?"

Her eyes narrowed, but she didn't rise to the bait

with one of her pithy comebacks that had become a hallmark of their relationship. Instead, she leaned in and let Damian expound.

By dessert, Jada was certain she'd lost her mind. Surely, Damian couldn't be the same arrogant man she'd been griping about the last two weeks. Some of the ideas he had for stories and how to take WLB-TV to the next level would assuredly get them nominations next year. Jada felt very shortsighted that she'd only focused on the negative.

"World War III hasn't broken out over here," Kyler said during intermission when Damian departed to mingle and the seat beside Jada became vacant. "I take it your evening isn't a complete bust?"

Jada shook her head. "Quite the contrary. I think McKnight and I have finally called a ceasefire."

Kyler raised an eyebrow. "Really? Though I shouldn't be surprised. You both have been engrossed in conversation for much of the night."

A crease formed on Jada's forehead. "We have not."

"Have too. I don't think either of one of you came up for air, that's until that producer came and spirited Damian away."

Was that true? Had Jada monopolized him the entire evening? It certainly hadn't been her intent. All she'd known was that he was right. They couldn't go on bickering, and now that she'd had a chance to listen to his ideas, he wasn't all bad.

"Well, then I should go mingle." Jada rose to her feet and was pushing back her chair when Damian returned to the table.

"Where do you think you're going?"

Jada smiled and reached for her clutch. "To mingle. If you'll excuse me."

DAMIAN WAS PERTURBED. He hated being interrupted from his and Jada's conversation. They'd finally waved the red flag for peace. She'd actually listened to him and vice versa. He had a lot of ideas about how to make the station successful and hadn't shared them with anyone until now.

Until Jada.

Damian usually kept his battle plan to himself, but he'd let his guard down tonight—maybe because Jada had finally lowered the walls around her enough for him to penetrate them.

Now, there was a word he shouldn't be thinking of.

All night, he'd sat beside her, smelling that uniquely Jada scent that was a mix of soap, perfume, and skin. It enthralled him, and Damian found himself softening his opinion of her. While he thought she was a spoiled, entitled princess, he also realized her degree in communications wasn't just window dressing.

And when she laughed at a joke he made, her long sable hair had cascaded down the length of her spine. Damian had wanted to run his hands through it and bring her mouth to his and finally have a taste of the forbidden, because that's exactly what Jada Hart was to him.

She was like the apple in the Garden of Eden that Adam should have stayed away from. Damian felt drawn to Jada when he shouldn't. He had to stop thinking about her. He walked over to another news group and made polite conversation even though his eyes followed her every movement.

He knew she was talking to a group of men, all of whom were fawning over her. *Ah, there's the other side of Jada—the flirt who wraps men around her baby finger.* Is that what she'd been doing to him tonight—drawing him into her web so he'd do her bidding?

But Damian wasn't so easily taken in. He turned his back on her.

He was determined to block her out.

DAMIAN HAD BEEN LOOKING at her. She was positive of it. And now he wasn't. Jada didn't know what made her walk up to several of the sportscasters, one of whom had asked her out at another such function. She'd given him the brush-off before because he enjoyed talking more about himself than finding out anything about her. Jada knew it would be the same if she went out on a date with him.

So why had she come over here?

Maybe to convince herself that Kyler was wrong. She wasn't monopolizing Damian. It was hard not to be taken in by the way those dark eyes looked into hers. He had a way of focusing entirely on her to the exclusion of everything else. It was heady and intoxicating, and perhaps Jada *had* spoken only to him during dinner. Well, she was making up for it now. During the intermission, she had made her way around the room talking to connections until she finally landed with the sportscasters.

"So, tell us, Jada, when are you going to have another one of your night on the town segments?" one of them asked with a smirk.

"I'd love to get in on the action and help you research," another of the men said and laughed out loud.

"Not tonight, fellas," a deep masculine voice said from behind her. "Jada is otherwise engaged."

Jada spun around just as Damian put his hand on the small of her back and led her away. "What the hell was that?" she asked, stopping midstride. She didn't appreciate him getting territorial.

"There's no need for you to fall back on your old standby."

Jada put her hand on her hip. "And what, pray tell, is that?"

"Batting your eyelashes and flirting with the first available man."

"Of all the—"

"I know there's more to you than this façade you show the world, Jada. Perhaps if you'd let someone see it. Be real. Be yourself—"

He didn't get another word out because Jada grabbed the bottom of her dress and stalked toward the exit. She had just about enough of Damian McKnight. First, he insulted their station, then he told her his Emmy ideas after staunchly ignoring most of hers, and now he was being a Neanderthal who thought he could control her. She couldn't figure him out and didn't want to. She walked quickly through the corridor. *How dare he say those things to me! He doesn't know me.* Just because he'd spent a couple of hours with her tonight didn't mean he knew a thing about what made her tick.

She was nearly to the stairs when Damian caught up to her and swung her around. "Let me go!"

"Not yet!" He grabbed her by the arm and strode to a secluded corner down the hall.

"I don't know who in the hell—"

Jada didn't get another word out because Damian hauled her to him. His hands threaded through her straight black hair seconds before he kissed her. It was a kiss meant to silence her, of that she was sure, but instead it *provoked* and intoxicated her. Angling her face, she allowed him to deepen the kiss. He devoured the softness of her lips, then his tongue darted through their moistness to duel with hers.

Jada had no choice but to respond to the passion Damian was rousing in her, especially when his hands roamed downward to cup her buttocks and he shifted her against his hard-on. She was stunned to feel just how hard he'd become from their deep, ravaging kisses and how wet she felt as he repeated the action again and again.

She gasped, groaning as she wound her hands around his neck and returned kiss for heated kiss. And when his lips left hers and moved to the column of her throat, placing hot kisses and gentle nibbles on her neck, quivers of pleasure surged through her. She felt the tips of her breasts harden and a low ache form deep in her belly. She didn't know what was going on. She only knew she wanted more of it.

And perhaps she would have gotten more, but suddenly they heard voices.

Instantly, they pulled apart as if burned. Jada couldn't look at him. How could she after the way she'd just made out with her boss! A man she disliked!

"I'm sorry. That shouldn't have happened." Damian's chest was heaving. Jada had gotten a glimpse of the man he could be when he wasn't in control.

"Well, it did," Jada said as she fingered her hair, trying to straighten it even though she knew she must look like a wreck. She reached into her clutch for a mirror and was stunned by what she saw. Her pupils were dilated and glossy, and her mouth was swollen from his kisses. And her hair—well, it looked like he'd been combing his hands through it as he'd plundered her mouth. "I-I have to go."

She had to get out of there before anyone at the station saw her or realized they were both gone. She couldn't take the gossip that would ensue.

"Jada, wait!" Damian cried out.

But she was already running down the stairs.

4

———

Damian jumped out of his bed in his boxer briefs and stalked out of his room. He headed down the hallway to the wet bar in his living room. He lived in a typical, stylish bachelor pad with modern décor thanks to the interior designer he'd hired to ensure it was cutting edge. The only thing atypical was that his "pad" was an ultraexpensive penthouse.

He poured himself a hefty drink of whiskey and sipped it as he sank into the leather sofa. He reached for the remote, but thought better of it. He didn't want TV. He wanted Jada.

Damn that woman for getting under his skin. He had no intention of kissing her tonight or ever, but every day for the last two weeks she'd been steadily egging him on, challenging him. And tonight, well tonight had been the final straw.

He hadn't realized he was jealous of Jada talking to those sportscasters until she'd run away from him. And then when they kissed, she was hot as fire. For him.

Oh yes, Jada Hart acted like she despised him, but when his lips touched hers, he'd felt fireworks and so had she. In that moment, he'd wanted to give it to her, moving her up and down his length. If they hadn't been interrupted . . .

Hell, what did it matter that they had been!

He should never have mixed business with pleasure. It was a cardinal rule of Damian's that he never went back on. Until now. The damn minx had him throwing out his rulebook. He wanted her so badly right now, he couldn't sleep. *Is she just as wound up?* he wondered. Or was she peacefully sleeping while he was sporting a painful hard-on and drinking himself to sleep?

What the hell am I going to do? Now that he'd tasted from the fruit of the forbidden tree, he wanted more. Damian gulped back another chug of whiskey.

He'd crossed a line from which there was no turning back. Damian wasn't altogether sure he wanted to anyway.

~

THROUGHOUT THE WEEKEND, Jada fretted. By Sunday night, she was a wreck and unable to sleep. She was out of her depth. She'd never, ever gotten involved in a workplace romance—certainly not with a man who was responsible for her future career as well as her paycheck. It was untenable.

How did I allow things to get so out of control? Yes, she thought Damian was attractive, but she'd never planned on acting on those feelings. But when he'd pulled her into that secret alcove and planted those full lips on hers, all thought of what was right and wrong had gone out the window. All Jada had been able to do was *feel*. Feel the soft pressure of his lips on hers as he coaxed a response from her. Feel the bristle of his goatee against her sensitized skin. Feel the hard ridge of his erection pressed against her middle as she shamelessly tried to ride him in her gown!

Oh Lord!

Jada clasped her face. She'd made a royal mess of her life. How was she supposed to go into the studio tomorrow and face Damian after what they'd done? After what she hadn't stopped him from doing? He may have initiated the kiss, but she could have pulled away, slapped him even, but she didn't. She'd indulged in her fantasies and made a colossal mistake that could cost her the career she'd been working so hard for.

Jada stared at her bedroom ceiling willing sleep to come. Instead, she tossed and turned until eventually sleep must have claimed her because the next thing she heard was her cell phone ringing.

She rubbed her eyes and glanced at her alarm clock. Four a.m. It was still dark. Who would be calling her at this hour? She reached for the lamp, flooding the room with light.

"Hello?" she asked blearily.

"Jada?"

"Yes."

"It's Andrew."

Instantly, Jada went on alert.

"Hilary came down with a terrible case of food poisoning and, needless to say, is becoming acquainted with the porcelain god. And I've been unable to reach Kyler, which means we need a body in the anchor seat in two hours."

"Alright. I'll be there in thirty minutes."

"How did you know I was asking?"

"C'mon, Andrew, you wouldn't be calling me at this ungodly hour if you weren't in a pickle. And even if I am your last choice, as you more or less said, you need a body in that chair to welcome our viewers to *Good Day, San Francisco.*"

"Yes, I do. So get your ass here." The phone went dead.

Jada's pulse raced. This was her opportunity to show Andrew Paxon and Damian McKnight that she was an asset. She threw back the covers and rushed toward the bathroom. After brushing her teeth, taking the quickest shower ever, and brushing her hair into a ponytail, Jada was out the door of her condo in fifteen minutes. She'd dressed swiftly in yoga pants and a tank top and grabbed her most appealing dress and shoes.

Another fifteen minutes later, with no traffic to beat, she arrived at the studio.

She strolled through the door looking cool and calm. Jada was ready for her opportunity. She hadn't majored in communications to stand on the sidelines. She was ready to be on the front line.

"Good morning," Jada said cheerily as she breezed through the newsroom to her desk.

"Thank God!" Andrew nearly wept when he saw her. "You're a godsend. I didn't know what I was going to do."

"Always happy to help." Jada placed her garment bag across her chair, but Andrew halted her. "There's no time for that. I'll have one of the interns take care of that. We need you in the conference room to go over today's show, and then we need to get you dressed ASAP."

Jada had to hide a smile and mask her true feelings. "I'm all yours."

She followed Andrew and anchor Jay and two other producers. Several curious sets of eyes peered at her. She caught their raised brows, but Andrew shook his head as if to say *don't ask*. Jada didn't care why she was there, only that she'd been asked to anchor the broadcast and she would do her very best.

Within the hour, she was up to speed on the morning segments. She would do the morning intro discussing the latest domestic and international news as well as interview a local actress starring in a block-buster movie, discuss shopping bargains, and then she and Jay would try their hand at a cooking segment with a vegan chef. Jada was thrilled beyond words with her luck.

She was leaving the conference room when Damian crossed her line of vision. Her stomach clenched as images of him pressing her up against the wall and kissing her senseless came to mind. She saw Andrew rush up to him and whisper something that immediately brought his gaze to Jada. She felt rooted to the spot and stood straight, pushing her breasts out. She wasn't going to cower. She wasn't the only one in the wrong. He'd been there too. And who cared if she wasn't looking her best in yoga pants and a tank top? Andrew called *her* to bail out the station. She couldn't be expected to arrive looking like she'd just walked off the pages of a fashion magazine. It took time to look effortless.

Jada turned on her heel and walked to the green room. She was happy that she wouldn't have to con-front Damian. It would give her time to think of a strategy and how to find her way out of this mess.

She toyed with the idea of ignoring the kiss, act like it never happened. Or she could confront Damian and hash it out, admit it was a mistake on both their parts, and agree to continue a professional relation-ship going forward. There was another alternative that was very attractive: They could pick up where they left off, and she could take Damian to bed. Her female intuition told her the man was good at everything he did, in or out of bed. *And then where will I be?*

Quickly, Jada flat ironed her hair, deftly applied her makeup, and got dressed. When she was done and admiring her handiwork, she turned around and found Damian standing in the doorway. Suddenly, her stomach lurched and flip-flopped at his perusal. He wore a charcoal suit that hugged his broad shoulders and made him look infinitely more powerful and unyielding than he had before—but equally as delicious as two nights ago when they'd kissed.

He took several steps into the room, and Jada sucked in a deep breath. She could smell the citrus scent of his cologne teasing her nostrils, could even see that he hadn't shaved and had a hint of sideburns. They made him look masculine and rugged. Jada's mouth watered, and she closed her eyes to will her erratically beating pulse to calm down.

She wished she knew what he was thinking. Was he remembering Friday night? Did he regret it? Had he come to talk to her and clear the air? What did he want? And why couldn't he stop staring at her?

He circled her for several moments before saying, "I don't like your hair like this."

Jada reached up to touch her straight locks. "You didn't seem to mind on Friday night." The image flashed of him running his fingers through it and bringing her mouth, her entire body, in close contact with his.

His eyes darkened, but he didn't say a word as he left the room.

~

Damian was fuming on the inside as he departed. It wasn't her fault that he'd woken up on the wrong side of the bed after a miserable night with barely any sleep the last few days. He'd been hoping to come to the station and get some work done. He hadn't known Jada was scheduled for this morning's news program, so it had come as a shock when he'd seen her in those body-hugging yoga pants and tank top showing a swell of her amazing cleavage.

Jada Hart had a body made for sin. And she knew it. Probably knew the effect she had on him too. Jada was a spoiled, distractingly beautiful woman. He doubted she knew the meaning of hard work or having to worry about where her next meal might come from. But it was impossible to deny that when he had stood in the doorway, she was simply exquisite, from her thick-mascara-coated eyelashes to her cute little nose and down to the natural pout of her sensuous lips that held a sheen of rosy gloss. And the simple asymmetric dress she wore curved over her bottom, stopping midway at her long legs. It had given him an amazing view of them; they seemed to go on forever in those four-inch heels.

Damian's mouth had gone dry at Jada's beguiling gaze. Was she some sort of mermaid sent to lure men to their deaths? Now that he was no longer in her presence, he looked for Andrew in the newsroom. "A word, please," he said after he spotted him and walked up to him.

"Of course, Mr. McKnight."

"Please call me Damian."

Andrew smiled. "Damian it is. What can I do for you?"

"Why is Jada Hart anchoring this morning's program?"

"Quite frankly, she was the only one available. Hilary came down with a case of food poisoning and Kyler, our backup, didn't pick up her phone even though we called nearly a dozen times." He glanced at Damian's annoyed eyes. "But if you like I can try again." He glanced down at his watch. "There isn't much time. Plus Jada is already prepped."

Damian shook his head. It wasn't Andrew's fault that he was out of sorts. "No, no. Leave it as is. I'm sure she'll do fine."

Two hours later, Jada had proven she was a natural. Damian had seen her on camera before during her entertainment segments, but he'd never seen her show such command and depth as she had this morning. She was poised and confident. There was no other way to say it: She'd brought her A game, and Damian was impressed.

"Well?" Andrew asked with a raised brow. "What did you think of today's show? Of Jada?"

Damian offered a half smile. "She did well. No, she did damn good. Was this her first time sitting in the anchor seat?"

Andrew nodded. "It was. Though I have to tell you, she'd been lobbying for quite some time for a crack at it, but they all love Hilary."

Damian glanced over at Jada. She was laughing and talking with the cameramen as she took off her mike. "They should have given her a chance. Perhaps a change of scenery would do the show some good. I would like Jada moved to the number-two position during Hilary's absences." He started to move away, but then paused. "No, scratch that. I have an even better idea. I want to try her out on Fridays. It's the least heavy-hitting news day of the week. I'd like to see how she fares in the anchor chair."

"Of course. I'll get right on it."

"Thank you, Andrew. And good call today." He palm slapped the man's back as he walked away. He needed to focus on other deals and areas of his business. As it was, he was already spending too much time at the station. Deep down, he knew why, though he'd never say it aloud.

Jada.

He glanced in her direction, unable to resist one last look. And when he did, their eyes connected from across the newsroom, and she rewarded him with one of her signature charming smiles.

Beguiling witch! Damian thought.

He frowned and immediately rushed out of the building.

~

WHAT IS HIS PROBLEM? Jada wondered when Damian scurried out the door. Several times during the broadcast, she'd found him watching her, but his eyes were shuttered and she couldn't read him. She should be feeling on top of the world. She'd finally managed to get into the elusive anchor's chair. So, why wasn't she happy? Had she been looking for Damian's approval? Had she been waiting for him to give her an attaboy?

Maybe.

She thought she'd done great. She hadn't flubbed any of her segments. In fact, if she did say so herself, she was warm and engaging with her interviews and knowledgeable on the subject matters. All in all, Jada was very proud of the effort she'd put forth despite Damian's lackluster response.

"Jada, you were fantastic!" Kyler gushed. She

rushed toward her as Jada made her way from the studio into the newsroom.

"Thanks, girl." Jada gave her good friend's hand a gentle squeeze.

"Were you nervous?"

Jada stepped back for a minute to regard her. "No, I wasn't. I was excited." She had been waiting for this moment for years, and fate had finally allowed the opportunity to fall in her lap. Kyler's misfortune had been Jada's gain.

"I'm so tickled for you."

"Really? I know they weren't able to reach you earlier this morning. Are you OK? "

"Of course," Kyler said without a moment's hesitation. "It's not your fault I forgot to charge my phone. When my body clock woke me up on its own, I was stunned to find it was six a.m. I didn't realize I had any messages until I checked my phone and realized it hadn't charged. So, how did it go?"

Jada tried to push down her large smile and act as if she was unaffected. As much as she wanted this, she didn't want to appear overeager. "It was great. I really enjoyed it."

"That's awesome, Jada." Kyler touched her shoulder. "I've always known you could do it. You just needed to be given the opportunity. Now, you've shown McKnight exactly what you can do."

Jada stared at the doorway Damian had just exited. She wasn't so sure. He'd made no move to come over and tell her what he thought of the program. Instead, he'd high-tailed it out of the station as if his pants were on fire. That pissed Jada off. This opportunity meant everything to her. It had been a chance to show him she had what it took.

"Jada?" Andrew came toward them. "My office, now."

Jada glanced furtively at Kyler. Had she done something wrong *again*? She prayed to God she hadn't blown her chance.

Kyler gave her a hesitant smile as Jada followed with leaden feet behind Andrew into his all-glass office. She closed the door behind her, hating that they were in a fishbowl. If he'd called her in here to chew her out about her performance, the entire crew would see. Somehow, she would hold herself together and show no emotion. She couldn't, wouldn't let anyone see her sweat.

Jada smiled at Andrew as she took a seat in the mesh chair in front of his cluttered desk. He sat down opposite her and steepled his fingers as he peered at her.

"I called you in here because I want to talk about today's show."

"Yes?" *Leave it at that*, she told herself, *and let him speak.*

"Mr. McKnight," Andrew began and then stopped. "I mean Damian and I have discussed your performance."

"And you thought I stunk?" Jada blurted. "That I tanked and I'll never be allowed to anchor the show again?"

Andrew chuckled. "Quite the opposite. Damian was very impressed with how well you did today, and he'd like to try you out on Fridays for the immediate future."

Jada sucked in a deep breath, and when she was finally able to release it, she said, "Excuse me?"

"You heard right, Jada. Your wish has finally come true, and Mr. McKnight, gosh, I mean, Damian sees potential in you. Undeveloped of course, but potential all the same, and he would like to switch things up a bit."

"I thought he wasn't going to make any sweeping changes."

"He's not. But he does want to try a fresh face, so we'll see what the ratings look like in a few weeks."

"Oh, Andrew, you don't know how excited I am for this opportunity."

"Excited enough to get up at three a.m. every Friday?"

"Heck yeah," Jada said, jumping to her feet. "And I promise you, you won't regret giving me this opportunity." She reached across the desk and pumped his hand furiously.

Seconds later, Jada walked out of the room with her head held high. Several curious stares were volleyed her way, but she didn't care. She was on cloud nine. Damian had ensured she'd get the chance to live her dream.

5

Damian stared at the facts and figures on his laptop. They were nothing but a blur of numbers. On and off for the last couple of weeks, he'd found himself daydreaming and unable to focus on his work. Today was no different. He'd become enamored with WLB-TV's new Friday anchor, Jada. Over the last few Fridays, he'd gotten caught up for two hours watching the morning news program—and not doing his work.

Jada Hart had captured his attention in more ways than one. Her outward beauty and sexy body haunted his dreams and made him think of all the things he'd like to do to her or her to him. He'd imagine that sexy, pouty mouth on his and how deliciously soft it would feel when he plundered it again, conquered it. And if that wasn't enough, he'd been pleasantly surprised that the woman actually was as sharp as a tack.

Just last week, he watched her tackle interviewing a school board member for closing a school in a poor district. Her interview had been tough and insightful. She hadn't allowed the member to get off scot-free and because of it, parents had started a petition to block the school closure. It was hard-hitting news, and Jada had delivered it in spades.

Damian had to keep his distance. He didn't want anyone thinking he had a favorite in the newsroom. It would do neither of them any good. But more than that, he was staying away because he didn't like the way he felt when he was near Jada. He was used to measuring his actions and feelings, but when it came to this woman, he felt out of his depth, anxious, and out of control.

He'd enjoyed casual relationships with many women that usually lasted one or a few dates. None of them had ever been able to hold his attention for long or understood his work ethic and ambition to be successful. How could they? Had they been raised on the streets? Left in a shelter by their crack-addict mother to fend for themselves?

Damian recalled his endless foster homes. None of the adults in them wanted an older kid with social and emotional issues. He'd always been a loner and more comfortable with his own company than other people's. That same quiet fortitude had allowed him to excel in high school and then in college because he focused more on his studies rather than going out to parties, getting drunk, or bedding women. Those things were all a distraction from his true agenda.

To be rich.

To be successful.

To never go without again.

It's why Damian knew he couldn't get too close to Jada Hart. She was a woman who'd never gone without. She'd been raised on a sprawling ranch in Dallas. Her father, Duke Hart, owned an oil company and her aunt and uncle Madelyn and Isaac Hart owned a high-end dude ranch, Golden Oaks, in Tucson. She had famous cousins-in-law like singer Chynna Hart and Oscar-winning actress Kenya Kingston. Jada wouldn't know the first thing about being poor, about failing, about going without. She'd had her every need in life catered to.

But it was impossible to ignore that when Jada was on screen, she shined. She was showing him what deep down he'd always known since he'd seen her picture and watched her videos amongst the other employee files.

She had star power—that certain something you couldn't name. You either have it, or you don't.

And Jada definitely had *it*.

Telling Andrew to give her an opportunity once a week to shine was only holding back the flame, but it wouldn't snuff it. Jada Hart was destined for great things. She would certainly be the next Kelly Ripa, and he damn well knew it. Now, if only she believed in herself as much. He'd seen self-doubt hiding behind the outward charm she projected to the rest of the world. He saw right through it. Through her.

Perhaps that's why he was so unsettled—because he didn't want to see it.

~

"WHEN ARE you coming home for a visit?" Jada's mother, Abigail, asked. Jada had just returned from Sunday brunch with Kyler and was looking forward to a quiet evening home before the workweek.

"For Bree's baby shower," Jada responded. "As baby girl Wells's auntie, I'm in charge and I'm planning something grand."

"How can you plan anything from San Francisco?"

"That's what party planners are for," Jada said evenly. "I tell them what my vision and color scheme is, and they set about creating it."

"Seems rather impersonal if you ask me. Bree's your big sister. I'd think you'd want to oversee things personally, and maybe even visit your mama. I miss my baby girl."

"Oh, Mama," Jada sighed. "I'm sorry I haven't been back in a while." She didn't realize Abigail was feeling neglected. She'd thought that since she and Duke had begun seeing each other again, her loneliness would have lessened. Her parents believed they were being coy, but Bree and Jada had suspected something was up back during Bree and Grayson's wedding. Their parents had been as thick and thieves, and it was just a matter of time before they were back together for good.

Jada couldn't wait for that day.

They should have never broken up to begin with, but her father, Duke, had been a rascal during the early days of their marriage despite how much he loved Abigail. He'd been weak one night, had too much to drink, and ended up impregnating her half-brother Trent's mother. After Abigail found out, she ended the marriage. Infidelity was a deal breaker. At the time, she'd been so young, Jada had been devastated by her parents' breakup. But now that she was older, she understood because she too would never let a man dip out the door on her.

It was all or nothing.

"It's OK," her mother was saying. "Just promise me when you come, you'll stay for a spell so we can catch up. I have no idea what's going on with you."

"I can bring you up to speed now," Jada said. "You know I've been wanting a shot at the anchor chair—"

"Yes . . ."

"I got the chance, Mama. I've anchored at least three shows."

"And why is this the first I'm hearing about this?"

Jada had walked right into that. She apologized again. "I'm sorry. You're right again, Mama. I've been a bit self-absorbed. But I'm anchoring *Good Day, San Francisco* on Fridays. I will send you and Daddy the videos of all the segments."

"I'd like that very much. And, Jada?"

"Yes?"

"I don't want to be the last to know about what's going on in your life. Don't make me have to come all the way to San Francisco and give you a talking-to."

Jada smiled as she thought about what Abigail's talking-to consisted of: a stern conversation over tea and cucumber sandwiches. She wouldn't mind one of those. Maybe she should stay in trouble. "Yes, ma'am."

Several minutes later, Jada ended the call. Her mother had a point. She hadn't been back to Dallas in a few months. Quickly, she went online and booked a first-class flight home. It was time she checked out things on the home front to see how Deborah Kenney, her event planner, was coming with Bree's baby shower. Bree's daughter was due in three months. Jada couldn't wait to become an auntie and spoil her niece rotten.

Who knew if she'd ever have any children of her own? After her relationship with Joshua blew up in her face, her career had become her focus. She supposed if the right man came along she might be convinced to have a child, but that day was a long way away. In the meantime, she would prove to Damian that she was the next face of morning television.

"I WANT to go to the Black Lives Matter rally," Jada said several days later on Thursday during a meeting with the other news correspondents. They'd all huddled around the television monitors when news hit about an unplanned rally later that afternoon.

"You?" Andrew chuckled. "I know you're anchoring the Friday show and have done a few newsy segments, but you're basically an entertainment reporter, Jada. You don't do hard-hitting news."

"And I'll never do more if I'm not given the opportunity," Jada responded.

"The street beat is mine," said reporter Nolan Reinhardt.

"Yes, it is," Jada replied. "And no offense, but do you honestly think you can get people to talk better than me?"

"Are you playing the race card?" Nolan asked. "Because if so, I would say it's beneath you."

"Now, now." Andrew jumped into the melee. "No need to get personal."

"This issue is real, current, and happening in our community," Jada said. "And we have to report it. We'll never win an award for standing on the sidelines."

"Is that all you care about?" said Nolan. "Fame and glory? Because if so, you're in the wrong business, and you might be better suited for one of those entertainment news shows."

Jada smarted in her suit. She was about to give him a piece of her mind when a deep masculine voice interrupted the conversation. "I agree with Ms. Hart. Black Lives Matter is relevant and is in the current news cycle. We can't act as if it doesn't exist. Having

Ms. Hart reporting from the rally isn't a bad idea. More supporters might be willing to speak with her."

"Because she's a pretty face?" Nolan surmised.

Jada blanched.

"No, because she isn't threatening," Damian said curtly.

Jada rose to her feet.

"Where are you going?" Damian asked.

Jada wanted to wipe the smug look off all of their faces. Damian was probably waiting for her to blow her top so he could give this story to someone else—to a serious journalist and someone far-less threatening. She bit the inside of her lip to refrain from speaking. "I'm leaving. We've talked about this *ad nauseam.* I'm getting out there."

"Someone's getting a big head now that she has a seat in the anchor's chair one day a week," anchor Jay Blair said underneath his breath.

The glare Damian threw in Jay's direction made Jada smile. Jay could see he'd been heard and immediately lowered his head.

"Jada, go make us proud," Andrew commented.

"I will." She turned on her heel and walked out of the room with her head held high. She wasn't going to turn back and give Damian a moment's notice. Just because he'd backed her up on the story meant nothing. He still thought she was just a pretty face and not a journalist worth salt.

She would show him.

An hour later, she and a cameraman were out at the rally where hundreds of Black Lives Matter protesters had taken to the street to speak out against the death of a young black student gunned down by police officers. He'd had a telephone in his pocket. The rally's leader today, a dynamic young woman from Los

Angeles, had flown up to San Francisco to talk about the injustice.

Surprisingly, Jada had even gotten a sound bite from her, which she knew would go a long way in showing Damian, Nolan, and anyone else who doubted her journalistic abilities, just how good she was. In the meantime, she weaved her way through the crowd to get small and wide shots as well as to interview several protestors. Their anger about the young man's senseless death was palpable. Jada found it hard to relate to because she'd lived in such a different world. But she was determined to show their experience, the injustice over what occurred, and what they hoped to change.

Jada completed her first live report from the scene of the rally. She was just finishing up her broadcast when several antiprotestors showed up and began yelling and screaming that "Police lives matter" to the Black Lives Matter group. The crowd began to get boisterous as both groups struggled to have their voices heard.

"We should get out of here," Tony, the cameraman, said.

"No." Jada shook her head and pointed at an antiprotestor who was getting in the face of a Black Lives Matter protestor. "Get that on film." When Tony did, Jada circled her index finger to indicate he should continue rolling tape—and she reported live from the scene. But the situation quickly spiraled and the next thing Jada knew, the entire crowd went crazy and she was being pushed and shoved. Eventually, she felt Tony's strong arm pulling her through the throng of people toward the camera van and hauling her inside it. Then he was pulling the van away from the curb.

"That was crazy," Jada said. Her heart was

pumping wildly as she glanced through the rearview mirror at the melee in back of her.

"You can't be doing that, Jada," Tony said. "You could have gotten hurt. Think of the liability to the station."

Jada shrugged. "C'mon, you have to admit that was great reporting back there!" She pointed to where they'd just left.

"Or damn stupid."

Andrew didn't share Tony's same opinion and congratulated Jada when they returned to the station. "Are you OK?" he asked. "That was a bold move out there."

"I know," Jada said with a huge grin. "It was awesome. I feel so energized."

"You should. You showed real promise out there, Hart," Andrew said. "And I have to admit that I underestimated your capabilities, but not anymore."

Jada beamed. "Thank you."

"I'd like you to edit the footage so we can rerun it on the six and ten o'clock news."

"Will do."

Jada forced herself not to let out a loud yelp of excitement because several eyes in the newsroom were watching her. She knew they all thought she'd had a lucky break today, but they were wrong. Now that Andrew had seen her potential, there was more where that came from.

~

Damian was livid as he drove back to the station. He'd been in a meeting during the four and five o'clock news hours and hadn't had the chance to see how Jada fared until the six o'clock broadcast. Jada had foolishly put herself in harm's way. *What the hell was she think-ing?* She should have gotten out of there as soon as the crowd changed, before things got out of control.

Sometimes, Damian didn't know if he wanted to strangle her or hug her tight.

He did know that he needed to see for himself that she was alright. He didn't know why, but he wouldn't be able to sleep if he didn't lay eyes on her.

With traffic, Damian arrived shortly after seven p.m. Most of the station had cleared out, but he noticed that Jada's car was still in the parking lot. *Good.* He could have a word with Ms. Hart. He jumped out of the car, sauntered into the building, and headed toward the newsroom, but Jada wasn't at her desk. His eyes scanned the room and caught sight of her leaning against the doorway talking with someone. He headed straight for her.

She looked up when she saw him approaching. "Mr. McKnight."

He frowned. She knew she was supposed to call him Damian, and given that they'd kissed and become quite familiar, he wouldn't think she had a problem with it. "May I speak with you?"

She stood upright. "Of course. Tony, I'll catch you later." She began walking toward the newsroom, but Damian grabbed her arm and pulled her into one of the breakout rooms for small meetings. She snatched her arm away, then folded both across her chest.

"What can I do for you, Mr. McKnight?" Her lips were pursed in the same way that always managed to rile him up, and Damian could feel the blood boiling in his veins. He inhaled deeply to calm himself. It's all he could do to avoid his instinct to pull her to him and bring his mouth down on hers, if for nothing else than to punish her for her insolence.

"I'm surprised you're still here. I would have thought you'd gone home to celebrate your achievement."

"And what achievement would that be?"

"Don't be coy, Jada. You know exactly what I'm talking about."

She burst out with an unabashed grin. "You mean that great piece of journalism I delivered for WLB-TV? Have you seen how much our segment has been retweeted, especially the sound bite I got from the speaker?"

"Yes, I've seen it."

"And?"

"And that was a stupid stunt you pulled out there today. Do you realize how dangerous that was?"

"I did what I had to do, what needed to be done."

Damian snorted. "C'mon, wasn't that stunt to prove to Nolan that you have *cojones* for serious reporting?

Jada's face flamed red, and Damian new he'd scored a hit in this neverending battle of wills between them. "N-no."

Damian moved closer toward her until he had Jada nearly backed up against the wall. "Don't give me that crap. You deliberately put yourself in harm's way to get a better story."

He noticed her breath hitched at his nearness. She was aware of him and was trying her best not to be. He watched her step sideways and out of his path.

"And it worked," she said. "You wanted hard-hitting stories, I gave it to you. What are you more upset about? That it came from me? I know you don't think I'm capable of more, just like everyone else." She turned her back on him as if she didn't want to look at him. It burned in his craw.

"That isn't true." He spun her around. "I'm about the only one who does believe in you. Or hadn't you noticed?"

"You have a funny way of showing it. You put me down in front of people in today's meeting and acted like I was nothing more than a pretty face. You embarrassed me."

"So they wouldn't know that I think you're the next big thing. So they wouldn't know just how damn much I want you."

Jada was stunned, wide-eyed.

"Nothing to say?" Damian asked. "I'm surprised. Usually, I can't shut you up."

"You, you—"

"You what? Don't believe me?" Damian's eyes penetrated hers, rooting her to where she stood. "Even you can't deny the chemistry between us." He stepped toward her once again. "That you don't feel it now." He took another step until they were a breath apart. "That you haven't thought about me, us, since that kiss in the hotel."

Jada turned her head away, refusing to look at him. Damian had his answer.

"Look at me," he ordered.

"Why?" She turned to glare at him. "You and I both know that it's pointless. You and me . . . it's too, too messy. Too complicated."

"Then we need to uncomplicate it. Come to dinner with me."

Jada shook her head furiously. "No. It's not a good idea."

"Yes, it is. I need to see. I need to be with you."

"Please don't say that." Jada tried to move away, but Damian grasped her hand. When she looked up at him with furtive lashes, desire coursed through his veins and he knew he would do anything to have her. Tonight.

"Yes," he said. "We're going to share a meal together and then ..." His voice trailed off.

Her almond eyes widened. "And then what?"

"I'll leave that up to you."

6

―――――

On the way to dinner, Jada sat beside Damian in his car with her heart in her throat. His declaration of just how much he wanted her had floored her. He'd thrown down the gauntlet, and Jada had to pick it up and accept it. She knew it wasn't the smartest or wisest move, but she couldn't deny that she was feeling the same emotions that were also swirling through Damian.

So, now she was throwing in the towel and giving in—to what, she wasn't sure. She would just have to see how the night progressed.

"Why are you so quiet?" Damian asked, taking a moment to glance at her.

"Am I?"

"Yes. Are you nervous about spending the evening with me?"

"I agreed to dinner. I never agreed to more."

Damian chuckled. "Sure, Jada. If that's what you need to believe, then so be it."

Jada wanted to comment on why he was trying to irk her, but she held off. It was time they put *this*—whatever it was—to bed. If going to dinner would accomplish that and get it out of their system, she would do it because the physical chemistry between them was dangerously strong and threatening to erupt at any minute.

They drove in silence, each deep in their own thoughts until Damian pulled up to Gary Danko's in Fisherman's Wharf. Jada loved the warm, enveloping atmosphere of the restaurant and the eclectic artwork lining the walls. Damian had good taste. She was exiting the vehicle on her own steam when he came around to close the door behind her.

"I didn't take you for a gentleman."

"That's because you don't know me," he whispered low and deep in her ear, "but tonight we're going to change that."

Jada hated that her stomach curled at the prospect of his words. He tucked her arm in the crook of his and led her into the restaurant. Since the restaurant took limited reservations, she was surprised when they were immediately seated at a table for two in the corner. "You must have some pull," Jada commented as the host placed a napkin in her lap.

Damian smiled. "Some."

While he ordered the wine, Jada allowed herself to truly look at him. With his dark good looks, smoldering eyes, tall stature, and excellent physique, Damian McKnight could easily be a model. Every woman in America would drool over him as Jada had since the day he'd walked into the conference room.

"Would you care for some wine?"

Jada blinked and realized the waiter was in front of her. "Yes, please."

Damian smiled from across the table as if he knew she'd been sizing him up. When the waiter had filled her wineglass and his, Damian held up his glass. "To a great night."

Jada held her glass up too and took a sip. Red wasn't her favorite wine, but she had to admit it was a delicious and robust vintage. She also noticed that Damian hadn't taken his eyes off hers *and* that his eyes had traveled to her lips. She squirmed. She didn't like his scrutiny even though she'd scrutinized him as well.

To throw him off, she said the first thing that came to her mind. "Why do you want me?"

He grinned and placed his glass on the table. "I would think that would be obvious. You're an incredibly beautiful woman."

"Whom you've clashed heads with since the moment we met."

"I'm sure you've heard that anger can, under certain circumstances, produce passion in its stead. You know the old adage that love is the opposite coin of hate."

"So, I'm an itch that needs scratching?"

"So to speak, but I would also like to know more about Jada, and not her representative."

"What the hell is that supposed to mean?"

"I mean I'd like to know the real you, not the one you portray to the world—the beautiful heiress with a penchant for flashy fashion."

Jada was appalled that he thought so little of her, thought her that superficial. "Is that really how you see me?"

"I did."

"*Did* as in past tense?"

Damian nodded. "The file on you was light with not much to go off of, and I made some assumptions which, thus far, you've proven wrong. You've shown more tenacity and spirit than I imagined a woman in your position would."

"Why does that sound like an affront coming from you?"

He stared at her from across the table with those deep, penetrating eyes. "I didn't mean it as one."

"Didn't you? That's the second time you've mentioned my position or heiress status. Do you have a problem that I'm rich, Damian? Because if so, I would say that's the pot calling the kettle black."

"*Touché*." He raised his wineglass and took a sip.

"But I'm right?" Jada pressed. She didn't understand why it was so important for her to know, but she wanted to know exactly what he thought of her. It would tell her whether this attraction between them would go beyond this dinner.

"I admit," he began, "that I had some preconceived notions about who you were and I was wrong. You're much more than a pretty face or a rich debutante. You've got heart and a lot more depth than I gave you credit for. You're extremely talented with a passion for your career, a talent which has been overlooked at the station for years. You're inquisitive. You're independent and charming. And the more I get to know you, the more I like you. Does that answer your question?"

Jada swallowed the lump in her throat. Damian had no problem being completely forthright. Could she be the same? "Yes, it does."

"I've surprised you, hmm?" He leaned forward and into her personal space. "Imagine my surprise to find that you both anger and enchant me, Jada." He reached across the table and tucked a strand of hair behind her ear.

"Stop saying things like that," Jada said as she looked downward. He was messing with her equilibrium, and she didn't like it. She was used to being in charge in her relationships, but Damian was changing all the rules.

"Why? Wasn't the purpose of this dinner to ease the tension between us? The *sexual* tension."

"Have you made your selections for dinner?" The waiter returned to their table to take their order, and Jada didn't have to answer Damian, at least not right away. She could compose herself and figure out what she was supposed to say and do next.

She opted for the scallops. Despite the fine dining establishment, Jada wasn't interested in eating much, not when there was a knot in her stomach the size of Mount Everest. Meanwhile, Damian went for the halibut. Once the waiter walked away, however, Damian returned his full attention to Jada.

~

DAMIAN WAS BEWILDERED. Outwardly, Jada portrayed herself as self-assured and queen of the jungle, but he could see now that it was all for show. There was a hidden vulnerability beneath her, and he was more intrigued that she appeared to be just as out of her depth in this scenario as was he. But that didn't stop him from pushing the envelope; he wanted, no, he needed her to come out of her shell. He needed to force her to confront this sizzle of passion between them that wasn't fading.

"Don't retreat from me, Jada. I want to know how you feel about me."

"I find you to be headstrong, arrogant, and bullish."

He rolled his eyes. "Ah, stop with the compliments."

Her face creased into a wide-open grin. She genuinely smiled for the first time since they'd sat down, and Damian sighed in relief. He was hoping she wouldn't be this defensive all night. "You're impossible, do you know that?"

"And yet that turns you on." It certainly did. He couldn't wait to strip her out of her black skirt and silk top and touch her. Each day, it had grown harder and harder to concentrate on work when her eyes would flare fire when she was fascinated by something or someone, like now. Her entire being came to life. It was something he wanted to capture, to taste.

Jada's face stilled and turned red. His directness embarrassed her.

"Do you always speak what's on your mind?"

"I do. And so do you, Jada." When she began to speak, he interrupted her. "Don't even try it. You do the same when it suits you. I'm doing the same now."

"It suits you to disarm me?"

"If it means you'll be real with me, then yes."

"Alright. Despite how insufferable I find you can be at times, I have found you to be fair, open to new ideas, and a man of integrity."

"Wow. Did that hurt you to give me a compliment?"

Jada held up her thumb and index finger. "Just a little."

He let out a loud belly laugh. "I think this evening is going to turn out to be more than either of us bargained for."

THERE'S NEVER BEEN *a truer statement*, Jada thought a few hours later after she and Damian had shared a delicious dinner and intriguing conversation. It had been a bit stilted between them initially, but once Jada got over her anxiety, she found Damian was good company and an excellent conversationalist.

Although he hadn't talked about his childhood or family, Damian had revealed his wide range of hobbies, from music and art to sports. He'd amused her when he offered to take her to a game and at his frown, she'd realized he was serious. He wanted to spend more time with her outside of tonight.

But do I want to spend more time with him?

She was asking herself that very question on the drive back to the station to pick up her car. It was nearly midnight, and the parking lot would be empty until the early shift came on at three a.m.

"We're here," Damian said as he pulled up beside her car.

"Thanks for a fun night." Jada turned toward him. "I had a good time."

"But?"

"I should go inside. I left a file that I need."

"Why are you running away, Jada? I didn't take you for a coward."

Her brown eyes flashed fire. "I'm not a coward. If you thought the evening was going to end with you taking me to bed, that's not my problem." She opened the door, hopped out, and began stalking toward the station door. She swiped her card and was entering when Damian's footsteps suddenly echoed behind her. She walked more quickly into the newsroom. It was empty with only the television screens in the background illuminating the room.

"Jada." She heard his deep voice behind her and spun around. He was several feet away, but it wasn't lost on Jada that they were alone.

"Why are you following me? Can't you take a hint?"

"I could if you weren't sending mixed messages," Damian said from where he was standing. "One minute, you're happy and relaxed at dinner with me. The next minute, you're coiled up as tight as a spring, jumping out of the car and running away from me. Which is it, Jada? Do you or do you not want this?"

Jada bit her lip and looked away. His sexual magnetism made him supremely desirable, but she was afraid of what might happen if she allowed herself to *go there.*

"What are you so afraid of?" Damian marched toward her. All the while, his steady gaze traveled over her face and searched her eyes for a sign. Jada felt a tingling in her stomach, and her heart jolted. He was disturbing to her on every level, and she knew she should take a step back.

But she didn't.

When Damian stood in front of her, he slowly and seductively stroked her cheek. "Jada, sweet Jada."

He said her name in a soothing *and* smoldering manner.

"Damian."

"Yes, baby?" His words were husky with desire.

Hot needles of excitement prickled Jada's flesh as she could no longer deny what was inevitable between them. She glanced up at him between lowered lashes. "Take me."

~

BLOOD ROARED in Damian's ears. Had he heard her right? "What did you say?" He needed her to repeat herself so that there would be no misunderstanding afterward. It would be very difficult to stop once they were in the throes of passion, though he would if that's what she asked him to do.

She smiled. "You heard me. I want you. So take me."

Damian grabbed Jada by the waist, and she slammed against him. He exulted in feeling her breasts squashed against his chest. Then he crushed her mouth beneath his. The kiss was fast and potent, sending pure fire directly to the pit of his stomach. When Jada wound her arms around his neck, Damian felt as if they were meant to be there. He tilted her back, and she made an inarticulate sound as he leaned in for a deeper, more fervent kiss.

Her mouth met his with equal ferocity, and in Damian's mind, the world ceased to exist. He just knew he had to have this woman. Tonight. Right now. He maneuvered her backward into a nearby office and closed the door. He surmised they were still alone, but he didn't want an audience when he finally was able to do the things he wanted to do to her.

His hands dug into her hair as he kissed her gently, seducing her mouth with slow, practiced kisses. Her entire body quivered underneath his as she rubbed herself against him. He loved the friction of her softness yielding to his hardness, the way her hands caressed the back of his neck, roving to his broad shoulders and downward to cup his buttocks and bind him to her. It caused something primitive and elemental to come over Damian because hadn't the seeds been sown between them since day one? Now it was time to reap the reward. He pushed her backward against the wall, driven by the need to explore this explosive physical attraction that he'd never experienced with another woman. He fumbled with the buttons on her silk shirt and cursed when he couldn't get the damn things loose.

She merely laughed and unbuttoned them herself, opening herself up to his admiring gaze. He'd suspected she had beautiful breasts. He was right. They were perfect twins and more than a handful. He pushed the fabric of her satin bra upward and lowered his head to take a nipple between his teeth. He heard her gasp. He liked the sound and that she was so sensitive. The next time, he put his mouth on her entire breast. He drew it in, rolling his tongue around her nipple before treating the other breast with equal attention.

"Yes, Damian," she moaned. "Yes."

He liked his name on her lips and planned to give her even more, but the little minx must have felt equally as needy because her hands were taking off his jacket while their lips never parted. His jacket, followed by his tie, fell to the floor. Then her greedy hands were on his shirt, tearing at the buttons causing them to fly in every direction. But Damian didn't care. He just luxuriated when her head lowered to flick her hot tongue across his nipple.

Sweet Jesus!

He reached for the zipper on her skirt that allowed him to glide it upward from her legs. The time was here and now for him and this woman to finally become one, but first, it was time for a long overdue feast. Slowly, he slid down her body and onto his knees.

DAMIAN'S FINGERTIPS slid upward to the cradle of Jada's thighs. She felt him kiss the hollows behind her knees and the back of her calves. She closed her eyes, waiting with tremulous suspense for the quivery sensations when he stroked her *there*, the place that ached for him.

"I need to touch you." Damian glanced up at Jada, and her breath caught in her throat at the lust in his eyes. His thumbs reached up and hooked into the waistband of her bikini panty. He drew it down ever so slowly until the scrap of fabric was at her ankle. "Step out of it."

She did as instructed and watched with amazement when Damian scrunched the panty and put it in the pocket of his suit jacket. "Spread your legs," he ordered. "I'm going to make you come."

Jada had no choice but to do as she was told—he'd reduced her to a quivering mass. One moment she'd been running away from him, and the next minute he had her up against the wall in the office, kissing her breathless. Every cell in her body responded and rejoiced to the rightness of this man in this moment. She wanted to be taken, possessed by him and vice versa.

Her blood was racing at the exhilaration of the pleasure he was about to give her. But the first touch of his tongue at her core was so profound, Jada damn near slid down the wall; but Damian held her up by gripping her waist. His thumbs held her open so he could blow, lick, and suck on her clitoris. She shuddered under the assault, and her senses became completely alive as need spun through her like a whirlpool. There wasn't a bit of her he wasn't encompassing with the skilled accuracy of his mouth and tongue. He clearly knew his way around a woman's body and how to give her the most pleasure.

"Oh yes." Jada let out a loud moan, trying to quiet

herself, but that only egged Damian on. He began tonguing her feverishly, thrusting in and out of her soaking core. Her sighs of pleasure became quicker, higher, and louder until soon she was in the grip of a mind-numbing orgasm. She cried out her release, and Damian lapped her up like she was the most delicious ice cream cone he'd ever licked.

Only when the spasms had lessened did he rise to his feet and begin unzipping himself, pulling his trousers down and freeing his bulging erection to life. He was incredibly beautiful. Jada went to reach him and take him in her mouth, but he pushed her hand away.

"Another time. I need to be inside you." She watched as he took a foil packet from his pocket and glided it on his burgeoning member.

And she needed that too. Although she'd loved the orgasm, she wanted to feel him and experience climaxing with him *together*. Arcing, she hooked her leg around his hip, opening for him and Damian answered. He positioned himself between her legs. She was so wet and ready for him that with one powerful thrust, Damian surged deep inside her. Jada gripped his shoulders as her body accommodated his size and the sensation of him filling her so completely. Then slowly, ever so slowly, he began moving inside her.

Jada was overwhelmed by the feeling of completion. "Damian."

And when he slid his hand under her butt and drew her closer, heat rushed through her, sending sparks through her core. "Omigod!"

The pleasure was so intense, especially when Damian increased the rhythm and began driving into her with wild abandon. He was hot and primal and out of control. Damian was riding her hard, his eyes locked with hers, drawing her to the edge. Jada tried to keep up, moving her hips, but her head fell backward, and Damian thrust into her while his mouth devoured hers in a hungry kiss. Soon, a violent climax took over her and all Jada could do was shudder and cling to Damian's slick shoulders, shattered by his fierce possession. Seconds later, sensations rocked her again as his orgasm rammed through him, hurtling him over the edge with her.

When Damian finally lifted his head to look at her, Jada's heart was pounding fiercely and her breathing was rapid and uneven. "Jada?" His voice was a husky whisper even though his hands were still clenched in her hair. "You OK?"

"I should be asking you that." He'd held them in position by his sheer strength until he'd driven them both to the peak. And he was still holding her.

"I liked holding you, but perhaps we should clean up."

Jada nodded as he loosened his grip, allowing her to slide down him. She hated that she hadn't been able to adorn his muscular body with kisses, feel his stomach contract as he'd made hers do, but there was no time. The need to mate with him had been so strong, almost elemental, as if she'd die if she didn't have him. Now that it was over, Jada felt like she was standing on unstable ground.

She moved away, keeping her back to him, and zipped up her skirt and buttoned her blouse. She glanced around for her underwear and flushed when she caught Damian watching her. Then he patted his suit jacket.

"I need those."

"Not tonight," Damian said with a smirk. He was already dressed and looking as flagrantly male as ever, especially with his shirt open due to the buttons she'd ripped off it in her eagerness to be with him.

Does he expect me to walk out of here without any panties on? Although there was something deliciously wicked about being naked underneath her skirt, Jada needed time to process what had just happened between them. She'd been with other men, but what she'd just shared with Damian had been more powerful than anything she had ever experienced.

It scared her.

"Come home with me tonight so I can make love to you properly." He walked toward her.

Jada took a step away from him and shook her head. "No, I can't. I, I have an early morning tomorrow, remember?"

Damian frowned. His dark eyes were like black coal and glowed fire at her. "Don't do this, Jada. You've been of two minds tonight. One minute, you're agreeing to dinner and what's on the table, and the next, you're running. But even you can't deny that what just happened between us was pretty damn spectacular."

"I—"

"There's nothing wrong with doing what pleases us, what comes naturally. Let's take what we want. And I want the rest of the night with you."

"And what then?"

"Excuse me?"

"You're my boss, Damian. Even you know that what we . . . what we're doing"—she pointed back and forth between them as her voice hitched—"what we did is dangerous and complicates everything. And I just need some time to think."

"Thinking is overrated," Damian said tightly. "I'd rather act."

"That's what got us into this situation to begin with —being impulsive." Jada walked backward toward the door. "And I really have to go."

Quickly, she dashed out of the room before she could change her mind.

That's what...into the situation to began with.

...being impulsive. Jada...also I had wanted to see his door. And I really have to...

Quickly, she dashed out of that room before she could change her mind.

7

Jada dragged in long deep breaths when she entered her vehicle. She would love nothing better than to close her eyes, lean back against the headrest, and replay the last hour, but she couldn't stay here. She glanced behind her to see if Damian had followed her out. He wasn't there. She was sure she'd wounded his ego by not agreeing to go home with him. But she was out of her element. He threw her off balance in their normal interactions, but tonight everything had changed because they'd had the hottest sex she'd ever experienced in her life.

Slowly, Jada turned on the ignition and pulled out of the parking lot. She had to leave before Damian convinced her to come home with him, but not before she pulled out her phone. The screen was dark. Her phone was dead. She plugged it in the dash and waited for it to charge.

Several moments later, the screen popped on and within seconds, her phone began beeping as text messages and voicemails appeared on her screen.

It showed multiple calls from Bree, one from Grayson, and another from her mother. Jada pressed play and listened to the most recent message.

"Jada, it's Mom. Call me immediately when you get this message. It's Bree. She's gone to the hospital with labor pains."

"Omigod!" Jada's hand flew to her mouth. *No, no, no.* It was too early. Her baby niece wasn't due to arrive for another three months. Bree must be scared out of her mind. Jada wasted no time calling her sister, but the call went straight to voicemail, so she tried Grayson. He picked up.

"Jada?"

"How is she, Grayson? How's Bree and the baby?"

"It's too soon to tell," Grayson said hoarsely. "We've been at the hospital a few hours, and they've given Bree some medication to stop the contractions. But, but . . ." His voice cracked, and Jada could hear the tension in it. "We just don't know."

"I'm sorry that I didn't get the calls, but I'll be there as soon as I can get a flight."

"Duke has already sent the Hart jet for you. It should have arrived or be there soon."

"OK. I'll call Daddy and get all the details. And, Grayson?"

"Yes?"

"Tell Bree I love her and I'll be there as soon as I can."

"Thank you, Jada. She needs you. She needs all of us. Please keep her and the baby in your prayers."

"I will." Jada ended the call and prayed for green lights. She had to get home to Dallas as soon as she could. A wave of guilt washed over her. If she hadn't been so involved with Damian tonight, she would have been home and received the call informing her that Bree needed her.

Jada had never been happier that the Hart family had more resources than the average person. As soon as she'd hung up with Grayson, she called Duke. He was heartsick over Bree's condition, but thrilled his baby girl, Jada, was coming home. The Hart jet had already flown to San Francisco that evening and was waiting for her arrival. Jada didn't bother packing a suitcase; she had clothes in Dallas. She just went home to pick up a few necessities, which she threw into her Louis Vuitton Keepall. When she made it to the private airfield, it was about three a.m., but the Hart jet was fueled and waiting to fly her to Dallas.

The three-and-a-half-hour flight home was interminable. Jada checked in with Grayson twice on the plane's phone only to be told that Bree's condition hadn't changed. Jada blamed herself for not being available during her sister's time of need. She and Bree had always been thick as thieves from the moment Jada had come out of the womb. She'd never for a second felt jealousy from Bree over being the youngest and spoiled.

In fact, at times, Jada had often felt envious of Bree and Duke's relationship. Bree was Duke's favorite. She was more like him than either Jada or her older sister, London. Duke and Bree's fiery temperaments often meant they butted heads, but there was always love there and always would be. Meanwhile, Jada had enjoyed a similar relationship with her mother. There wasn't anything Jada couldn't confide in her. Until now.

Jada wasn't sure how her mother would feel about her getting involved with her boss. Heck, she wasn't even sure how *she* felt. All Jada knew was that this time apart, away from Damian's circle of influence, would do her good. She wouldn't run into him day in and day out or see his surreptitious glances in her direction and the enigmatic stares he bestowed when he thought she wasn't looking.

She'd seen them because she too hadn't been able to stop staring at Damian McKnight from the moment he'd bought the station. Nothing she'd said or done had seemed to change what must have been destined to happen.

They would become lovers—though Jada wasn't sure she would necessarily call what they'd done against the wall of the studio lovemaking. No, she called that hot, unadulterated, sinful S-E-X. Since she had nothing but time on her hands on the flight, she replayed the images of the two of them together, clutched tight, as her legs had twined around his waist and he'd plunged deep inside her. The place between her thighs still pulsed, attesting to the fact that he'd branded her. Made her his.

There hadn't been any soft kisses.

Just heat.

And passion.

She wished she could take it for what it was—sex of the purest kind—and make no apologies for taking what she wanted. It was just . . . Jada didn't know where they could go from here. Damian had indicated he wanted to take her back home to his place and make love to her properly, but Jada feared what might have happened had he gotten the opportunity.

Jada didn't get easily attached to any man because she usually found them all interchangeable. But Damian had a way of pushing all her buttons to make her react. Anyone could have come back to the studio and seen them up against the wall going buck wild!

She would have lost all her credibility. She'd made the right decision to take a step back and think things through. Jada had a lot more to lose than Damian. He owned the station. There was no blowback for a man in his position. He'd get an attaboy from most of the men there for having conquered what none of them could. Several of her colleagues had tried to put the moves on her and been promptly dismissed. Meanwhile, Jada's reputation would be trashed. They would say she was sleeping her way to the top.

Jada refused to be a laughingstock. She hadn't left her family, friends, and home in Dallas to be the butt of anyone's joke. Ending their one-night encounter before it really began was best for all parties, especially Jada.

The plane touched down, and Jada peered out the window and saw her cousin Caleb standing beside his truck.

Seconds later, the pilot opened the cockpit and walked out to the passenger seats to greet her. "Ms. Hart, welcome back home."

"Thank you. It's good to be back."

While he lowered the stairs, Jada grabbed her Pochette Metis and Keepall and followed him outside. The pilot helped her down the steps, where Caleb waited for her. Her cousin was over six foot tall and all brawn. His years of riding bulls had kept him fit, but he still looked the same with a bald head and a touch of mustache and goatee.

"Jada." He smiled when he saw her and pulled her into his embrace. "How are you, cuz?"

Jada leaned backward to glance up at him. "I'd be better if I knew how Bree was."

"She's hanging in there." Caleb took her bags and threw them in the cabin of the truck. "She's a tough cookie, and she's fighting as hard as she can to keep your niece in her belly."

Tears sprung to Jada's eyes. "I know that. It's just too, too soon."

"Aww, come here." Caleb roughly hauled her to him and enveloped her in a bear hug. "It's going to be OK. We just have to believe that."

Jada nodded and sniffed. Caleb moved away to open the passenger door of the truck. She hopped inside and seconds later, he was in the driver's seat and pulling away from the airfield.

"Duke wanted to get you himself, but I knew he didn't want to leave Bree at the hospital. So, I offered to get you."

"I understand. He's right where he needs to be at Bree's side. And it's where I'll be too."

Caleb snorted. "If you can pry Grayson away. The man is a wreck. He's usually so solid, ya know? But to see his wife, the love of his life, fighting to save their daughter—well, needless to say, he's beside himself. And I know how he feels. If anything were to happen to Addison, Ivy, and Ethan, I'd lose my mind."

Thinking of Caleb's beautiful children made Jada smile. "How are my adorable little munchkins?"

"Getting bigger every day," Caleb said as he guided the truck along the freeway and toward the hospital.

"I can't wait to see them." It seemed like just yesterday Addison had given birth.

"Time flies," Caleb said. "Before you know it, you're looking at life through the rearview mirror."

"That's why you have to live every day like it's your last."

"Is that why you can't settle down, li'l cuz?" Caleb said as he glanced at her. "You know you're not getting any younger."

"What are you trying to say, Caleb—that I'm getting old?"

"No, but I know when someone's got that wander-lust, and you have it. Same as me. I was never able to really commit to any one person or thing."

Jada frowned. "That's not true. I've committed to my career."

"Your career won't keep you warm at night, or help you when you're sick, or listen when you've had a bad day. And I understand Joshua did a number on you, but eventually you've got to get back in the saddle."

"It's hard to believe how far you've come," Jada said. "To think you were once a ladies' man and the hottest bull rider this side of Texas."

Caleb chuckled. "I don't know about all that, but I was successful. And I'd give it all up in a heartbeat for Addison and my family."

"You're a changed man, Caleb Hart."

"Yeah, well, when you meet the right person—the person who makes your heart go pitter-pat, the one you can't stop thinking about and who sets your soul on fire, you'll know what I'm talking about. Trust me."

FRIDAY MORNING, Damian tossed the newspaper on the table and stood up from his chair. He walked over to the balcony and stared out over the bay. He was still in disbelief over the events of last night and the evening's abrupt end. How could Jada have left the studio after what they'd shared? How could she have walked away so easily?

Damian was surprised by his own questions. Typically, after one night with a woman, he would begin looking for greener pastures. But last night with Jada had only whetted his tongue. He wanted more. He wanted Jada.

He would not be denied.

He showered and dressed for the office. Jada wouldn't be able to ignore him at the studio.

A few hours later, he found out he was wrong.

"What do you mean *she's gone*?" Damian asked as he glared at the beleaguered station manager. He wasn't upset with him per se. He was upset with the situation. He'd been intent on calling Jada into his office so they could talk, so when he heard she'd flown the coop, he was not pleased.

Damian saw red. He didn't like his plans being thwarted.

"I'm sorry, Damian, but Jada left word this morning that a family emergency arose and she had to leave town immediately," Andrew said. "It sounded like life and death. I'd never heard her sound so distraught, so frantic."

Damian's brows drew together as he pondered Andrew's report. Jada's official employee profile had put Damian under the impression that her parents were in excellent physical condition. "Did she say who it was?"

Andrew shook his head. "No, the call didn't last that long, but I could tell she was on the up and up."

Damian nodded. "Of course. Do you know if she was going home to Dallas? Perhaps we could send flowers."

"Most likely. I know she's from there, but she didn't say."

"You're a good man, Andrew, and I'm sorry for raising my voice."

"No worries. She's your new protégé, and I know how important she is to you." He spun around and walked away.

How important she is to me?

Damian turned and circled the room. *Is that what everyone thinks—that Jada's my protégé?* He thought his interest in her success had been backed up with clear proof of her charm and poise on camera. Had they seen more? Did they realize just how far his feelings for this woman went?

Do I?

JADA WALKED QUIETLY DOWN the hall of the maternity ward. She didn't want to wake any mothers or babies with the click of her stiletto heels. Grayson had just come to get her from the waiting room, where she'd been huddled with her parents hoping she'd get word that she could visit her big sister. Waiting through the morning hours for any change in Bree's condition was nerve racking. Medical staff had restricted visits so only Grayson was allowed into her room.

Since her arrival, she'd learned more. The pregnancy had brought on high blood pressure for Bree, something called preeclampsia. Jada hadn't understood how this was possible because Bree was the picture of health and hardly ever gained weight. They'd both been blessed with excellent metabolisms like their mother, who was petite. Grayson had explained that diet wasn't the only factor, and that genetics and her autoimmune system played a role too.

In the afternoon, when medical staff finally approved a visit, Jada took a deep breath then pushed the door open. Bree was sitting on the bed, looking fragile and weak. Her normally bouncy curls hung like limp rags around a pale face. Instantly, tears filled Jada's eyes, but she willed them back. Bree needed her to be strong.

"Jada." Bree smiled and stretched out her arms. As soon as Jada made it to the bed, Bree hugged her in spite of her expanded belly. Jada realized it should be the other way around, but she accepted the show of affection nonetheless.

"I'm so sorry that I wasn't here and didn't come sooner, Bree."

"It's OK." Bree pulled back and pushed her hair aside to look at Jada. "You came when you could. That's all that matters."

"How are you and the baby?"

Bree tried to smile, but it didn't quite meet her eyes. "We're hanging in there, Jada. I'm doing my best to keep this little girl inside me, but she seems determined to come out."

Jada reached for Bree's hand and squeezed it. "You can do this, Bree. I know you can."

A tear trickled down her sister's cheek. "I don't know, Jada. If the contractions don't stop . . ."

Jada leaned over and hugged Bree. "I've got you, sweetie. I've got you."

"I want our little girl to have a fighting chance, and every hour she stays in the cocoon of my womb gives her that chance."

"Is that what the doctor said?"

Bree nodded. "I'm twenty-four weeks. The highest chance of survival is twenty-eight weeks, though he did say he's seen babies survive as early as twenty weeks, but they have health complications." Bree's hand flew to her mouth. "I, I don't want that for my little girl. I want her to be healthy." She rubbed her stomach. "I just don't know what else to do."

"Please be calm, Bree. Worrying won't help. You have to focus on the positive and that the baby will pull through this."

"Thank you, Jada. I'm so glad you're here. I need my sister."

"Well, you have another," a familiar female voice said from behind them. Jada leapt up and was thrilled to see London standing in the doorway. London rushed over and gave Jada a firm yet gentle squeeze before setting her aside and moving quickly to Bree.

"How's my baby sis?" London sat down on the bed and wrapped Bree up in her one of her signature hugs.

At five foot nine, London was taller than Jada, who needed the assistance of four-inch heels to achieve her height. London was beautiful and full-figured and had the confidence to go along with it. She was killing it in her hip-hugging jeans and wrap top.

"I would be a lot better if being in the hospital wasn't the catalyst for bringing us together," Bree said as she glanced at London then at Jada. Their relationship hadn't always been close. London had been raised by her biological grandparents in New Orleans, so they didn't have the same bond until a few years ago when all three sisters had made a determined effort to do better. And they had. They were closer than ever.

"Well, we're here now," London countered, "and that's all that matters."

Jada felt powerless to help in this moment, but she forced herself to remain hopeful. She walked toward the group. "London's right. Family sticks together, and we wouldn't want to be anywhere else."

She and London remained in Bree's room for nearly an hour until Grayson returned and kicked them out to spend time alone with his wife. In the corridor, Jada sighed and leaned against the wall.

"Didn't realize how hard that was going to be, did

you?" London asked. She had picked up on Jada's distress.

"I, I've never seen Bree like that." She glanced at the closed door. "She's always so invincible. And now—"

"You realize she's human like the rest of us?" London said with a lopsided grin.

"Yes, I guess I have."

London touched her shoulder. "Whatever happens, we will get Bree, Grayson, and our niece through it. We're Harts, right?"

Jada nodded.

"We're strong. We're fighters. We never give up. Remember that."

Jada knew London was right. She just supposed the saying that goes something like "It always seems darkest before the dawn" was true. Or was it, "It's hard to see the forest for the trees"?

"Your sister is giving sound advice, Jada," a deep masculine voice said from several feet away. "You should take it."

Jada's heart jumped. That voice didn't belong here, in *Texas*. It belonged in San Francisco, in another time and place that was far removed from her family and Bree's plight. But she would know it anywhere because last night that voice had whispered wicked things to her as its owner made her come against the wall at the television station.

That voice.

Belonged to Damian.

8

Damian hadn't meant to intrude on a family moment. When he'd exited the elevator, he spotted the Hart family huddled together. He had only given them a cursory glance, recognizing Duke and Caleb because they were the most well-known Harts. Once he realized Jada wasn't with them, he'd gone off to search for her.

Chasing after a woman was utterly ridiculous, but as soon as the Harts' housekeeper, Miriam, had told him Jada's sister Bree was in the hospital, he felt he had to come. He had called the Hart residence in his search for Jada. He couldn't explain why, but deep down something had told him she might need him. So, he had canceled some appointments to free up his calendar, called the pilot to fuel his private plane, and had flown straight to Dallas.

He wondered if he'd gotten it wrong because Jada was staring at him as if she couldn't quite believe he was standing there. Then she charged toward him . . . and flung herself at him.

Damian caught Jada in his arms, enveloped her in his embrace, and rested his head against hers. He could feel her entire body shaking. "It's alright, Jada," he whispered. "I'm here."

She didn't speak. He just heard her quietly sobbing into his jacket.

"I'll give you both some privacy," said the other woman who was standing beside Jada. Damian acknowledged her with a nod and heard her retreating footsteps.

After several minutes passed, Jada pulled away and wiped at her nose with the sleeve of her shirt. "I'm, I'm sorry. I, I don't know what came over me."

"It's alright." He wiped her tears away with his thumbs. "You've had an eventful night. I would expect nothing less."

She glanced up at him with a wry smile. "For me to cry into your Amani sweater? I doubt that very much."

"I don't care about the clothes, Jada. I care about you."

"Is that why you're here?" She frowned as if the thought had just occurred to her. "Why *are* you here?"

Damian could ask himself that same question. He'd come on instinct and because he couldn't deny that, in some way, he cared for Jada. "I, I—," he started, but was interrupted.

"Jada?"

Duke Hart stood behind his daughter with a scowl. Damian didn't particularly relish meeting Jada's father under these circumstances—hell, under in any circumstance. He'd never been with a woman long enough to meet her family. He was definitely in foreign territory.

"Yes, Daddy?"

"Would you care to introduce me to your *friend*?"

Duke's tone wasn't lost on Damian. And his stone-cold face showed he didn't appreciate having an outsider disturb their family at a time like this. At six foot five, Duke was an enormous man with a football player's build. He could easily tackle Damian if he chose to.

Damian watched Jada walk over to her father and slide her arm through his. She glanced up at her dad with a genuine smile—a smile he wished she'd bestow on him. "Daddy, I'd like you to meet Damian McKnight. Damian, this is my father, Duke Hart."

Duke stared at him for several seconds as recognition dawned. "Are you the same Damian McKnight that *Black Enterprise* magazine is hailing as the next coming in the communications world?"

Damian shrugged. "I don't know about all that."

"Don't be modest. You have quite the reputation for a man so young."

"Thank you, sir."

Duke offered his hand. "Great to meet you, Damian. You don't mind if I call you Damian, do you, especially if you're dating my daughter?"

Damian stared at Jada. Had she told her father about him? He wouldn't have thought so. And he'd be right because her face was flushing with embarrassment.

"Aww, don't go looking at her," Duke said, humor in his voice. "I have eyes, and as I walked up, I saw the two of you cozied up awful close. It doesn't take a scientist to figure this out."

"I suppose not," Damian offered. "But it's a little early in the relationship."

"Yet, here you are."

Damian chuckled. He liked Duke. He was a man who spoke his mind. Damian could respect that. "Yes, I'm here because I felt like Jada might need me."

"She does." Duke stepped away from Jada, and she seemed surprised by the action. "Don't go holding on to your father when you've got a perfectly good man to hold on to. Go on."

Damian smiled as Jada stared at her father incredulously as he ushered her toward Damian. Reluctantly, she came back to stand at Damian's side.

Duke began to walk way, but then he stopped and turned back to look at them. "Don't think our conversation is over, Damian. When my daughter Bree is settled, you and I will have a talk man to man, *capiche*?"

"Yes, sir."

Once he walked away, Jada rounded on Damian. "What the hell was that? Daddy just handed me off to you like it was nothing, when he's meeting you in a hospital, of all places."

Damian shrugged. "Perhaps he realizes you're in good hands."

"Am I? Because what I said back in San Francisco still remains true, Damian. Nothing has changed."

Damian frowned. "Everything has changed, Jada, and you damn well know it."

Jada glared at him but then lowered her voice. "Now is not the time or place to discuss this."

"I know that," Damian hissed. "Which is why I wasn't going to get into it now."

"Then why are you here?"

"As I said before, I care about you, and when I heard about your sister, I was concerned and thought you might need a shoulder to lean on."

"And you hoped that would be you?" Jada folded her arms across her chest. "So what? So you can get me back into bed?"

"Don't do that, Jada," he warned. He didn't like the defensive posture she'd taken. "Don't try and rile me up to make me turn away from you when I know you want the opposite."

"You can't know that."

"I do," Damian contested hotly. "The way you flew into my arms when I got here told me all I need to know."

"Which is?"

"That you want—no—that you need me."

~

He was right.

She did want him.

Did need him.

But Jada refused to admit it. Because if she did, it would mean Damian meant more to her than she was telling herself, and she couldn't deal with her burgeoning feelings for this enigmatic man right now. Not when Bree needed all her strength, all her prayers.

Jada was relieved when Grayson walked out of her sister's room and interrupted her talk with Damian. She looked at her brother-in-law for any sign of hope, but his worried features held none. "No change?"

Grayson nodded. "You should go back to the ranch, Jada. Get some rest. You flew all the way here in the middle of the night and have been here for hours."

"I can't leave, Grayson. Not when Bree needs me. I would never forgive myself. So, if it's all the same to you, I'll stay, but I'll head back to the waiting area so you can spend time with Bree in peace."

Grayson gave a half smile. "Thank you, sis." He walked over and gave her a quick hug, which Jada returned as she patted his back.

When they pulled apart, Grayson glanced at Damian, so Jada felt compelled to make yet another introduction. The men shook hands all while assessing each other. Jada chuckled inwardly that the men in her family seemed keen on figuring Damian out.

"I'm heading back inside," Grayson said, keeping his comments to himself, "but I'll come out soon with an update." Seconds later, he was gone, and Jada and Damian were alone again.

"Let's go." Damian placed his hand on the small of Jada's back and led her down the corridor, but she stepped away from him to walk on her own. He wasn't happy about her recalcitrance, but he didn't say anything and she was thankful.

She didn't want him touching her. The chemistry between them was so palpable, she'd felt the zing of attraction just from his hands. And Jada felt guilty thinking about anything other than Bree and her niece.

When they arrived to the waiting area, several sets of eyes focused on them—her father's knowing ones as well as the rest of her family's curious stares. "Everyone, I'd like you to meet Damian McKnight." She motioned to the group. "Damian, this is my family, my mother, Abigail, my sister, London, my cousin Caleb, and his wife, Addison."

"Pleasure to meet you all." Damian nodded in their direction and followed Jada. Then he took a seat by her side across from London.

Jada hated that all her business was on display. Now, her entire family knew that she and Damian were an item when she herself hadn't figured out what was going on between them.

"Relax," Damian whispered in her ear.

He wanted her to relax? She had a hard enough time doing that in a normal environment. Add the pressure of her niece's potential arrival and her entire family staring at them—well, it was all just too much. Anxiety flowed through her veins, but there was nothing she could do to change the situation.

Jada rose from her seat. So did Damian. "I'm going to the chapel," she announced.

"I'll join you," Damian said before anyone else could.

Jada was irritated. She was hoping for some peace in the sanctuary of a safe place, but it appeared she wasn't going to get any. And she wasn't about to make a big deal of Damian joining her, especially when they had an audience. Instead, she left the waiting area and approached the nurses' station for directions. Once she knew where to go, she headed there with Damian at her side.

He was surprisingly quiet. When they found the chapel, he pushed open the double doors and Jada walked in. It was a small unadorned room with several church-style pews. A cross stood at the front surrounded by candles. Jada walked to it and took a candle from the box and lit one. Then she took her seat. Damian was quiet and just sat beside her. Jada bowed her head, closed her eyes, and said a silent prayer for Bree, praying that God would keep her niece safe in the womb for just a little while longer.

When she felt large hands encompassing and squeezing hers, tears welled in Jada's eyes. She blinked them back. Damian just squeezed her hand even harder as if he were trying to give her his strength in the face of trauma. In that moment, despite not knowing where their relationship stood, Jada accepted the comfort and compassion he was offering.

Jada didn't know how long they sat in the chapel, just that they did. Damian didn't attempt to strike up a conversation, and Jada was glad because she was too lost in her thoughts to notice. Eventually, she must have dozed off. When she awoke, she found herself sleeping on Damian's lap. When she glanced up, she could see he'd been doing the same because his eyes were drowsy.

"Hey," he said.

"Hi." Slowly, she levered herself up and scooted several inches away from him.

"You didn't have to do that. I kind of liked where you were."

Jada offered a small smile. "Thank you for being my pillow."

"My pleasure."

They stared at each other underneath their lashes, neither saying a word until the chapel doors opened and London walked in. "There you are. I was looking everywhere."

Jada was instantly on high alert. "Is everything OK?" Her heart thumped, and she could feel her pulse quicken as she searched London's face for a sign.

"Bree appears to be out of the woods. The medication they gave her has stopped the contractions, and she's resting comfortably. Everyone is going back to the ranch for some rest and a bite to eat. We thought you might like to join us—that is if you don't have other plans." London glanced in Damian's direction.

"Of course not," Jada said indignantly. "I came here for Bree."

London smiled. "Alright, well, we're heading back. Do you need a ride?"

"I've got her." Damian inserted himself into the conversation. "I'll drive Jada to the ranch."

Jada looked at Damian, but his expression was neutral.

"Alright, we'll see you there." London left the chapel.

"I could have driven back with my family," Jada said as she stood up.

Damian did the same. "I know that. But as I stated before, I'm here for you."

Jada tried not to melt at such a statement because she wasn't sure what Damian's intentions were, but she was too exhausted to argue. As she glanced down at her watch, she realized she'd been at the hospital for nearly twelve hours and could use a hot shower and a good meal, exactly in that order. "Alright, let's go."

9

D amian was happy Jada didn't argue with him since that appeared to be one of her favorite pastimes. He suspected that the stress and anxiety over worrying about Bree and the baby had made her a little more easygoing when it came to him. She didn't complain when they left the hospital and walked to the garage. She merely climbed into the passenger seat when he opened the door to his rented Range Rover, the only vehicle he could obtain on short notice, and placed her head against the headrest. Within minutes, she was knocked out while Damian navigated his way to her family's ranch. He had learned the address on the same call with the housekeeper, Miriam, when he found out Bree was in the hospital.

All Damian could do was think about Jada's virtues. She was easy to talk to when she wasn't infuriating him, a temptress who burned up when he touched her. Her uninhibited response to him and the way she came alive had him fired up on all cylinders. There was no way he was not going to have her again. But more importantly, she'd shown she was a woman who loved her family and would drop everything in a heartbeat to be there in a loved one's time of need.

He wanted to know more.

More of Jada.

He wasn't leaving Dallas until she gave in to him.

He enjoyed the drive to the ranch because it afforded views of the Texas countryside. The ranch sat on hundreds of acres that Duke Hart had held in his reins for decades. The house itself was a sprawling estate with four wings and an indoor solarium with a pool along with hundreds of acres of land. Damian didn't know how many bedrooms it held, but it looked massive. He wondered what it must have been like for Jada growing up here surrounded by all this luxury and beauty, but most importantly, with family.

When he pulled up, several vehicles were already parked outside. He reached across their seats to stroke Jada's cheek. She jumped and glanced around. Realizing where she was, she wasted no time climbing out of the Range Rover. Damian watched as she closed her eyes and breathed in the Texas air. She was happy to be home.

The front door opened, and Duke walked along the wooden porch to look down at them. "Well, don't just stand there, baby girl. Come on in so we can get to know this man of yours."

Damian sucked in a deep breath. Things were about to get real.

~

JADA WALKED inside her family home a bit uneasily. Never in a million years would she have imagined that she would be introducing Damian to her family—and certainly not in this situation with *all of them*, all at once. She stood in the foyer, twisting her hands.

"Is there a problem?" Amusement danced on Damian's face. He might be amused now, but she wondered how long he'd feel that way when her family roasted him over the coals.

"Apparently not." She rolled her eyes and walked ahead of him into the main living room, where her family was congregated. Her parents were sitting on a sofa together, which Jada was happy to see. They were well on their way to a reconciliation. Addison and Caleb were snug on a loveseat while London sat in a chair and watched them. London had it much easier because her husband, Chase, hadn't met the entire clan until their relationship was a done deal.

"Do I need to make another round of introductions?" Jada asked as she found an empty seat on the sofa opposite her parents.

"No, I think we all remember Damian," Abigail said softly. "Please have a seat."

"Thank you, Mrs. Hart." Damian slid beside Jada on the couch. It was impossible not to feel the heat emanating from him. "It's a pleasure to meet all of you. I'm sorry it's under such trying circumstances."

"We're hopeful that it's behind us," Abigail said with a small smile. "Bree is a fighter, and she will keep our grandchild safe. But in the meantime, we'd like to make sure our youngest is safe as well."

Damian sat upright. "Of course." He glanced in Jada's direction. "I want the same."

"If that's true, then you won't mind telling us about yourself." Duke folded one leg across the other. "And before you go giving me some song and dance, I'd like to hear something I can't find in the press."

"How about getting the man a drink first before

you interrogate him, Daddy," London said with a chuckle. Jada shot her big sister a grateful smile.

"Sounds like a mighty fine idea," said Caleb as he rose. "What can I get you, Damian?"

"A whiskey if you don't mind, and a bourbon for Jada."

While Caleb took care of the drinks, Jada watched her father stare Damian down. But Damian held his own, returning her father's hard stare with equal ferocity. Caleb returned moments later with a bourbon for her and a whiskey for Damian. Jada quickly took a sip, desperate for something to alleviate the tension and butterflies swarming in her stomach.

Damian took a liberal drink and then dove right in. "Many people know that I grew up in shelters and was taken in by a kind older couple who helped me during those critical teenage years before I eventually went to college."

"Yes, I read that," Duke said. "I believe they've passed on."

"Yes, sir," Damian answered and put his drink on the coffee table. "Mr. and Mrs. Lockett were the closest thing I had to parents. They took me in when most folks would have passed me by. You see, I was an angry young man with behavior problems, and most foster families wanted no part of that, but the Locketts saw beyond it."

"Sounds like they were great people," Abigail said.

Damian smiled fondly, and his eyes became wistful as he stared off into the distance before looking back at Jada's parents. "They were, and I will forever be grateful for the opportunities they gave me, but what most people don't understand . . ." He paused for several beats before he said, "Well, they don't know that my mother was a drug addict. She was always on the hunt for her next fix, and a young child was a hindrance to her getting high."

"That's awful," London said.

But she couldn't be anymore horrified than Jada, who, while she had researched Damian, had not uncovered the severity of his experience growing up. Damian had never shared his backstory with her, and she was shocked he was doing so now and laying himself bare in front of her entire family.

"I grew up not knowing when or where my next meal would be. I had to scrape food together to make a meal most nights and that's when my mother remembered to shop for groceries. I never knew when we might be put out of our apartment because she'd spent our rent money on her habit."

"How did you survive it, Damian?" Abigail asked.

Damian shrugged. "I don't know."

"He was resilient, Abigail," Duke interjected. "It takes fortitude to withstand life's adversities and still come out on the other side."

"How did you end up with the Locketts?" Caleb asked.

"Eventually the day came that the sheriff came and put our things out on the street. We lived out of my mother's car for a while until she sold it for drugs. I wasn't surprised when she forgot to pick me up from school one day and never came back."

Jada reached across the small distance between them and grasped Damian's hand. She was thankful he felt he could share his story with her family without being judged.

"I was put in the foster care system in the hopes I'd get adopted. When I was nine, I thought the day had come because I was with a family of educators. But once they got pregnant, I got put back in the system.

It's where I stayed for years. The last foster home I was in, the father was a drunk who didn't mind beating the children. I was older and wouldn't be pushed around, so I was told to get out."

"Omigod!" Abigail said. "What did you do?"

"I lived on the streets for a few weeks, but I was a sophomore in high school and made sure I went to class each and every day. I stayed at the odd shelter until one day an elderly woman—Mrs. Lockett—saw me sifting through the trash for some leftovers at the local neighborhood diner. She took me home for a hot meal. One day turned into two, then a week, then months. Mr. Lockett wasn't too happy when she brought me into their home, but he came to love me and teach me how to be a man. I wouldn't be where I am today if they hadn't taken me in and shown me I could be more than my mother's son."

"That's quite a story of survival," said Duke. "Thank you for your honesty and candor. It takes a man of integrity to be comfortable in his own skin and tell his truth. I respect you for that. It shows me you just might be good enough for my daughter."

Caleb coughed loudly, and Abigail hit Duke's knee.

He shrugged. "What? Damian understands a father's love. Don't you, son?" He returned his dark eyes on Damian.

"Yes, sir."

"Good, then why don't we retire for a bite to eat because," Duke said, glancing up at the doorway to see the housekeeper, Miriam, standing there, "it looks like dinner is ready."

Everyone took their leave and headed for the dining room. Damian rose as well, but Jada held back. "Damian?"

"Hmm." He glanced at her quizzically.

"Why didn't you ever tell me about your past?"

"I just did." He started toward the door, but she touched his arm.

"I know, but—"

He placed his index finger on her lips. "No buts. Your father wanted to know what kind of man I am."

"He knows now."

"Yeah, he does. C'mon," he said, inclining his head toward the door. "Let's go eat. I'm starved."

The rest of the evening went swimmingly in Jada's opinion. Damian's forthright nature served him well with the Hart family, and he fit right in as if he had been a part of it his entire life. Now that her father understood his roots, his questions were more conversational in nature rather than Spanish Inquisition style. Jada found herself relaxing and enjoying the evening with Damian at her side.

She didn't miss the smile and glances London and Addison lobbed her way throughout the evening, so when they asked for her help to make coffee, she took the hint. They wanted to chat, and once the three women were alone in the kitchen, London and Addison went in for the kill.

"Where have you been hiding him?" Addison asked.

"And why is this the first time any of us are hearing about him?" London added.

"I wasn't hiding him," Jada said as she leaned against the counter. "Our relationship, if you can call it that, is still very new. Matter of fact," she said as she grasped both their arms and pulled them deeper into the room, "we just became intimate last night. We didn't have time to figure out what it all meant when I got the call about Bree."

"Yet, he flew all the way from San Francisco to be with you," London said. "That tells me that he's way more invested than just wanting to hit it and quit it."

Jada chuckled. "I know, which is why this is all so confusing. I don't know what it means."

"It means he's into you," Addison said. "Trust me, I see it in his eyes. That man is sprung, so whatever you did last night worked. Keep it up." She gave Jada a little smack on the behind.

"Addison!"

"What? Just because I'm a happily married woman doesn't mean I don't remember what it was like during those early days with Caleb. The man was insatiable. Hell, he still is."

"I hear you, girl," London added, and the two women high-fived. "Now that we're married, Chase is even more into me."

"I'm glad to hear you both have active sex lives," Jada said. "So, what am I supposed to do with him?"

"Well, if I were you, I'd hop on him and—"

"London!" Jada blushed. She couldn't believe her older sister. "I'm going back inside."

London and Addison followed behind her *sans* coffee, and no one said a word.

"Well, it's late," Duke said, smothering a yawn. "Your mother and I are going to retire upstairs. Damian, do you have accommodations for the night?"

"Yes, I do. I have a room in town."

"That's much too far," Abigail said. "We have plenty of room here, don't we, Jada?" Her mother gave her a conspiratorial wink. "Why don't you show him to one of the guest rooms."

Jada watched her parents disappear, followed in quick succession by Caleb and Addison, then London.

"Well, I guess that just leaves us," Jada said. "Whatever are we going to do?"

"Oh, I can think of a few things." Damian's voice was husky with desire, and his words stirred Jada's blood and had her imagining all sorts of things they could get into.

DAMIAN WALKED behind Jada as she led him up the stairs of the Harts' ranch-style home after he'd returned to the Range Rover for his overnight suitcase. He'd been honest and forthright with the Hart family, and they hadn't smarted over his background. Instead, Duke respected the fact that he'd talked about his mother's drug addiction. Usually, Damian hated revealing anything about his past, but something told him he could confide in these warm, kind people who looked after their own. He envied them. He had always wished he could be part of a large family instead of a fractured one. Tonight was the closest he'd ever come to feeling like he was part of one, though he believed Duke Hart wasn't done with him yet; he had a feeling he was just warming up.

As he suspected, the home was quite massive and had several wings that went in various directions. When they stopped in front of a large oak door, Jada opened it and Damian stepped inside. The room was the size of his penthouse in San Francisco. It held a massive four-poster bed done in grays and blues. He watched as Jada came to another door: behind it was an *en suite* bathroom.

"You'll find everything you need in here," she said as she pointed to the room. "Towels, toiletries, and such."

"Thank you."

"It's the least we can do since you flew all this way." He could sense she felt uncomfortable being alone in the room with a massive bed just waiting for them to enjoy it. "Anyway, I should go."

Jada headed toward the door, but Damian was quicker and caught her hand on the doorknob. She glanced down at it then up at him. His eyes took in her frozen expression. She didn't know what he was going to do. Tension had been rising inside him since last night, all pent up . . . until this moment.

He sandwiched Jada between himself and the door. Then he slid his hands around her neck and let his fingers glide through the silky mass of her dark hair. It felt soft to his touch, so he leaned in and took a whiff. Then he curled his fingers around a strand and tugged, forcing her to tilt her head so he could finally do what he wanted to do since his arrival in Dallas— kiss her long, hard, and deep. He did that until he felt her arms circle around him and she responded to his fervor. He pressed her backward into the door, shifting his hips to come into contact with hers. She released a soft moan, and he felt her surrender.

With strength he didn't know he had, Damian levered himself away from Jada slightly to look down into her eyes and the whole of her face. Her lips were red and plump from his kisses. "You have no idea how much I want you right now, but you've been through an ordeal. So, I will let you go tonight, but don't expect me to do it again."

10

___

Jada woke up Saturday morning feeling well-rested. It had taken awhile for her to fall asleep knowing Damian was just down the hall. It would be so easy to tip-toe into his bedroom, slide between the covers, and let him make love to her all night long, but she couldn't do that. She'd already made a mistake by having sex with him, and doing it again would only compound the problem. Yet, Jada couldn't deny that she wanted the man. After that soul-stirring kiss, she literally ached between her thighs. She had become slick—from just a kiss.

Suddenly, a knock sounded on her door, interrupting her musings. "Come in."

She was patting down her bed hair when Abigail walked in carrying a mug of what Jada hoped was coffee. "Good morning, sleepyhead," her mother said as she approached her. She extended the cup, which Jada happily accepted. She took a few sips.

"Have I been sleeping long?" Jada glanced at the clock. "Omigod, is it really nine a.m.?"

"Yes, ma'am. Though I have to say I'm surprised to find you alone."

Jada blushed. "Mom—"

"What?" Abigail bunched her shoulders. "I'm not blind. I saw the way that young man was looking at you."

"How was he looking at me?"

"Like a man who has it bad for my daughter. And from the looks of it," her mother said as she stared into her brown eyes, "the feeling is mutual."

Jada shook her head. "It's not like that. We barely know each other and—"

"Who are you trying to fool, young lady? Me or yourself? It's obvious Damian McKnight cares for you or he wouldn't have come all this way."

"He just doesn't like to lose or to be told no."

"And is that what you did? You told him no? He doesn't strike me as the stalker type."

Jada chuckled. "He's not stalking me."

"Are you sure about that? Because if you need your father and Caleb to run him out of town, you know they'd have no problem with that."

"Yes, I'm sure. Damian and I just need to talk is all, clear the air."

"I SEE I'm not the only early riser," Duke Hart said to his daughter's paramour as the young man stood outside on the porch and watched the ranch come alive.

"I'm a morning person," Damian said. He didn't turn around but felt Jada's father join him at his side.

"Impressive, isn't it?" Duke asked.

"Yes, sir. You have quite an operation here," Damian said between sips of his coffee. "I never realized just how many people it takes to have a working ranch."

"A helluva lot. But I've been fortunate to have more than one generation of ranch hands working for me."

"Says a lot about the boss." Damian gave him a sideward glance. He noticed Duke was in much the same outfit as the day before: Wrangler jeans with a large cowboy belt buckle, plaid shirt, a cowboy hat, and some seriously worn cowboy boots. *Do all cowboys dress the same?* Damian had opted for jeans and a black T-shirt.

"A man has to stand for something, ya know. Have integrity in everything he does."

"Yes, sir. I agree."

"If yesterday was anything to go by, it appears you could be the same kind of man," Duke said, turning to face him.

"Why would you say that?"

"Oh, I don't know. Maybe the way you looked after my daughter—cared for her. I saw her leaning on you for support, and you gave it unconditionally. She hasn't done that in a long time."

"That's why I'm here."

"Is that the only reason you came?"

"I don't follow."

"Exactly what are your intentions where my daughter is concerned, Damian? I'd like to know, man to man."

"Well, sir." Damian turned to find Duke's midnight eyes laser focused on him. He was surprised to find him glaring. The man was protective of his daughter, and he had every right to be. "I'm interested in Jada."

"Define *interested*."

"We've spent some time together outside of work, and I enjoyed it. I'd like to get to know her better, but Jada isn't making it easy. She ran away just as things were heating up between us."

"So, you work with Jada?"

Damian shook his head. "No, Jada works at the television station I own."

"Interesting little predicament you've gotten yourself into getting involved with an employee."

"I'm aware that it's unorthodox."

"Yet, you still intend to pursue her?"

"Yes." Damian was honest. He saw no reason to lie, and his presence in Dallas clearly indicated that he was giving chase. "I want to see where this goes."

"And what does my daughter want?"

"I'm not sure, which is part of the reason I'm here: to support her as well as figure out where we stand."

"You're a brave man to come on Jada's turf surrounded by her family with your hat in your hand."

Damian chuckled. "Yeah, I don't know if I'd call it brave or just plain stupid."

Duke laughed right along with him. "You're a good man, Damian. Once again, you're impressing me with your forthrightness. But you should know that Jada's affection won't be easily won. She had a heartbreak that's hardened her heart against love. So I would say your odds are fifty/fifty."

"I've bet on less, Mr. Hart, and still won."

"Then may the odds be forever in your favor." Duke tipped his hat at Damian and, without another word, stepped inside.

Damian liked Jada's old man. From his outward appearance, he appeared tough, but Damian suspected Duke Hart was a lot softer when it came to his girls, who Damian could see were his pride and joy. He also knew Duke had a point. Jada was a tough nut to crack. He would have to take control of the situation and force her to face what was happening between them. She was already halfway there. Last night, underneath the surface, the unrestrained passion was still there; it was just waiting to be unleashed.

Surely, once they had sex again, maybe more than once, he could get some perspective because right now the only thing he could think of was how he wanted to merge his body with hers again. He would take his time and savor every inch of Jada. And she wouldn't be able to deny the truth, which was that they were damn good together.

AFTER TALKING WITH HER MOTHER, Jada called Bree to check in. Grayson informed her that Bree was doing much better and due to be released later that morning. He would be taking her home, where Jada could visit later. She was so relieved that her sister and niece were going to be OK.

After the call, Jada showered. Then she dressed in her usual attire when she was on the ranch: jeans and a button-down jean shirt. She found her favorite pair of cowboy boots in the back of the closet of her room. They were worn and rugged after years spent mucking out in the stalls and working the ranch, but she loved their familiarity. Deciding on practicality, she wore her hair slicked back into a neat ponytail, grabbed a cowboy hat from one of many on the rack in her closet, and went in search of breakfast.

The house was already well underway for the day when Jada finally made it to the kitchen. She found that Miriam had left a plate in the warmer with some bacon, eggs, and grits. Jada opened a drawer, pulled out a fork, and began munching while leaning against the cupboard. She was nibbling on a slice of bacon when Damian walked in.

He looked sexy as usual in dark jeans that clung to his muscular thighs, a black T-shirt that did little to hide his bulging biceps, and his casual tennis shoes; but he did look a bit overdressed in this atmosphere. "What?" he asked as Jada stared at him.

She laughed and took another forkful of eggs and grits. "Oh, nothing."

He looked chagrined. "Something's on your mind. Just spit it out."

"You look out of place in this environment," Jada said. "If you hadn't noticed," she said, motioning down to her attire, "I've adapted."

A slow smile spread across his face, and it was obvious he had noticed. He didn't hide that fact and let his eyes roam from the top of her cowboy hat to her pointed-toe cowboy boots. "You look like a cowgirl."

"That's what I am."

"Oh, really?"

Jada placed her plate on the counter and stood straight. "Don't get it twisted, Damian. Just because I like dresses and high heels doesn't mean I can't get dirty with the best of them. I grew up on this ranch, you know. And Duke ensured every one of his girls knew how to get by. Matter of fact, I bet I could show you a thing or two about ranching."

"Is that so?"

"Yes. Are you up for the challenge?"

He grinned. "I've never backed down from one."

"Good." Jada turned her back on him and tossed the contents of her plate into the garbage. Then she rinsed her plate off in the kitchen sink before placing it in the dishwasher. Miriam would have her head if she left dishes in the sink. She spun around to face Damian. "First thing we're going to do is get you some proper clothes. I can't have you walking around in those duds and embarrassing me."

Damian chuckled. "I wouldn't want to do that. Lead the way."

~

WITHIN MINUTES, they were in Damian's rented Range Rover and driving into a neighboring small town that held a bank, grocery and clothing store, post office, dry cleaners, and barbershop.

Damian frowned when he got out of the vehicle and glanced up at the storefront. "Are you sure about this?" It wasn't a place he'd ever frequent for attire, let alone be caught dead in. But Jada seemed to think his appearance needed improvement, so he was going to play along. If it meant they could spend time together and she would feel more comfortable, then he was game—because eventually, they were due to have a long talk about what happened in San Francisco.

"Absolutely," Jada said with a smile. "Don't be a snob."

He followed behind her as she walked into the clothing store. "Hey, Hank," Jada called out to an older gentleman standing behind the counter in much the same outfit Duke Hart had been in that morning.

Does everyone in Texas dress alike with no fashion sense? Damian wondered.

"Come on." Jada motioned Damian over to a rack of unimpressive and similar-looking plaid shirts. She began pulling several hangers from the rack and placing them against his chest. He watched her concentrate on finding the best shirt. Eventually, she settled on one, then she moved to the jeans section. It amused Damian. He'd never been shopping with a woman and had always been content to let a personal shopper handle his attire.

"What're your measurements?" Jada asked as she peered through different colors and varieties of jeans.

He rattled off a number and watched her pick up several pairs and place them, along with the shirts she'd been holding on to, into his arms. "Go try these on."

"Why do I have a feeling you're enjoying bossing me around?" Damian asked as he walked ahead of her toward the fitting rooms located in the back of the store.

"Because you've taken great pleasure in telling me how to wear my hair and what looks good on me. It's about time I returned the favor, don't you think?" There was humor in her tone, and Damian couldn't help but chuckle.

"I suppose turnabout is fair play." He swept the curtain back with his free arm and caught the sparkle in her eyes as he closed the curtain behind him. He would be a good sport and give her a fashion show. He selected the first shirt, which had taken Jada some time to select, along with a pair of distressed blue jeans.

"Don't forget this." He glanced down and saw that Jada was holding a belt with an enormous buckle through the curtain opening. Rather than take it, he pulled Jada into the fitting room with him.

"What do you think you're doing?" she huffed when his arms encircled her waist and brought her face within inches of his.

"I'm giving you a proper kiss as I should have done first thing this morning." Damian lowered his head and followed through on his words—soft at first, then deeper. He devoured her, plundering her mouth with his tongue so he could fully taste her, perhaps tempt her to be naughty. She didn't protest when he hauled her closer and she was damn near sprawled against his chest. Jada moaned and shivered against him, winding her arms around his neck so his mouth could pillage hers.

Damian felt himself swell in his jeans, and he pressed the steel of his erection against her, pushing her backward into the mirror. When Jada began rubbing against him, Damian's heart walloped as everything began to blur except him and Jada. But he'd only meant to have a quick kiss, not a total assault on his senses.

Slowly, he pulled away and looked down at Jada. Her eyes were dark and glazed with passion, and it made Damian want to take her right there and then, but this was neither the time nor the place. "I'm sorry. I probably shouldn't have started something I can't finish."

Jada chuckled softly. "You're probably right. This shirt looks good. I'm going to leave now before we do something embarrassing. Try on the others."

"You don't want to help me with that?"

"Oh, I think I've done enough in that department."

JADA COULDN'T BELIEVE how reckless she'd just behaved. She was happy to not have an audience when she left the dressing room. If anyone had seen her, well—there would be rumors all over town that would no doubt make their way back to her father. She wasn't ready to deal with Duke's questions because she wouldn't have an answer for them. She and Damian had circled each other for a month, and now that they'd opened Pandora's Box, they couldn't put the lid back on.

Jada knew what it felt like to be kissed by Damian, to have him *inside* her, *deep inside* her. She couldn't forget that moment, and as much as she hated to admit it, she wanted it again. Their first encounter had been hot and heavy, but rushed. Jada wondered what it would have been like if she had gone back to Damian's and let him make slow, sweet love to her.

"What do you think?" Damian asked from behind her.

Damn, the man could make jeans and a plaid shirt look like he was decked in Armani. "It looks good," she said nonchalantly, having turned to face him. "You're just missing one thing." She started walking away from him and heading down another aisle.

"Oh yeah? And what's that?" Damian glanced at himself in a nearby pedestal mirror. "Because I think I look like every other Texan."

When Jada returned, she held a large shoebox. "You're not a real cowboy without some boots. I didn't know your size, so I took a wild guess."

He glanced down with a smile. "You're right."

"Thanks. Give those a whirl."

Fifteen minutes later, Damian was decked out in his new attire with some weathered-looking cowboy boots and a cowboy hat.

"Now that I'm not embarrassed to be seen with you, we can go back to the ranch and go riding. It's been ages since I've been home."

Jada stopped in front of the Range Rover and waited for him to open her door, but Damian didn't move from the sidewalk. "I don't know about that. I've never been on a horse before."

"That's OK. I've got you." Rather than wait for him,

she swung the door open and climbed inside, leaving Damian no choice but to follow her. Jada was doing everything she could to put off the inevitable—spending time alone with him.

Horseback riding was just a distraction to ensure she didn't throw herself at Damian and beg him to take her like she'd done before. But she was tempted. Every time they were within a few feet of each other, the very air around them sizzled with unbridled sexual excitement.

Damian made Jada more aware of her sexuality than she'd ever felt before. She'd always thought she was aware of her abilities as well as her wants and needs, but when she was in Damian's presence, all her judgment went right out the window. She acted recklessly and on impulse with no thought for the consequences. Yet again today, she'd allowed the kiss between them to go from zero to nine on the Richter scale. And Jada knew there was little she could do to stop the quake. They were headed for a seven on the scale. She just wasn't sure what condition she would been in after the shaking was over.

11

Jada returned with Damian to the ranch and immediately set off for the stables. He was ready to be exposed to the other side of her. She knew he thought she was prissy and into how she looked, and that was true when she was in work mode at the station. But when it came to spending time at the ranch with her family, Jada could let loose and just be herself.

As they walked through the hay-strewn stables, Jada said hello to one of the stable hands. "How are you, Steve?"

"Very good, ma'am."

"How's Christy and the boys? I haven't seen them in ages."

"They're doing great, Miss Jada. My oldest, Mark, is graduating from high school this year, and my youngest two are still in middle school."

Jada shook her head. "Is that right? It seems like just yesterday that Mark was following me around. Is he going to college?"

"Yes, ma'am. He's following in your footsteps and going to the University of Texas at Austin. With him playing football, several coaches scouted him at the end of junior year, but he wanted to stay closer to home."

"Really?" Jada's mouth widened. "That's so fantastic. You tell your Christy that I said hello, ya hear? Do you have any carrots I can feed Thunder?"

"Sure thing." Steve walked over to a small cooler and pulled out a bag. "Thunder hasn't seen you in a while, so he might be a little bit antsy. You be careful."

"Don't you worry about me, Steve. There's not a man out there I can't handle."

"Now *that* I believe." He tipped his hat and continued his task of mucking out the stalls while Jada walked over to her favorite Arabian, who stood grazing some hay. She turned to Damian, who stood with his arms folded, watching her.

"What?"

He shook his head. "I don't know. I'm just seeing a different side of you. I didn't expect it."

"Don't judge a book by its cover, Damian. Perhaps you should open it and read what's inside." She turned away and opened the stall to walk into it. She made kissing noises, which Thunder heard and he immediately came over to nuzzle her. Damian stood at the door of the stall. "Don't just stand there. Come in."

"That's a big animal that can easily trample me."

Jada laughed. "The name is deceiving. Thunder is as gentle as a lamb." She reached inside the bag and pulled out some carrots, and Thunder began chomping on them eagerly.

"That's not what Steve said."

"Not everyone knows how to handle him, but he's my horse. I know him better than anyone else." She walked over to grab one of the brushes hanging on a hook and came over to Thunder and brushed his coat. "He trusts me. Don't you, boy?" She kissed the horse.

~

Jada had surprised Damian yet again. There were so many facets that he'd yet to uncover in this amazing creature. There was concerned Jada who'd do anything, drop anything, to be by her sister's side in her time of need. Then she was gentle and caring with the horse and downright charming to the stable hand.

The way she was brushing the horse's coat and whispering things to calm him made Damian eager for her to whisper things to him. But he didn't want gentle Jada. He wanted the wild and untamed Jada who he'd made love to in the office.

"Would you like to come over and feed him?" she asked as she glanced over at Damian. At his reluctance, she said, "Don't be a chicken."

Since he was no coward, Damian walked over, then he took the carrot and dangled it in front of the horse's mouth. The animal smelled his hand at first before happily accepting the treat.

"See, that wasn't so hard." Jada patted the animal's back. "You ready to try riding?"

"No, not really, but I expect I'm not going to get much choice in the matter."

"Nope." Jada whispered something to her horse, then grabbed his reins and led him out of the stall. "We're going regardless." When she saw Steve, she yelled, "Can you get Lady for Damian? We're going out for a ride."

"Yes, ma'am."

Damian followed Jada toward the stable exit and watched her saddle up the horse. There was lots of tying and buckling, but Jada was in her element and knew exactly what she was doing. It was clear she was an accomplished horsewoman. "How long have you been riding?"

"Since I was four. I had my very own pony."

"Sounds like fun."

"It was. I couldn't get enough of it. I competed throughout my teens."

"What stopped you?"

When Jada turned around to look at him, her eyes were clouded with regret. "Dreams changed. I fell for my high school sweetheart. Thought I was getting married and having some babies."

"Sounds like there's a story there."

Not one she wanted to share today. Jada was happy when she saw Steve leading the horse toward Damian. "Ah, here's your horse," Jada said, and Damian spun around to see an enormous animal coming toward him.

Lady had a well-chiseled head on a long neck, a dark-brown lean body, and long legs. Damian had a look of sheer fright. Jada tried to calm him by saying, "She's gentle."

"It's a she?"

"I thought you might be more comfortable with a woman." She winked at him. "Thanks, Steve." She took Lady's reins and tied her next to Thunder.

After Jada finished saddling both horses and ensuring they had water in their cantina, she looked at Damian. "You ready?"

"As I'll ever be."

"Alright." She walked him over to his horse. "Put your foot in the stirrup and swing yourself over."

He did as instructed and found himself on top of the large animal. Lady grunted and made noises, but Damian watched Jada sooth her with words before handing him the reins. "Lead her, and she'll follow."

"Wish that were true of all the ladies."

Within seconds, Jada mounted Thunder and made tisking sounds that prompted Lady to follow her out of the stables. As for Damian, he felt odd horseback riding. He was a city kid, raised on the streets, and he was riding out into the open as far as the eye could see. They rode for a time in companionable silence before Jada yelled, "Give her a kick." Then she was off galloping.

Damian did the same, and Lady took off after Jada and Thunder like a bat out of hell. Lady caught up with Thunder quickly, and Jada smiled at Damian as her hair flew in the wind. She looked carefree and uninhibited. It made him wish she could always be like this.

After they'd run some energy off both horses, they stopped for a break so the horses could graze. Damian swung himself off the horse and found he had some trouble walking, which made Jada burst into a fit of giggles. "It's not funny. Don't laugh at me."

But it was, and soon he was laughing right along with her. Damian couldn't recall the last time he'd truly laughed and had a good time, certainly not with another woman, but Jada brought out that side of him. He reached across the short distance between them and pulled her into a kiss.

Hungrily, he fused her lips with his and kissed her open-mouthed. His tongue slid against hers, rough and wild, just like he wanted her to be. Her body instantly responded to his, and she pressed herself against his already primed erection. It didn't take much for her to light a fire in him—he was that hot for her. He savored every minute of the delicious kiss, cupping her bottom and pulling her more firmly against him.

When she finally lifted her head, she moaned. "Jesus, I can't think straight when I'm around you—"

"No thinking is required."

She muffled a laugh. "That's right. You only want me naked."

"I do, but that's not the only reason I came here. I'm here because I was worried about you."

A beep sounded, and Jada pulled out her phone.

"What is it?" Damian asked.

"Grayson just texted me. Bree was released from the hospital. I'd like to go check on her. We should get going." She turned toward the horses, but Damian placed a hand on her arm.

"And our talk?"

"Later." She moved away and began tending to the horses. He followed her.

"I think you know me well enough to know that I don't like being put off, Jada." Damian would drop the conversation for now, but it was far from over.

He and Jada had a reckoning coming.

~

"OMIGOD, YOU LOOK SO MUCH BETTER," Jada said when she sat beside Bree on the oversized couch of the Wells's mansion in Preston Hollow. She and Damian had arrived a few moments earlier and found her sister downstairs resting in the living room with her husband and his brother, Cameron.

"Really?" Bree pinched her cheeks. "I thought I looked a bit ashen."

"You've never looked lovelier," Grayson said from a chair by her side.

"I was so frightened for you," Jada said.

"So was I," Cameron chimed in. "But Bree's going

to be OK, right, Grayson? She's not going to go to the hospital and not come back like Mom?"

Bree glanced at Grayson, and he immediately stood and walked over to his brother on the loveseat. "That's right, Cam. Bree and the baby are going to be OK."

"I'm so glad." Cameron turned to Damian, who was sitting next to him. "I'm going to be an uncle, you know."

"And I'm sure you'll be a great one," Damian said with an indulgent smile. Jada hadn't shared with him that Cameron was autistic, but he must have picked up on it. He'd been humoring all of Cameron's questions about who he was, why he was here, and how long he was staying.

"How about some lemonade for the ladies and a beer for us?" Grayson glanced at Damian.

"Sounds good." Damian rose from the loveseat. "I'll join you."

"Cam, why don't you help us out?" Grayson asked.

"But I want to stay with Bree," Cameron complained with a frown. "I missed her."

"She's not going anywhere," Grayson said. "Plus, I think Bree and Jada want some time alone."

"Oh, so they can have girl talk," Cameron said, and everyone chuckled. "OK, then I'll go too."

Jada watched as the three men exited the room. She was thankful that Grayson recognized her need to spend some quality time with her big sister. Jada reached across Bree and pulled her into a small hug. "I'm just so . . .," Jada said, her voice breaking, "happy. My prayers were answered." She pulled back to look at her sister. "I don't know what I would have done."

"Let's not think about that," Bree said and patted

her hand. "Me and this munchkin," she said, patting her swollen abdomen, "we pulled through."

Jada inhaled deeply, trying to center herself. "I know, I know." She jumped up from the couch and began pacing the room.

"Why do I have a feeling my condition isn't the only reason you're so jumpy?" Bree asked.

"Why would you say that?"

"Because you're as jumpy as a cat."

"Am not."

Bree stared at her incredulously, then patted the seat Jada had just vacated. "C'mon over here and tell me what's really going on."

Jada sighed. She could never fool Bree. Somehow, her sister could always sense when something was wrong and would always call her out on it. Jada walked back over to the couch and gingerly took a seat beside Bree. "If you must know, I'm conflicted."

"About Damian?"

Jada nodded.

"I'm not surprised. I've never seen you bring home a man before other than Joshua, and he doesn't count. We grew up with him."

"I didn't bring him home. He followed me here to Dallas."

Bree raised a curious brow. "Do tell."

"Damian and I work together," Jada started, then stopped. If she couldn't be honest with Bree, who could she be honest with? "Damian is my boss. And we've had a somewhat combative relationship over the last month until a few days ago when—"

"When what?"

"When we had sex," Jada blurted. "At the studio. Up against a wall."

"Well damn!"

Jada glared at Bree.

"What?" Bree bunched her shoulders. "Don't get all high and mighty now when you've been getting freaky with your boss. And at the office, no less."

"Don't rub it in, Bree. I've been trying to figure out what's going on with me."

"Lust, plain and simple. You've finally found a man who has you all hot and bothered, a man that you cannot manipulate with a bat of those beautiful brown eyes of yours, and it's got you running scared."

"Thanks a lot, Bree."

"You wanted someone to give it to you straight," Bree said, folding her arms across her chest. "And I've always done that for you, Jada. I'm your sister, and I'm going to speak the truth. You may not like to hear it, but you know I'm right. And what's really got you on the ropes is that the man cares for you."

Jada frowned. "Why would you say that?"

"He flew to Dallas to be by your side. And he's here now spending time with your entire family. Looks like he's a man who is not afraid of commitment."

Jada shook her head. "This isn't commitment, Bree. Damian wants what happened at the studio to happen again."

"Don't you?"

Jada colored, and Bree pointed to her. "See? I'm right. You want him too. So, why don't you go after what you want? I've never seen you shy away from living life on your own terms. Why start now?"

Because Jada was afraid if she wasn't careful she could lose her heart to Damian.

~

To prepare the beverage tray, Damian helped Grayson take some beers out of the stainless steel refrigerator in the large kitchen. He had to admit he liked the feel of the breakfast bar's spacious counters and large rectangular table in the nook facing the pool. It had a homey lived-in vibe that lended itself to family meals with everyone gathered around the table.

"So, you're into Jada," Grayson said conversationally as if they'd been talking about the weather. He placed a pitcher of lemonade on the beverage tray.

"Yes, I am," Damian said as he looked at Grayson. "Do you have a problem with that?"

"Not at all. As the youngest of the Hart clan, I've heard Jada can be a handful and not easy to manage."

"No kidding." Damian chuckled.

"Sounds like you've experienced it firsthand."

Damian nodded. "But no one can say she's boring."

"Neither is Bree," Grayson said. "This pregnancy may have sidelined her a bit, but Bree is just as stubborn as the rest of the Harts. Must be genetic."

"Yeah, Duke can be pretty intimidating," Damian said, "but lucky for me I grew up on the streets of Los Angeles, so I'm used to standing up for myself."

"Couldn't have been easy, and I can commiserate. My father died when I was young, so I had to be the man of the family and look after Cameron and my mother. Well, now just Cameron, since Mother passed."

"I'm sorry."

Grayson shrugged. He reached for one of the beer bottles, screwed off the top, and handed it to Damian before reaching for another. Damian watched as Grayson joined him in tipping their bottles back for a swig. Both men were contemplative. Then Damian broke the silence.

"How long have you and Bree been together?"

"Less than two years."

"Any insight you can give me on Jada?"

"Not really. Jada has always kept herself somewhat apart from the family living in San Francisco, but she's fiercely loyal. She wasn't too happy when she found out why I'd initially sought Bree out. Heck, most of the family wasn't, but eventually I gained her respect. She does, however, strike me as a woman who is ruled by emotions. If you can touch the right chord, you can win her over."

"Thank you, Grayson," said Damian as he tapped his beer bottle against the other man's, "for the words of wisdom."

"Don't thank me yet. The Hart women are tough nuts to crack, so be prepared to pull out all the stops."

Damian took Grayson's advice to heart, and while Grayson joined the women in the living room, Damian stepped away to make a few phone calls. Grayson was right. It was time he went for the full-court press. And tonight, he intended to do more than just talk with Jada.

12

"Where are we going?" Jada asked when she noticed that Damian wasn't driving toward her family's ranch. They'd just left Bree's a short while ago. Jada felt much better seeing that her sister was OK. She would wait another day or so before returning to San Francisco just to make absolutely sure her sister was on the road to complete recovery.

"You'll see," Damian responded.

"Excuse me?" Jada turned to glare at him. "I thought we were going back to the ranch."

"Not tonight. I have other plans."

"Would you like to clue me in on those plans? Or am I supposed to remain completely oblivious?"

Damian cocked his head to look at her. "Something like that."

Jada fumed in her seat but saw no point in escalating the conversation because she was a bit curious as to what Damian had up his sleeve. It wasn't like they were dressed for a night out on the town. She was in jeans and cowboy boots for God's sake, as was he.

Jada found out what his plan was when they drove into the heart of Dallas's central business district and he pulled the Range Rover to the curb outside The

Joule. Damian came around to open her door, and Jada had to admit she liked his style. The neogothic building turned hotel was a landmark in the city and known for dramatic artwork that adorned its walls. It was quite chic. Jada would never have thought Damian would go for a place like this. She'd pictured him in the Ritz or Four Seasons.

She didn't gripe when he took her hand. Instead, she tried not to focus on the burst of sensation that traveled up her arm at his touch. She tried to jerk her hand away while she still could, but he wouldn't budge. Instead, his larger, warmer hand enveloped hers, leading her to the elevator. He pressed the button for the Penthouse West. She was happy when he released her hand because the ride up to his suite was uncomfortably tense. She should be angry at his presumptuousness and want to ring his neck. Damian thought it was a given that she would go to bed with him tonight.

She would show him he was wrong.

When the door swooshed open to the penthouse, the ultrachic sophistication of the contemporary interior bowled Jada over. Her boot heels clicked on the marble floor as she followed Damian in. She loved the variety of colors ranging from blue to gold to deep red to plum and silver. Two large gray sofas with comfortable cushions and rich blue chairs were sprinkled throughout the large living area, and a long, sleek dining room table and a stunning chandelier abutted the room and the adjoining full kitchen.

"Would you like a drink?" Damian asked. He moved toward the wet bar that had been tucked on the far side of the living room and faced a terrace that wrapped around the entire penthouse.

"Yes, thank you. A bourbon if you have it."

"I have a full bar," Damian said as Jada made herself comfortable on one of the sofas while he set about making their drinks.

When he was finished, he handed her the bourbon but instead of joining her on the sofa as she'd expected, he sat in one of the blue chairs across from her. *Better to read me from there?* she wondered. It didn't matter. Jada only intended on staying here long enough for Damian to get off his chest whatever was on it and go home. If he didn't want to drive her, she had any number of people in town available to give her a ride.

She sipped her drink and waited, but Damian seemed to be in no hurry to speak. Instead, his onyx eyes continued to fix on her, making Jada squirm in her seat. Was his intention to keep her off kilter?

Jada placed her nearly finished bourbon on the sleek, white coffee table and folded her arms across her chest. "Well?"

"Well what?"

"You brought me here, Damian, I presume to talk. So here I am. Talk."

He sipped his drink, and Jada couldn't read his eyes as he glanced at her above the rim of his glass. "Where would you like me to start?"

Jada shrugged. "I don't know. You tell me." She felt like a caged lioness.

"Alright, Jada. Let's start with the fact that we've been orbiting each other for weeks, no, make that a month."

"I don't know what you're talking about."

"Would you like me to remind you?" Damian started to rise, and she put her hand up.

"Stop. Alright. I admit there has been a certain

level of sexual tension between us that erupted and we had sex."

"Sex? That's all you felt?" Damian stared at her boldly.

His glare made it uneasy for Jada to continue, but she had to end this once and for all so they could move on. "Yes, sex, which I've come to realize was a mistake."

"I see."

Damian slammed his glass down on the table, rose from the chair like a sleek panther, and was now stalking toward her as if she were his prey.

"Stop right there, Damian." Jada jumped to her feet. "Even you must see that this, this *situation* between us is not ideal. You're my boss, and I'm your employee. It would be too complicated, too messy for us to become involved, not to mention what this would do to my career."

"This *situation*, Jada, is all I have thought about for days."

Jada wasn't prepared for his honesty. She didn't know what to say.

"All I've thought about is the abrupt end to our evening when you ran away from me." Damian moved toward her, and just like the last time, Jada moved away. "All I've thought about is how I can't wait for it to be messy and complicated again because maybe then I can sleep at night without picturing myself buried deep inside you as you come and moan my name."

Jada colored at his bluntness. This was a bad idea. She should never have come upstairs with him. She started toward the elevator, but she didn't make it far because Damian blocked her path. She glared at him, and his dark eyes burned bright and hot, damn near searing straight through her.

"You can't stop this," Damian said quietly. "And I won't let you. You know that you've never had it so good with another man. You've never felt the kind of passion we shared that night with anyone else. That's why you ran scared and left me with a raging hard-on, I might add."

"I would have thought we'd solved that after our interlude," Jada responded huskily.

"Not in the least," Damian said. "I was just getting started. That wasn't even the appetizer."

Jada swallowed and looked down because she didn't want to see the naked hunger lying in the depths of his eyes. "Please move aside, Damian, and let me go. This isn't good for either of us."

DAMIAN COULDN'T LET Jada leave him. Not now. He was hungry for her. He had been for days and he'd done the right thing, waiting in the background until her sister was out of the hospital and out of danger. But it was his turn now. Their turn. He didn't want her to turn away from what was developing between them.

Their physical chemistry was so strong and surprising given from the start they'd agreed about very little. But she was just so damn beautiful. Her black hair cascaded down her lovely shoulders, and that heart-stopping lovely face and her full sensual lips had filled his dreams for days. Damian strode up to Jada until they were almost close enough to touch. He heard her sharp intake of breath, but he didn't back down. She was aware of him. That was good.

She glanced up at him, and Damian felt her eyes were filled with infinite depth that he could lose himself in. If he was honest, she'd dazzled him from the moment he'd met her. He'd tried to push down the attraction, but he couldn't any longer. He wanted to uncover every hidden secret he saw in her eyes.

Damian reached across the short distance between them and hauled Jada to him, cupping her ass. "Damian—" She didn't get out another word because his mouth fastened on to hers. His tongue searched and left her with no doubt as to what he wanted and what they both would have. Tonight.

Instead of fighting him as he thought she might, Jada shifted recklessly against him and began rocking her hips as his hands moved from her ass upward to cup her weighty breasts. Her nipples were already tight and aching for him to take them in his mouth. So he did. He sucked on them through her plaid shirt and bra and heard Jada moan softly just as her legs gave way as if she couldn't stay upright anymore. He caught her taking them both down to the floor in a tangled mass of limbs.

They kissed and touched as if they were starved for each other. Damian *was* starved. He couldn't ever remember wanting someone so badly that he physically ached. He didn't care that they were on the floor. He wanted Jada *now*.

They quickly kicked off their boots and tore at each other's clothes, eager to be naked and this time there would be no running way. When Jada was down to her panty and bra and he was down to his boxer briefs, Damian smiled. She was finally his to feast on all night long. His hands circled behind her to unclasp her bra and toss it aside. He was free to look his fill, and Jada was a sight to behold. Her round breasts and chocolate nipples were waiting for his touch. Damian lowered his head and took one in his mouth. She caught his head as she fell backward onto the heap of clothes.

God, she tastes so good. He laved, teased, and suckled her into his mouth and watched her writhe on the floor. His fingers slid down her abdomen until he reached the ridge of her panty. His hands swept along the fabric. "You're wet for me." He lifted his head to look at her.

Jada's hand slid to his erection in his boxer briefs. "And you're hard for me." She smiled.

"I think it's time we did something about that."

"Oh, please do," Jada begged.

So, Damian answered her bequest and made her wetter, swirling and teasing and stroking her with his fingers north of where she wanted. He played with and petted her until she whimpered, only then did he bury his fingers inside her hot heat. Pushing her legs as wide as he could, he worked his fingers faster and firmer inside her, tormenting her with his clever fingers and then he replaced them with his mouth.

Jada jerked upward when he nuzzled her intimately, intensely, licking and teasing her with his skilled tongue sucking deep on her clitoris. "Oh God, yes," Jada moaned when his fingers returned along with his mouth to rub her. Her orgasm struck her like a lightning bolt, and she cried out.

Her body trembled in his hands.

~

JADA COULDN'T BELIEVE how loud she'd been, but then again she'd never experienced an orgasm quite like this . . . except for maybe the one she'd had hardly even two days ago at the television station. Damian brought out a sensual side of her nature better than any other lover had. Sensations were still coursing through her, but he didn't appear done with her yet.

She watched him strip out of his boxers and don a condom. From where he had retrieved it, she didn't know and didn't care. She could no longer deny the inevitable. He slid on top of her, and they kissed just as his hips settled between hers and she felt the silken tip of him pressing into her wet entrance.

He surged forward, filling her in one stroke and causing Jada's entire body to lift off the floor at feeling him push deep inside her. Damian stilled, pulling back and nearly out of her. Jada wanted to protest. She wanted more, but she didn't have to wait because he thrust in again, this time harder than he had before and she let out a raw, jagged cry.

Her eyes fluttered closed. *Sweet Jesus, he feels so good.*

But then he retreated again. She moaned and circled her legs around his waist. She needed him to go faster. There would be time for slow lovemaking later. She urged him on, and he surged forward yet again, hitting her at just the right spot that her breath hissed and she clutched at his broad shoulders. When she glanced at him, he was deep in concentration and focused solely on her and her pleasure.

He slid out again and back and Jada wanted to dig her heels into the carpet, but there was nothing but cold marble against her bare bottom and Damian's hot body on top of hers. There was nowhere to go but to accept his slow, torturous lovemaking. It was almost unbearable. Almost. Just when Jada thought she could stand it no more, Damian thrust into her again and this time she screamed.

Shudders racked her body as wave after wave of pleasure engulfed her causing her to contract around him, squeezing him, but Damian didn't stop thrusting inside her. Instead, her orgasm spurred him on, and he began pumping harder and faster into her in a frenzied rhythm until she heard a groan above her as Damian found his own release. His body sprawled across hers, and Jada ran her hands down his back, slick from sweat, but just as swiftly he reversed positions and she was on top of him.

He glanced up at her with a rueful smile. "Wow! That was more incredible than the first time we were together."

"Ya think?"

He grinned and swept her damp hair away from her face so he could look at her. "I *know*. But alas, this floor is a bit too cold for me, babe, plus I'm ready for round two."

Jada's eyes grew wide. "Already?"

"I have an insatiable sexual appetite—one that you've just unleashed."

DAMIAN CARRIED Jada to the bedroom, swooped back the covers, and laid her down on the king-sized bed. Then he set about showing her his ravenous sexual appetite. He spread her body before him and began his own exploration. It was the most intense and erotically charged experience Jada had ever had.

His mouth and hands worshiped every part of her as they roamed the length of her curves. Eventually, when he came to the place she wanted him most, he spent an inordinate amount of time centering his attention just there. Jada thrashed her head about on the pillow as he sucked, licked, and tongued her deeply. And when she screamed, he knew exactly how the very essence of her tasted.

But he didn't stop there. He worked her breasts and nipples, massaging and toying them with his hands and fingers and then with his tongue, working them faster and faster, making sure Jada was so hot and hungry for him that she climaxed a second time and he hadn't even entered her yet. She was still convulsing when he rose to lie over her. Tilting her hips, his hard length filled her and she clenched around him, her muscles milking him. Damian continued thrusting inside her, claiming her, possessing her, and Jada arched upward to meet his each and every thrust. She completely opened herself up to him, and he answered by going harder, deeper, and faster until they both climbed the peak and went hurtling over into oblivion.

13

The next morning, as sunrays creeped through the penthouse's windows, Jada woke up as did a pulsing ache between her thighs. Last night, Damian had fulfilled every sexual fantasy she'd ever had and then some. After their second time together, they'd dozed off for a while, but she'd only been half asleep because she'd been wired and fully aware of Damian sleeping beside her.

Eventually, he'd awoken to pull her into a massive shower designed for two. They'd stood under the multiple showerheads as it glistened them with water before Damian had begun soaping his hands. He'd lathered her back and buttocks before gliding downward to soap her thighs and calves, all while driving her crazy with deep, relentless kisses. It made Jada not only want more but demand he give it to her. His kisses became more urgent, more relentless, inspiring a need in her she hadn't known she had.

Then he lifted her, gripping her against the slick, wet tile, and entered her hard and fast. She'd cried out and clutched the corded muscles of his arms to keep from falling. He'd bitten her neck as his pelvis had pistoned into her. He'd gripped her hips and pumped into her, and she'd given in and given up all control.

She remembered telling him, "Please, Damian. Please don't stop."

He'd done as she'd asked, tipping her up to meet him and she'd drawn him in deeper. She'd given him everything, and he'd taken it until they both reached a shattering climax that had her screaming yet again. Damian's hoarse cry ricocheted through his powerful body, and she felt the shudder shoot right through her.

Afterward, they'd returned to bed, and Jada had fallen asleep in his arms only to be woken in the middle of night to Damian massaging her buttocks as her backside lay nestled against his burgeoning erection.

"Can't a girl sleep?" Jada had asked.

"There will be plenty of time for sleeping later," Damian had said. "I have lost time to make up for." Then he moved, angling her exactly how he wanted and took her from behind, thrusting so deep, he'd brought her pleasure that had been beyond anything she'd ever experienced. She'd moved sinuously with him even though his pace was slow—slow enough to keep her teetering on the edge and just shy of the abyss she craved. He'd played her well, toying with her breasts and teasing her clit until he'd finally pushed them both over the edge and they'd climaxed violently.

It was a wonder Jada could even move after being made love to so thoroughly and completely into the wee hours of the morning. Her body felt the evidence of a night of lovemaking and was sore in all the right places. Jada smiled and started to snuggle up closer to Damian when reality hit her and she sat upright in bed. Dear God, she'd never called her parents to tell them she wasn't coming back home. After everything going on with Bree, they must be worried sick.

Her abrupt departure from his chest startled Damian awake. His slumberous eyes opened to peer at her. "What's wrong?"

"I didn't call my parents." Jada started to scoot from the bed, but Damian caught her around her middle and tumbled her back down onto the pillows.

His eyes were dark, yet serious. "You're a grown woman. I'm sure your parents realize you're with me."

Jada stared at him incredulously. "You can't know that."

"I know because I texted your father and told him that you were spending the evening with me."

"You did what?" Jada bolted upright again. She couldn't believe his audacity.

"C'mon, don't be angry," Damian implored with an impish grin. "I just figured it was better coming from me than you. And it was. He merely told me to take care of you."

"You mean to tell me my father approved of me staying the night with you?"

Damian laughed. "I didn't say that. I merely said that he knows you're in good hands."

Jada glanced down at Damian's warm, massive large hands—hands that had become intimately familiar with every aspect of her body.

"Listen," Damian said as he scooted upward into the sitting position, "I'm not going to apologize for wanting to spend uninterrupted time with you, not when I know that you wanted me as much as I wanted you."

"That's not the point. You should have told me."

"I'm sorry I didn't, but are we really going to argue

about something this trivial? Because I doubt you wanted to leave my bed anymore than I wished to let you go. Am I right?"

Jada sighed. "Yes."

"Good, so let's stay in bed."

IT WAS NEARLY noon when Jada and Damian finally made it out of the penthouse's bedroom and then it was only because they were both ravenous. Having burned hundreds of calories, Damian ordered room service. The server delivered it to them out on the terrace underneath an umbrella with Jada dressed in nothing more than a robe. Damian had sent her clothes to be laundered.

She'd never done anything like this before. She'd had other lovers but had always kept them at arm's length. After Joshua, she didn't want anyone to get too close, but Damian had—close enough to meet her family, the people nearest and dearest to her heart. Despite it all, Jada realized how very little she knew about Damian other than what she'd read in the papers and what he'd told the Hart family in their living room. She wanted to know more.

"What was it like for you growing up?" Jada wondered aloud.

"Why do you want to know?"

Jada cleared her throat and shrugged. "Is there something wrong with getting to know the man I've spent the last day with?" She sensed her intrusion was deeply unwelcome.

"No, of course not."

"Then talk to me, Damian. I know so little about

you other than what you told my family. You mentioned growing up in foster care. Was that in—"

He didn't give her a chance to finish her question. "It was in Los Angeles."

"Was that when you met the Locketts?"

Damian nodded as he tore off a piece of crusty bread and slathered it with butter. "Yes. Mrs. Lockett was very kind to me when I was nothing more than an angry kid. She saw value in me."

"Every person has value."

"You really think so?" Damian asked as his dark eyes bore into hers. "Or maybe you do because you grew up in an ivory tower, but for some of us . . . sometimes all people can see is what we are, not what we have the potential to become."

"I can understand that."

Damian frowned. "Well, I couldn't. Not when you're nine years old and hoping some foster family thinks you're worthy of a home, of a family. But for me, they never did. All they could ever see was that I was raised by a drug addict who pimped herself out to the highest bidder, and when that wasn't enough, she tried to sell her own son."

"No!" Jada's hand clamped to her mouth.

"Yes, Jada. When you live on the streets you learn the world is an ugly, ugly place. Some people can't wait to get their hands on a young man, but I was scrappy for my age and fought them off. Not everyone can. So, is that the story you wanted to hear, Jada? Does it make you feel better to hear my sad tale of woe?"

"Of course not. I don't know why you think it would," she huffed as she shuffled to her feet. "Just because we grew up with different backgrounds, Damian, doesn't mean I don't have empathy, that I can't feel sad for that lonely nine-year-old boy who wanted to get adopted." With that, she turned her back and headed into the living room.

Damian stalked after her and caught up with her in the living area. He spun her around. "Jada, I'm sorry."

"For what?"

"For making assumptions about you and how you might feel about my past. I don't talk about it, not with anyone."

"Clearly."

"Can't you give me a break?" He tugged on her arm.

"Why? You haven't given me one. You came here when I didn't ask you to, being all kind and sympathetic until finally I gave in, yet you won't give an inch. And when I ask, you turn on me. I don't have to stay here to be treated like this. I won't let another man take me for granted." She struggled to get out of his grasp, but he held her firmly.

"Jada, please," he implored. "I don't want our night, our day, to end like this. I'm sorry for how I spoke to you. I'm not used to sharing my feelings."

"I'm just trying to get to know you, Damian. I thought that's what you wanted, unless it's just me flat on my back that interests you."

His eyes darkened. "That's not fair."

"Fair? No. Accurate? Yes."

Tension flared between them as she looked at him with disdain, but he didn't look away. Instead, he gave a short, scornful laugh. "Alright. I admit that I want you. I've only tried to get you to acknowledge what's between us."

"And now that we have? Now what? What happens when we get back to San Francisco?"

~

DAMIAN DIDN'T HAVE an immediate response, so Jada jerked away and headed toward the bedroom. He caught up with her and found her picking up the clothes that had been dropped off while they'd been lunching. "I'd like to continue seeing you."

Jada turned to glare at him. "That sure took you long enough to say."

"I don't know how to do this, Jada."

"I can see that. Well listen, I get it, OK? You got what you wanted: me in your bed. And now you're done. Don't make it worse by saying things you don't mean."

"Don't presume to know what I'm thinking, Jada," he said curtly.

"Of course I shouldn't, because I don't know you. And all of this," she said, waving her hands in the air, "all this patience and kindness you've shown to me and my family has all been a means to an end."

She stalked toward the bathroom, but he beat her to the doorway and blocked her path.

"Move," she ordered.

"Who's going to make me?"

Jada snorted. "Kindly let me pass so I can do what I need to do to get the hell out of here."

"Not like this." Damian's tone had changed to one of softness. "Not after the amazing night we shared."

"We sated our lust, which is all we have."

Damian believed it to be more than that, but he wasn't ready to say the words out loud—at least not until he had a chance to evaluate the time he'd just spent with Jada and her family. Not until he could figure out what the hell kind of spell Jada had put him under.

"Fine. If lust is all we share, then we should damn well enjoy it for however long it lasts." Damian reached for the clothes in her arms and tossed them away. Then he pushed her backward into the bathroom and toward the shower stall.

"Damian . . ." Jada's eyes were large and stunned when he untied the robe she'd been wearing and it pooled at her feet. Then he quickly flung his robe off to reveal an erection. Jada looked downward and blushed. "Have you no shame?"

"None when it comes to you." Damian pushed her inside the shower. Then he leaned over to turn on the taps, and soon the water began to steam around them. Damian tried to grab her, but Jada moved away and ducked her head under the showerhead. He watched the water sluice over her shapely curves, and he groaned. He needed to be inside her. Needed to claim her and make her his. Despite her protests to the contrary, Jada was not immune to him and he wasn't about to let her treat him like one of her boy Fridays.

He sidled up behind her and heard her gasp when she felt the hard length of him on her ass. He kissed her neck and shoulders, but she didn't speak, didn't even look at him. He let his fingers glide south to cup her breasts, rubbing them with his thumb and forefinger until they puckered for him, but still she said nothing. And he wasn't having it. He eased her backward against the marble, then knelt before her.

Her eyes were large and flaming. She knew what he was about to do, but still she asked, "What are you doing?"

"I'm going to taste you." He gripped her hips, spread her legs, and lowered his head between her thighs as visceral need filled his loins.

"Damian." She groaned his name, but he could

barely hear her. She'd stirred a passion in him that had unleashed the beast. His mouth began worshiping her, arousing her until she began to shake and quiver and toss her head from side to side, but still his tongue continued going deep. He slid between her damp folds to find her tight nub, and he centered there on the sensitized flesh until she couldn't breathe and began to protest, "I, I can't—"

"Yes, you can," he growled. "Come for me, baby." His hands worked north to work her nipples, teasing them as his tongue slid faster in and out of her core. Her hips rocked against his mouth until shudders racked her body and he tasted her very essence.

AFTER THE SHOWER SESSION, Jada toweled off and dressed in the clothes she'd had on the day before. What kind of mind game was he playing? Was he trying to show that he could make her a quivering mass of limbs? Well, he'd succeeded. He knew exactly where and how to touch her until she couldn't bear it anymore and had cried out in his arms. Jada couldn't make sense of the emotions he aroused in her.

When she heard his boots hitting the floor, she turned to find him coming out of the bedroom. Damian was no longer in the cowboy gear she'd bought him. He had returned to the sophisticated Damian she knew in San Francisco. He was dressed in dark trousers and a black silk shirt with a few buttons opened. He looked scrumptious. Jada willed her riotous emotions to calm down.

"Are you ready to go back to the ranch?"

"Yes."

"I'll drive you."

They were silent when they left the penthouse and hardly spoke on the car ride back to the ranch. Jada was lost in her thoughts. She was starting to understand the past that had shaped Damian into the man he was today. It's also what drove Damian to succeed at all costs and made him such a feverish workaholic and a loner. But it had stunted his emotions. The only way he knew how to show Jada how he felt was in the bedroom.

Jada couldn't allow their relationship to operate according to Damian's rules only. Yet, she hadn't exactly figured out what she wanted either. He wanted to see her once they were back in San Francisco. Did she want the same? If they continued the relationship, it would complicate her work life and she'd just found her footing at the studio. Maybe she should leave the incredible lovemaking they'd shared here in Dallas and move on?

When Damian drove the Range Rover past the Hart family insignia on the ranch's gates, Jada realized she didn't have to decide today. She would spend another day or so with Bree and her family, then figure it out.

Damian cut off the engine and leapt out of the car to open her door. Jada accepted his hand as she exited. "Thank you."

"I'll walk you inside." Damian started walking in step with her, but Jada placed her hand on his chest.

"There's no need. I can take it from here." She was trying to get some distance from this man who had set her blood on fire.

Damian's eyes were cloudy and faraway. "No, I'll walk you inside. I promised your father I'd bring you back safely, and I'd like to say my goodbyes if it's all the same to you."

"Of course." Jada was suitably chastised and walked up the steps to her family's home. She let them inside and walked down the hall to see if anyone was in. She found her father in his study with his reading glasses, poring over papers. "Daddy." She walked behind his desk and gave him a peck on the cheek.

He glanced up. "Baby girl, you're back home."

"As promised," Damian said from the doorway.

Duke grinned. "Good to see you're a man of your word."

Damian nodded. "I am." He stepped toward the desk. "I've also come to say goodbye."

"So soon?" a female voice said from behind him. That's when Jada realized her mother was sitting in Duke's oversized chair knitting. She hadn't even seen her there. How could she when the two men in her life filled the room with a buzzing energy?

"Yes, ma'am," Damian said with a sincere smile. "I have to get back to my businesses."

"I'm sorry you have to go." Abigail stood up and walked toward him with outstretched arms. "But I'm so glad we got to meet the new man in our daughter's life."

Abigail hugged Damian, and Jada saw his eyes find hers across the room. Clearly, Damian wasn't used to being treated so affectionately, but eventually he returned her mother's spontaneous hug. When they parted, he looked toward Jada. "Walk me out?"

Jada glanced at her parents, who were beaming with approval. "Yes, I'll be right back."

She walked ahead of Damian until they reached the front door. She was opening it when he pushed it firmly shut. She spun around to face him.

"Can I get a kiss goodbye?" He didn't wait for her to answer. He covered the ground between them in a split-second, causing Jada's heart to race as one of his arms circled around her waist and crushed her against him. Her eyes fluttered closed just as his lips descended on hers. The kiss ignited an electric spark, and at first it was soft and gentle, with his tongue flicking over the seam of her lips seeking entry. Jada eagerly gave in even though she was conflicted about her feelings. But her body wasn't. It wanted more, deeper sensations that only he could give. Jada surrendered her mouth to the intimate connection.

This wasn't just any kiss. It was a branding, and when their mouths burst apart, they were both breathing unevenly and Jada's heart was pumping so hard, she thought she might pass out. But Damian seemed to be very much in control.

He stared down into her wildly dilated eyes. "I'll see you when you get back to San Francisco." He pulled away, and she watched him as he walked out the door.

Despite herself, Jada followed and saw him hop into the Rover, kick the engine into gear, and speed off. She couldn't reason away what was going on. She was falling hard for Damian and wanted him more fiercely than anything she'd ever desired. *Including my career?* Because when she got back to San Francisco, she would be put to the test and find out how much she was willing to sacrifice to be with him.

"You're in love with him, aren't you?" Jada heard her mother ask from behind her as she closed the front door.

"Mom, how long have you been standing there?" Jada was trying to evade the question.

"Long enough."

Jada blushed as she imagined Abigail catching her and Damian in the heated liplock a moment ago. "You're mistaken."

"I know love when I see it," her mother said with a knowing look. "And you're head over heels for that man."

Jada shrugged. "Mama, I think you have stars in your eyes because of you and Daddy."

"Excuse me?"

"C'mon, Mama, we've all seen it." Jada nodded in the direction of the study. "You and Daddy have been inseparable for over a year, yet you're keeping him at arm's length. And you haven't told your children what's going on between you two."

"Because it's grown folks' business."

"Ah." Jada smiled. "You can use that excuse, but I can't?"

"It's different and you know it, Jada Hart. Your father and I have decades of history. Children. A divorce between us. If we're being cautious, surely you must understand why."

"I do, Mama. I know what Dad's infidelity did to this family. It tore us apart, but don't you know what having a reconciliation between you would do for all of us? It would give us faith to believe in love—that two people can make it work despite their differences and the past."

"Is that what's holding you back from admitting how you feel? Because of your father and me?"

"No, not entirely, but it has affected my view of happily ever after. I've seen what can happen when two people love each other yet still manage to hurt one another."

"I admit that forgiving your father hasn't been easy."

"And?"

"But I have forgiven him because I love him—always have and always will. He's the only man for me, Jada."

Jada smiled. It warmed her heart to hear her mother speak about Duke this way. She and Bree had always hoped for a reconciliation between their parents, and now the day had come. "I'm so happy for you, Mama."

"So am I. I think the last time I felt this giddy was when Duke and I first met. I was so enamored with him. He was so strong, confident, and powerful. I was immediately drawn to him. I imagine it's the same with you and Damian."

Jada nodded reluctantly. "It is, but we've also butted heads since day one."

"Because you were fighting the attraction between you."

"Well, in case you haven't noticed, we've stopped fighting or at least we've called a ceasefire the last few days."

"I noticed."

"Mama." Jada looked upward. "I've never felt this way about a man before, not even Joshua. Looking back, I think that was puppy love in comparison to this . . . and it scares me. The intensity of it frightens me."

Abigail smiled knowingly. "That's what happens when you meet the *one*. You're unable to deny the force of nature that draws you to them."

"I've tried." Oh, how she'd tried. And look where they'd ended up: a charged encounter at the television station against the wall, and in Dallas at the penthouse for the last night they'd sexed each other crazy. "I don't know what to do. Damian's my boss. This is complicated."

"It always is," her mother said, "but you can't be afraid, Jada. You're a Hart. Go after what you want."

Abigail's words reverberated with Jada long after they parted, leaving Jada to wonder if she had the courage to do as her mother had suggested.

~

WHEN DAMIAN'S jet landed in San Francisco, he was happy to be on solid ground, literally and figuratively. While in the air, he tried to concentrate on work, but it had been fruitless. Instead, he thought about Jada and the last few days he'd spent in her company. He'd never seen such solidarity in a family. The Harts were a tight bunch. He envied them because since the Locketts had died, he'd felt alone.

But Jada, she had divorced parents who were clearly in love even though they tried to hide it. And the deep affection she had for her sisters was undeniable. Damian longed for what they had, and he hated that because it made him feel weak. If he didn't allow himself to feel, he could cope with life's inequities. It's why he always kept himself removed from forming any real attachments. Yet, as soon as he met Jada, something in him that he thought was dead had come to life. Suddenly, he was feeling more than he'd ever allowed himself.

He'd started to care about what happened to Jada.

Care about her sister and be invested that she and her baby pulled through and thankful when they had. Damian never prayed, but he had when he sat by Jada in that hospital chapel. He silently prayed to God or whoever was listening that life shouldn't be so cruel and take Bree's baby when she was so close to delivering a healthy child. When his prayers were answered, Damian had released a long-held sigh of relief.

After Bree's drama was over, his deep feelings for Jada had come bubbling to the surface. She was more than a breath of fresh air—Jada Hart was an original.

In Dallas, he'd seen a pluckier, down-to-earth Jada who wasn't afraid to be seen without makeup, who wasn't afraid of putting him in his place by making him wear Western clothes and forcing him to face his unease about horseback riding. He'd been out of his element but had played along because he'd loved seeing Jada's smile. Loved watching her black shimmering hair blowing in the breeze underneath her cowboy hat as she'd kicked the horse into galloping and left him in her dust. And when she'd become relaxed around him, softening toward him, he'd gone in for the kill. Jada hadn't been able to deny what he'd known since he laid eyes on her: They were joined by some invisible thread, and the chemistry between them was electric, culminating in the most incredible lovemaking Damian had ever experienced.

Damian had thought if they were together again, he could exorcise Jada out of his system, but that didn't happen. Her almond-brown eyes haunted him and made him want to see the smile on her teasing, pert mouth, a mouth that had brought him pleasure over and over last night.

But today was another day, and they would have to figure out how to navigate their workplace in lieu of their sexual relationship—because Damian wasn't about to stop being Jada's lover. If she thought she could relegate him to the backburner when she returned, she would find out that she was mistaken. He intended to be a fixture in her bed for the foreseeable future.

But he worried over just how much Jada would fight him and herself on this inevitability.

~

"Jada, you're still here?" Bree asked when Jada stopped by the Wells mansion later that day.

Jada frowned. "Of course I am. Where else would I be right after my sister nearly suffered a miscarriage?"

"I'm sorry. I just assumed you had to get back to work, plus Duke mentioned that Damian had already left."

"And you assumed I went back with him like a

good little puppy dog?" Jada snapped. "I don't follow behind any man. I follow my own path."

"Jeez, I know that, Jada," Bree said tightly. "What's got you so riled up?"

"Nothing." Jada busied herself fluffing pillows that didn't need fluffing.

"I would beg to differ. You're wound up as tight as a drum."

Jada rolled her eyes. "I'm sorry if I came off abrupt. I came to check on you is all. I have to be sure you're OK before I leave."

"And I am." Bree patted her large belly. "The baby and I are fine."

Jada's brow turned up questioningly.

"We are. You can get back to your life."

Jada knew what Bree wasn't saying. "You mean get back to Damian?"

Bree grinned. "If the shoe fits."

"What do you think you know, Bree?"

"I know you stayed out all night and didn't come home."

Jada laughed. "Do you have spies at the ranch? You haven't lived there in almost two years."

"Yeah well, I'm still a Hart and I hear things. Anyway, don't try and be coy with me, sister. Just spill the beans and admit you got busy with Damian."

"Alright, we spent the night together."

"And? Why am I having to pull this out of you? I'm six months pregnant, and you know how some women feel horny at this time in their pregnancy. Well, I don't. I just feel like a big beached whale. So spill, damn you."

"Alright, alright." Jada held her hands up in defense. "It was good. Real good. No, correction: It was great. Fucking great. The best I've ever had. There, are you satisfied, Ms. Hot Mama?"

Bree grinned. "Actually, I am, but it sounds like that took a lot out of you to admit. Why? What's going on?"

"I don't know. I'm just confused. You know we work together."

"So did Grayson and I, but we made it work."

Jada remembered, but it wasn't without drama. Grayson had hurt Bree with his lies and deception, and it had taken months for him to win her back. "It's more than that. Damian is not open. When I tried to get him to talk after our amazing night together, he clammed up. It was as if I was only good for one thing, but not to go deeper."

"And that hurt you?"

"Of course it did. I know I may put on an air of 'I don't care,' and with most men that's usually true, but—"

"But Damian is different?"

Jada nodded. "I've never felt this way, and it's unnerving. I'm used to setting the pace with men, and when I'm done with them, I move on to the next one."

"But you're not in control with Damian?"

Jada snorted. "Not in the slightest. And the funny thing is, I think neither is he. I think he's scared too by the depth of feeling we bring out in each other. I'm not sure I should explore it—not when he clams up like a tortoise."

"I thought I heard he grew up on the streets. Maybe it's hard for him to show emotion. I can't imagine he could show fear when he was out there."

"I can understand that, but I'm also not willing to be his booty call. It's only going to get worse when I get back to San Francisco. Before, we didn't know how good it could be, but now we've opened that door. It's damn good, Bree. How can I possibly work with him when he's seen me naked? When we've done all sorts of—"

"Spare me all the details. I just wanted a little gossip, not the full enchilada."

Jada burst into laughter. She missed having her sister close by. "I love you, Bree." She reached across the distance between them and embraced her. "I promise I'll be back as soon as I hear you're in labor."

"You'd better be." Bree pointed her index finger in Jada's face. "You promised you'd be in the delivery room with me and Grayson. Keep him on the straight and narrow."

"I promise."

And I mean every word, Jada thought as she drove back to the ranch an hour later to prepare for her flight back to San Francisco that evening. Her mother had tried to convince her to stay until morning, but now that Bree was out of danger, Jada needed to head home and face the music.

ON MONDAY, Jada was nervous as she walked into the bustling studio with morning broadcasts already underway. Would Damian be there? What would their first encounter be like? Would he treat her differently now that they'd become intimate?

Despite all her worrying, Damian was nowhere in sight.

The good news: All her colleagues were happy to see her. Many approached her to find out if everything was OK. Jada was happy to report that mom and daughter were doing great and she expected a healthy niece in three months.

"Jada, welcome back," Andrew said when he visited her desk.

"Thank you, Andrew. And I'm sorry for the short notice on my departure." She'd finally gotten caught up on all her emails and voicemails and was ready to dive back in.

"Couldn't be helped. Family is family. We did have to fill your Friday anchor slot."

"I know, but Kyler is here. She handled it, didn't she?"

"Here's the thing," Andrew whispered, grabbing Jada by the shoulders and leading her away from the newsroom. "Her numbers were abysmal compared to yours."

"Really? But she's always been the backup."

"Well, the tide has changed. You know how fickle the public can be. Mr. McKnight indicated that Friday will be your permanent spot going forward."

"Did he?"

And where was the elusive Mr. McKnight? He'd been MIA even though she texted him last night to say she'd made it back to San Francisco. He'd replied with a brusque, "Glad you made it home safely" text. Was that it? Was that all he had to say after their time in Dallas?

"Yes, Mr. McKnight believes in your talent, despite your rocky start with him," Andrew said. "So, whatever you're doing, I would tell you to keep it up." He tapped her lightly on the shoulder before departing.

Keep doing what I'm doing?

Which was what exactly? Lie on her back whenever Damian McKnight said so. Well, he could think again. She wasn't his beck-and-call girl. He couldn't just have her whenever *he* wanted. What about what *she* wanted?

And what do I want?

Hell if she knew. But she certainly wouldn't find out if he didn't contact her. Annoyed, Jada stalked back to her desk determined to put Damian further out of her mind. If that's the way he wanted to play this, as if she was insignificant and no more than another notch on his bedpost, then so be it.

Two could play that game.

J ada was ignoring his calls.

Damian didn't like it. He didn't like it one bit.

Since returning from Dallas, he'd put out several business fires that had required his immediate attention, which necessitated putting all thoughts of the raven-haired beauty aside until he had resolved the issues. Additionally, a major deal that had been on the verge of coming through had indeed proved successful over the last several days. He was now the proud owner of a new radio station in Los Angeles.

But he was also tense as hell. He needed an outlet.

Usually, he would burn it off in the gym—run five miles, swim multiple laps, or spar with a boxing partner. When none of that worked, he'd call one of the women he kept on standby for just this type of situation. They'd help him relieve some stress in the bedroom, and he'd leave sated.

Tonight, none of those options appealed to him.

He only wanted one thing. Or should he say, one woman.

Only Jada could put out the flame growing inside him, but she was refusing to acknowledge his presence. Could he blame her? He hadn't exactly pulled out the welcome mat. It wasn't his fault he couldn't indulge her text messages, beyond acknowledging she was back home. He'd had other more important priorities, but he doubted she'd see it like that. Women always wanted to be the center of attention, especially this woman.

My woman.

When had he begun thinking of Jada as his? Since she'd turned his world inside out one night against a wall of a television studio and again in that Dallas penthouse. There was no way he could think of any other woman. There was only Jada.

But Damian didn't know how to make this right. He didn't do relationships. He had sexual encounters, but Jada wasn't having that. He knew she would want more. He didn't know how much more he could give her, but he had to try. And so, now he was in his Tesla and heading for the studio.

Damian was unprepared for the sight that greeted him: Jada walking arm in arm through the parking lot with another man. Meanwhile, Jada saw Damian slide his Tesla into his reserved parking spot, and in that moment, Damian saw a smile form on those damn delicious lips of hers. Fury raged inside him. He wanted to get out of the car and beat the man to a bloody pulp for taking his woman, but he couldn't. He hadn't made sure she understood in every way imaginable that he didn't share. Wouldn't share. She was his and his alone.

He watched her get in the other man's car and drive away. She'd made her point. She would not be trifled with.

Then again, neither would he. He would show Jada Hart just the kind of man he was.

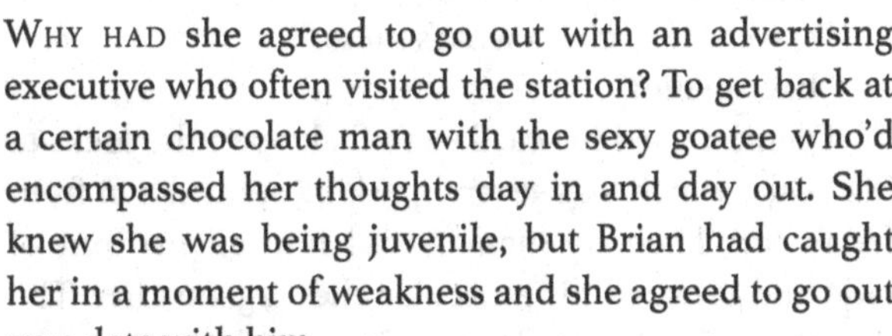

Why had she agreed to go out with an advertising executive who often visited the station? To get back at a certain chocolate man with the sexy goatee who'd encompassed her thoughts day in and day out. She knew she was being juvenile, but Brian had caught her in a moment of weakness and she agreed to go out on a date with him.

Jada was just thankful the evening had ended and he was driving her back to the station, where her car was parked. After he found a spot close to hers, he walked her a few steps to her Jaguar. Then he leaned in for a kiss, but Jada tipped her head to the side to present her cheek instead. "Thank you for dinner, Brian."

"So, we can do this again sometime?"

Jada shook her head. "No, I'm sorry. I'm getting over a bad breakup, and I'm just not ready to jump into anything new." That was partially the truth—she wasn't ready to start dating anyone, not until she cleared Damian out of her head.

"I appreciate your honesty, Jada. Take it easy," Brian said. Then he left.

Jada stared after him for several seconds as he walked away. He was decent, just not the guy for her. She was about to jump in her car when the hairs on the back of her neck stood up. She didn't have to turn around to know who it was. She could smell his cologne. Jada spun around on her stilettos. "What the hell, Damian? You scared me half to death."

"I doubt that," he said smoothly and stalked toward her. "You knew it was me."

Jada blanched. Had he read her mind? "It's late,

and you could have been anyone," she deflected. "What are you doing here anyway?"

"I've come to claim what's mine."

"Excuse me?"

Damian used his car key to flick open the locks to his Tesla, which was several parking spots down from Jada's car. Then he maneuvered himself in front of Jada and brushed his muscular chest against her. The tips of her nipples hardened. "Come with me."

"You don't get to order me around, Damian."

"You're trying my patience tonight, Jada." The edge in his voice gave her pause. "I know you saw me pull up tonight, yet you still chose to go out with . . . with that other man." There was no mistaking the hurt in his tone.

"I have every right to go out with whomever the hell I want. I'm a grown woman, and I'll do—"

In seconds, Jada was flat against the wall of Damian's chest. He'd hauled her hard against him. "You're going to get in my car, or I'm going put you there myself. Which is it going to be?"

Jada shot daggers at Damian and pushed against him until he slowly released her. But she couldn't help herself. She found herself walking with him to his car. When she was safely in the passenger seat, he slammed the door closed and joined her moments later in the driver's seat.

He revved the engine to life and pulled out of the parking lot. Damian emanated a barely unleashed fury as he gripped the wheel. Jada had no idea where he was taking her. She wanted to ask but thought better of it. She'd already rattled his cage enough tonight and evoked his ire. But it's not like she'd known he was coming to the station. He hadn't called her all week.

Nearly twenty minutes elapsed before they pulled into the garage of a high-rise building, and Damian turned off the engine. Jada didn't wait for him to open her door. She jumped out on her own accord. He didn't speak. Instead, Damian headed for the bank of elevators and pressed the call button.

"How long are you going to ignore me?"

He turned his head and smirked at her. "Perhaps as long as you've ignored me the last couple of days."

The elevator door chimed, and Jada stormed inside but not before saying, "It goes both ways, Damian."

"I know that." He entered the car with her and pressed the button for the penthouse floor.

"Really? You could have fooled me." Jada folded her arms across her chest. She was partly angry, but she also needed to cover up her nipples. They seemed to have a life of their own. Or perhaps they sensed the one man who knew how to caress, suck, and kiss them?

"I realize that I inadvertently caused this," Damian acknowledged from the other side of the cab, "but it was unavoidable. I had some pressing business matters to attend to."

"That's all I get?" She stared at him incredulously. His eyes smoldered with desire back at her. "You just used high-handed tactics to get me to come with you. And where the hell am I, anyway?"

The doorbell chimed again. Jada hadn't even realized they'd moved because she was so in tune with this man.

"You're at my home."

Jada blanched. "Why?"

"So we can talk—uninterrupted."

Jada glared at him. "I already know what you're

going to say. We had a good time in Dallas, but we're back in San Francisco."

"And?"

"And what?"

"We work together. So this," she said, pointing back and forth between them, "is going nowhere because it can't."

"Who says it can't?"

That response surprised Jada. She didn't have a comeback. The elevator doors opened, interrupting their conversation. A large open-concept apartment with modern contemporary furnishings and high ceilings greeted Jada. The place was obviously the work of an interior designer. She saw the pops of color amidst the dark masculine blacks and beiges as well as the eclectic mix of artwork that adorned the walls. "Nice place," she commented as she stalked through the rooms. She stopped when he did at the bar.

She watched him pour himself a glass of bourbon and another. He handed her one. "Drink."

She accepted the glass because he remembered what she liked to unwind to.

"The bourbon should relax you. Hell, relax us both."

"So you can get me into bed?" She eyed him warily.

"Although I would love to take you up on the offer, that's not solely why we're here."

Jada took a large gulp and felt the burn going down her throat. She leveled him with a dark gaze.

"I don't like how we left things in Dallas," he began. "I'd like to clear the air."

"Do you always have to be in charge?" She pointed her pinky at him while still holding her glass. "Do you always have to try to set the pace? Why can't we let things happen organically? That would be too much, huh? I can assume that if Dallas wasn't a one-time thing, you brought me here for one reason: to resume our physical relationship."

"That's right. I'm willing to offer a committed sexual relationship in which both of us agree to be mutually exclusive and not sleep with anyone else."

Jada snorted and rolled her eyes. "What's in it for me?"

"I would imagine the multiple orgasms you've been having," Damian quipped.

Color rushed to Jada's cheeks. She didn't appreciate his frankness, but she was nothing else if not honest. "I own my sexuality," she retorted. "So yes, I loved every minute of those orgasms."

Damian smiled, and Jada realized he'd lured her into a web of his own making. "And I assume you'd like more?"

"What girl doesn't?" She eyed him as he circled around her, and she blew out an uneasy breath. If he was trying to disarm her, it was working. It had been a long day, and with the glasses of wine at dinner and the sips of bourbon, the liquor was having the desired effect.

"Then my offer benefits the both of us."

"And what do you get out of this arrangement?"

Damian paused from circling her and stepped toward her. Jada moved backward, and the back of her legs hit the settee. "You. In my bed. *Exclusively*. Are you in or are you out?"

～

DAMIAN HAD LET his imagination run wild for days, picturing Jada in every conceivable position as he took those full curves deep and hard in his hands. He knew he couldn't offer her anything more than a committed sexual relationship. It was all he was capable of. Her brown gaze burned into him, and she didn't speak. She merely nodded and accepted his terms: to be his *exclusively.*

Instantly, he reached for her, fastening his mouth on those luscious lips. His tongue searched for all the secret spaces Jada tried to hide from him. Any vestige of anger he'd had over her date with another man tonight was quickly extinguished as the flame of desire engulfed them both. His hands covered her body, weighing her tight breasts and nipples that begged to have his hot mouth on them. She shifted and restlessly moved the lower half of her hips against him.

Damian lowered his head and took a nipple in his mouth. It caught her off guard, and she swayed against him so he moved them backward to the couch. He began tugging at the zipper on the back of her dress, eager to get her naked. She seemed equally as desperate and helped rid him of his clothes. When they were both naked, he quickly slid on a condom. Then he kissed her again while his hands found a path down her arms, hips, and thighs until he came to the place he sought. "I love how wet you are for me."

She stretched her legs wide, giving his fingers easy access to swirl, stroke, and tease her slick flesh. But while he thought he was mastering Jada, the little temptress was giving as good as she got. She had his hard length in her clever hands and was squeezing and pumping her hand up and down his shaft. The tables had turned, and his breathing was just as choppy and uneven as hers.

Damian feared he would come without being inside her. He grabbed her hand to stop her from tormenting him, then he swung her atop him to straddle him. "Ride me."

"With pleasure." Her hips settled on his, and he felt the head of his erection just as she took him inside her silken, wet entrance. Damian threw his head back as she began to undulate against him. Back and forth. Up and down. She was relentless. At one point, she'd nearly retreated and he was all the way out, but he wouldn't let her go. He grasped her hips and surged hard upward, desperate for release. She got the hint and spread her fingers on the broad bunches of his shoulders and began moving faster.

"Jada, sweet Jada," he muttered. His breath hissed, and he tipped his head back and watched her. She was entirely focused on riding him harder, and he met her by pistoning his hips upward. When her orgasm hit her with full force, she screamed out his name "Damian!" Then she fell forward on top of him.

Damian was nearly at the edge, and he flipped her onto her back so he could take over. He placed her legs on each of his shoulders and surged forward in one powerful stroke. Her eyes fluttered open as yet another cry came from her lips, but he didn't stop. Instead, he thrust hard and fast, his breathing coming uneven and his heart beating so rapidly he thought it might burst from his chest, until eventually shudders racked his entire body as unbearable ecstasy washed over him. Jada contracted all around him, squeezing him tighter and tighter until he could no longer deny that this woman had him wrapped around her little finger.

16

Jada awoke on Friday morning in a foreign place. It took her a few minutes to figure out she wasn't in her condo but at Damian's penthouse and that the man was asleep right beside her. They hadn't exactly discussed how this "committed sexual relationship" was going to work in or out of the office. He'd just taken her straight to bed, or rather to the living room couch since they'd been so passion starved.

Damian must think her some sort of nymphomaniac, but that was far from the case. She didn't sleep indiscriminately with men. But since she'd met Damian, they'd done it up against the wall, on the floor, on the couch, in the shower, or on whatever surface was available.

"Stop thinking so much," Damian said from beside her.

Jada jumped. She hadn't realized he was awake. Slowly, she turned toward him. "Good morning."

He reached behind her and pulled her toward him. He kissed her. "Now that's a proper good morning."

Jada gave a half-hearted smile. "I should get going.

I'm not too late and can still make the staff meeting." She pushed back the covers and scooted to the edge to escape, but Damian stopped her.

"Jada, nothing has to change at work. You'll be you, and I'll be me."

"How's that going to work with us sleeping together?"

He sat up and leaned on an arm. "It can work as long as we're both honest with each other."

"I don't know ..." Her voice trailed off.

"How not to jump my bones when you see me?" he offered with an unabashed grin.

She couldn't help but smile because that would definitely be a problem. "Sort of. I mean, there's no denying there's an attraction between us. What if other people notice? I don't want them thinking my Friday morning anchor slot came via the casting couch."

Damian bolted upright in the bed. "You got that position because you were the best person for it. And we weren't sleeping together when I gave you the try-out. Yes, we had kissed, but that's all."

Her eyes lowered. She could hear the whispers. "They won't know that. They'll speculate." She paused. "Can we keep this under wraps?"

"If it makes you feel more secure, then yes."

Jada nodded. "Thank you. I just never really thought about the two of us past Dallas." She hadn't dared to think about more than the moment. San Francisco had seemed far off in the distance, but it wasn't anymore. They were here, now.

He stared at her. "And after last night, you're having second thoughts?"

She heard the edge to his voice, but they had to

face that they were in muddy waters. "It's clear there's something between us," Jada replied. "I don't deny that."

"But—"

"It won't be easy hiding my feelings toward you." Feelings she didn't clearly understand, and sleeping with Damian wasn't going to make it any easier. "I don't like being sneaky, but right now I don't see another way." She'd begrudgingly begun earning her colleagues' respect. She didn't want to lose it. Yet, she didn't want to give up the amazing connection she had with Damian, even knowing she could fall deeply in love with him.

"Then it's settled."

Jada shrugged. "I guess so."

Damian threw the covers back and walked toward the bathroom. When he made it to the door, he said, "Then what are you waiting for? Let's get clean."

AN HOUR LATER, Jada was sitting at her desk, staring blankly at her computer screen reliving her own movie trailer of the morning's highlights: Damian hoisting her up against the wall and ramming into her in the shower. Damian's kindness when he'd pulled a box from the closet to reveal a designer dress with matching shoes and the most beautiful lingerie from La Perla. He'd purchased them with the hope she might stay over and wear them one day. And since he didn't want her to be late to work, she'd generously accepted the gift.

Now, she was wearing the dress Damian had personally handpicked for her along with the sexy lace push-up bra and knickers that were mere wisps of fabric and left nothing to the imagination. Just knowing he'd be thinking of her in them was a heady feeling.

"Earth to Jada." Kyler stood in front of her cubicle and leaned over her desk.

Jada blinked back. "Oh, hey girl. How are you?"

"I'm fine, but you looked far away. Everything OK? Are Bree and the baby alright?"

Jada smiled. "Oh yes, they're fine. Thank you so much for asking. I'm sorry if I was preoccupied."

"It's OK. I just thought we might catch up later. You know, maybe have girls' night out."

A flash of black caught Jada's attention, and Kyler followed her gaze. It was Damian. He'd just walked into the newsroom and was talking to Andrew.

"Boss man is here. He's been MIA all week," Kyler said. "I thought he might have tired of us already. No such luck."

"He's not that bad."

"Hey, I thought you were with me in thinking he might not be good for WLB-TV. But then again, maybe you're not. He did give *you* the Friday morning anchor spot. Maybe you were onto something by speaking your mind. Clearly it didn't hurt your career."

"I'm just as surprised as you are. I wasn't his favorite person when he bought the station."

"But you are now." Kyler winked. "Have any tips?"

Jada's mind wandered to when she'd taken him in her mouth last night and watched Damian fall apart. "Umm, no, I don't. Guess I was just lucky."

"I hope your luck rubs off on me. How about cocktails tonight? It's been ages since we hung out on a Friday night."

"Of course." Her life couldn't revolve around Damian and their next booty call.

When Damian called later, asking if they could have dinner, Jada turned him down. "I'm sorry, but I made other plans."

"Please don't tell me we're back to square one and you're going out with some other joker. I thought we agreed to be exclusive."

"And we are. I'm going out for girls' night and having cocktails."

"Girls' night?"

"You know, when women get together, have cocktails, and talk about men, work, and family. Oh, and did I mention men? I'm sure guys do it too."

"I don't."

"C'mon. You don't have any male friends who you hang out with and shoot the breeze?"

"No, I don't." He sounded affronted that she'd asked him. "I'm much too busy for that sort of thing."

"Well, I'm not," Jada whispered into the phone so no one would hear her. "I have a life, friends, and family, and I'm not going to give them up simply because we're sleeping together."

"I never asked you to. I, I just thought that since we'd made it official, we'd spend our first night together as a real couple. But clearly I was wrong, and I'm sorry to have bothered you. I will be sure and contact you in advance to make sure your calendar is clear."

Click.

Jada stared down at the phone. Had he just hung up on her? The sound of the dial tone told her he had indeed ended their call. She'd had no idea he would be so sentimental about their relationship. It was just sex after all. But she supposed she could make an effort to be more considerate of his feelings in the future.

~

DAMIAN STARED DOWN at the phone in his hands. He shook his head in consternation. He couldn't believe he'd actually behaved so childishly and hung up on Jada. He'd just been so annoyed that she wasn't available this evening. He'd given great thought to their first night together. He'd even made reservations at his favorite restaurant in San Francisco to impress her. But he'd gotten his signals crossed.

Jada wasn't as invested in this little relationship of theirs. Well, if she wasn't going to give him the time of day, he would do the same. He had business to run across the country. He didn't have time to cater to this fascination he had with Jada. When the time came that Jada finally found herself available and ready for him, he would show her exactly what she'd missed.

~

"I CAN'T BELIEVE we're finally hanging out," Kyler said when she and Jada were seated on a plush velvet sofa in a nearby martini bar later that evening. "You've been so busy lately."

"I'm sorry if I've been incommunicado."

"You couldn't have predicted Bree's pregnancy scare."

"I know, but I have been a bit self-absorbed with my own drama. How are you?"

Kyler shrugged. "I would feel better if I knew what

I'd done wrong and why Damian doesn't want me to be Hilary's backup."

"You know I had nothing to do with his decision."

"Yes, of course, I know that, here," Kyler said, pointing to her head, "but here," she said, pointing to her heart, "feels a bit wounded. Damian sees something in you that I'm missing, and I wish I knew what it was."

Jada felt guilty because although she deserved the spot—she'd been at the station longer than Kyler— she wasn't entirely sure Damian's decision had nothing to do with the relationship they shared. "You're a great news correspondent, Kyler. You mustn't let this ruin your confidence."

"I just wish I knew what he was looking for so I could prove how invaluable I am."

"You'll figure it out."

Kyler nodded. "Enough about work. Let's talk about something more upbeat, like *who* has you preoccupied."

"Wh-what are you talking about?" Jada feigned ignorance.

"C'mon, Jada. We've known each other for years, and I know what you look like when you're smitten. So spill. Are you seeing someone?"

"No one."

Kyler raised a brow. "Bull. I've seen that starry-eyed, glazed look before. Remember when you were seeing that football player, what's his name."

"Brady Smith."

"Yes." Kyler pointed to her. "Exactly him. You were so sprung on that fella. Lately, you've been acting the same way."

Jada weighed what she could tell Kyler. She couldn't

spill her guts and tell her she was seeing their boss, especially given Kyler's feelings of inadequacy. It would
be like pouring salt on her wounds, not to mention that
Kyler might think Jada had the upper hand because she
was sleeping with Damian. No, no, she couldn't tell her
the truth, but she could give her a portion of it.

"OK, OK. I admit I recently began seeing someone,
but it's much too early to call it anything other than
hooking up."

"Must be damn good given the glazed look I
caught on your face today."

Jada chuckled. "I admit he's been putting it
on me."

"Oh really?" Kyler lit up with a smile.

"To be honest with you, I think he's the best I've
ever had." Jada blushed as she sipped her martini. "He
knows exactly what buttons to push, if you know what
I mean."

Kyler fanned herself with her hand. "Damn, it's
like that? Wish I could get some of what you're having." She picked up her glass and liberally sipped her
drink.

"He's got me twisted. I can't think straight."

"Tell me more. How did you meet? What does
he do?"

"We met at a work function. I don't remember
which one," Jada lied. She couldn't exactly tell Kyler
that she'd met the man about a month ago. It might
give her away. "He's a businessman."

"That doesn't tell me much. Do you mean to tell
me that's all you know? Are you sure he's not married,
Jada? I'd hate to see you get in over your head."

Jada shook her head. "He's not married, Kyler. I
checked him out online."

"Good girl. I always background check men these days. You can just never be too careful."

"Have you given up on Tinder?"

"Girl, please." Kyler sighed. "I've given up on dating entirely. It's just too hard to find a good man. That's why I'm living through you, vicariously getting tasty snippets about your love life because mine is nonexistent. If it keeps going like this, I'm going to be as dry as the Sahara Desert down below, if you get my drift."

Jada burst out laughing. She placed her martini glass on the table. "C'mon, let's get out there and dance. We've got to lighten up the mood." She didn't like having to keep secrets from Kyler, but Jada had been the one who'd suggested keeping her and Damian's relationship a secret because she didn't want any fallout at work.

So, she had to live with her decision.

～

DAMIAN GLANCED down at his phone. Three missed calls from Jada. He'd proven his point that he was just as busy as she was, but he felt hollow. He'd like nothing better than to have Jada come over tonight. It would be a salve given that he'd wanted to spend the evening with her.

But he realized Jada had no illusions that this fling, although monogamous, would eventually end. She was preparing herself for the eventual fallout by staying at a distance from him. In the past, that wouldn't have mattered because when Damian was done with a sexual relationship, he moved on. But being with Jada wasn't so cut and dried. She was not just in his body . . . she had also creeped her way into his heart.

Maybe seeing less of her was just what he needed to clear his head. The old adage "out of sight, out of mind" might just be right. It was for the best because he was years away from being ready for the demands of a serious relationship, let alone marriage and children. He doubted he was even cut out for fatherhood after what he'd endured.

Damian had mastered the art of being alone—understood the nuances, never let anyone close. He shook his head, dismissing the topic from his mind and determined to focus on McKnight Media. Yet, he couldn't stop himself from feeling a mix of unhappiness and frustration at Jada's choice of companion for the evening.

JADA CALLED Damian on her way home, but the call went straight to voicemail *again*. *What is this all about?* He'd said he wanted to spend time with her, but now he wasn't picking up? She'd thought they were over these childish games. If she knew where he lived, she'd drop by and give him a piece of her mind. But last night had been so steamed, she'd barely noticed any landmarks on the way there.

Well, if he wanted them to have a committed physical relationship, he was going to have be more open with information, especially something as simple as his address. Jada wondered if Damian even knew how to open up. He was great in the bedroom and knew how to express himself with his needs and desires, but take him out of that arena and he was completely inept.

Maybe she should have given more thought before accepting his terms. Instead, she'd given in immediately because she was powerless to defend herself against the man's charisma. Damian had a way of upending her that no other man before him had. That scared her. She didn't want to fall in love with a man incapable of offering love.

17

By Saturday afternoon, after yoga and running a few errands, Damian still hadn't called. So, Jada took matters into her own hands. She headed to the station. She was a reporter after all and was sure she could find some information with his name and address. The parking lot was half full with only a minimal crew for the weekend shows, but she spotted Damian's Tesla sitting in the reserved spot and she pulled her Jaguar beside his.

Jada hopped out of the car and stormed into the station toward his office on the second floor in her yoga gear. When she reached his door, she swung it open with a thud. Damian looked up from his laptop.

She drank in the sight of him from the doorway. He was wearing jeans and a Polo shirt and, heaven help her, he looked good enough to eat. For his part, he stared at her intensely until eventually Jada broke the eye contact by folding her arms across her chest. "Look who we have here." She walked toward his desk, then glanced down at his phone and grabbed it. She swiped it back and forth. "And guess what? It works."

Damian's obsidian eyes glared at her from across the desk. "Jada."

She tossed the phone down. "Do you have anything to say for yourself?"

He shrugged. "No, why would I?"

"Because!" She stomped her foot. "I called and texted you half a dozen times with no response."

"I was merely giving you your space. I wouldn't want you to feel like you were at my beck and call or that I was crowding you."

"Really? I didn't have to come here, but I was foolishly trying to . . ." Her words trailed off. Why would she put forth the effort if he didn't want to make this work? If all he wanted was a bed buddy, he could find someone else. She was done.

She spun on her heel and started toward the door. Lightning fast, Damian caught up with her right outside his door near the stairs. "Jada, wait!" He moved closer into her personal space. Her breathing shortened, and Jada felt herself flush at his nearness. "What?" She lowered her eyes to avoid looking at him.

"Don't leave."

"Why not? You don't want to speak to me, so what's the point?"

His forefinger lifted underneath her chin, forcing her to look up at him. "I'm sorry."

She hadn't been expecting an apology. "Excuse me?"

"I'm sorry," he said again. "I was acting like a child. I was upset that you weren't available last night. I let it get the better of me because I wanted to spend time with you. There! Are you happy?"

Jada couldn't resist a grin, and her anger immediately evaporated. Damian was admitting his true feelings, and she knew how hard it was for him to open up. "Was that truly hard for you to say? It's OK to miss me, Damian. I missed you too, which is why, if you'd picked up your phone last night, I would have told you so and come over."

"Can we start over? Jada, would you like to have dinner with me tonight? Say seven p.m.? I can pick you up from your place."

"On a date?" Jada glanced down the stairs. No one was watching them, but they were out in the open. "Are you sure that's a good idea?"

"I have a very private place in mind."

Jada nodded. "Alright then. I'd love to have dinner with you."

"And *dessert*?" He raised a mischievous eyebrow.

She chuckled. "Yes. I'll bring my overnight bag."

Damian leaned in closer to her ear and whispered, "Good, because I'm going to need the whole night to make up for yesterday."

"All night?" Jada's tongue slid out to wet her lips.

"That's right. So, you'd better get some rest." He swatted her on the behind as she bounded down the stairs.

DAMIAN ARRIVED at her doorstep at seven o'clock on the nose after she'd texted him her address. He whistled when she opened her door. She was wearing a rose-colored strapless number bedazzled with studs and crystals, paired with gold stilettos. The fit of the dress gave her defining curves that would leave Damian salivating for the evening. Her hair was down, curled simply, just the way he liked it.

He gave her a once-over down the length of her

body. His unspoken message was clear: He intended to ravish her *all* night long. "You look hot!"

Jada beamed. "Thank you. I try."

"You don't have to try too hard." He brushed his lips across hers. "You're beautiful. Is that your bag?" He inclined his head toward her Keepall a few feet away.

"Yes."

He grabbed it and her hand and led her to the elevator. Once in the lobby, Jada noticed that they were the center of attention. Outside, Damian's Tesla was parked by the valet stand, and after helping her inside and depositing her bag in the trunk, Damian slid in beside her. Then he surprised her by reaching across and taking her hand. When she tried to snatch it back, he captured it with his own and held her tight. She glanced at him, and his eyes were warm. Jada's heart thudded as she waited with baited breath as he leaned over and molded his mouth perfectly to hers.

Jada released a low moan that Damian swallowed as he claimed her lips. He drenched her senses so thoroughly that she wanted to protest when his mouth finally pulled away from hers.

"We can pick that up again later," he said huskily and started the engine.

The drive was a half hour with all the weekend traffic, but when they arrived at their destination, Jada was shocked to find the restaurant empty.

She turned to Damian. "What's going on?"

"I wasn't able to reschedule the dinner for last night that I'd arranged, so I thought this would be the next best thing. The entire restaurant is ours for the evening."

"You bought out the restaurant?"

He grinned. "Yes. You wanted privacy. We have it."

"Don't you think that's a little excessive?" Jada laughed. "I only meant some place secluded or off the beaten path."

"This is better. Come." He led her toward a table set for two in the middle of the restaurant.

He pulled out her chair, and Jada sank into it. She couldn't believe the magnitude of how far Damian had gone to get her alone. She didn't want to admit it, but it made her heart turn over. Could his feelings be deeper than she thought?

A waiter approached them with a bottle of champagne that Jada knew cost an exorbitant amount. She watched Damian as a glass was poured for him to taste. With a slight nod, Damian indicated his satisfaction and the waiter continued filling their glasses.

"To a wonderful evening." Damian held up his flute.

After clinking her flute with his, Jada barely recalled the rest of the evening. A flurry of servers carried delectable bites for them to try. A world-renowned chef even came out, and Jada did her best to summon enough excitement at having his Michelin-starred food, but she'd barely eaten any of it. Her thoughts were on one thing: the enigmatic man in front of her.

Was Damian a closet romantic showing her his interest? Or was he the powerful media mogul intent on ruling televisions and radios in every household? Or maybe he was the kind and caring man who'd sat by her side at the hospital and chapel when she'd prayed for Bree. She'd made the decision to be with Damian. He wanted her and cared about her, but with him, love wasn't on the menu. Despite the ambiguity, she would have to roll with it. She was here, and that would have to be enough.

"Penny for your thoughts?" Damian said as they sipped on cappuccinos after finishing dinner.

"Hmm?"

"You've been introspective tonight. Did you not like dinner? Was this too over the top?" He motioned around the empty restaurant.

Jada noted the hint of doubt in his voice. It was unusual for Damian not to be completely sure of himself. She reached across the table and placed her hand over his. "This was absolutely wonderful. Thoughtful even."

"But?"

"You don't have to do this to win me over," Jada voiced what she'd been thinking most of the night.

"That's very perceptible of you."

"How so?"

"When I was in and out of foster homes, I always tried to please in the hopes that one of the families would want to keep me."

Jada couldn't believe Damian was telling her something so deeply personal without her pulling it out of him. They were definitely making progress. "Except that day never came." It was a statement, not a question.

Damian fingered the rim of his mug back and forth. "That's right."

Jada noted the telltale sign that he was nervous and didn't like the direction the conversation was going in. "You don't have to try and please me, Damian. You're going to get lucky tonight either way." She teased because she didn't like the somberness that had come over him.

"Am I?" His eyes pierced hers from across the short distance, and something intense flared between them.

"Yes. So, why don't you get the check so we can get out of here?"

Damian sprang to his feet within seconds. "No need. It was already taken care of." He extended his arm to her. "Let's get the second half of this evening started."

Jada rose and accepted his arm. "Can't wait."

The subsequent ride to Damian's place was filled with prolonged anticipation of what would come next. The elevator ride up was nearly unbearable, so Jada said, "You know, I have no idea of where you live. I mean, I don't have your address. So, last night, I—"

Jada never got another word in because Damian eased one hand around her waist and kissed her.

JADA'S BODY aligned perfectly with Damian's, making desire explode in his veins and heat his skin from the inside out. From the moment he laid eyes on her in the station conference room, he'd felt a fast-burning lust that only she could slake. He tightened his arms around her and angled for a deeper kiss that better suited him.

Jada's lips softened under his, and Damian used it so he could explore her properly even though they'd yet to make it to the penthouse. The kiss was so damn hot, he wanted the clothes between them gone. She detonated a need in him that made his heart jolt and his pulse pound.

The elevator door chimed, and slowly Damian pulled away. "We're here."

Jada glanced up, and he scanned her eyes. She was just as thrown by the dizzying currents racing through them as was he. He didn't waste any time with pleasantries. He knew what he wanted and grasped her hand. After entering the penthouse, he walked her directly to his bedroom, where he deposited Jada and her Keepall. Not that she would need any clothes—he intended on keeping her naked for as long as possible.

"Don't I even get a drink?" she asked.

Damian removed his suit jacket and began unknotting his tie. "Do you need one?" When his tie was sufficiently loosened, he tossed it away and toed off his shoes. Then he began attacking the buttons on his shirt all while Jada stood there in that daring rose dress that fit her like a bandage. He'd wanted to tear it off all night, and he couldn't wait a second longer. His shirt had the same fate as the tie. When he was bare-chested, he walked toward her, and she melted into him. Her soft lips came alive with his kiss, and her body snuggled right into his. He groaned as hot spikes of desire surged through him.

He didn't think he'd ever find a woman quite like Jada who intrigued him, mind and body. And Lord, her body he knew intimately with all its nuances. He was looking forward to heightening the experience tonight. All night.

Damian felt Jada's fingertips as she slid them up his sensitized back . . . and lower. When she reached his butt, she gave him a firm but gentle squeeze and his groin swelled. If she kept that up, their first time tonight would be over quickly.

"Wait." He lowered his head to kiss her nape and shoulder while his fingers walked down the curvature of her back until he found the hidden zipper. He drew it down until, eventually, the dress fell in a puddle on the floor and bared her breasts to his hungry gaze.

"I could look at you for hours," he whispered. He took one round globe in his palm. He massaged and kneaded it until her nipple puckered for him, then he lowered his head and swirled his tongue across her flesh. He latched on and sucked her with quick little pulls. Air whooshed out of Jada's lungs as she threw her head back, allowing him to take liberties. The action made her nipple drive deeper into his mouth, and he scraped it with his teeth, tonguing it until he switched to her other breast to lick and suck, alternating his movements until she squirmed in his arms. Only then did he let up, but only as far as to walk her backward to the bed and tumble them both onto it in a mass of limbs.

When he raised his head, his gaze raked her, then he quickly went to his knees to aim for the juncture between her thighs. He needed to taste her. When he reached her panty and ran his hands across her, Damian grinned when he found purchase. His hand dipped inside the elastic edge to the soft fuzz of hair between her legs, and Jada let out a low moan. She was already slick and wet for him. It made Damian crazy. With a tug, he ripped her panty off.

"Damian!"

He said nothing. He simply put his mouth over her center. She nearly bucked off the bed. He placed firm hands around her hips to hold her in place so he could tongue her properly. When she tried to pull away from his exquisite torture, he gripped her rear and shoved her closer against his mouth. He tunneled her bare flesh and drove deep into her core. Jada arched off the bed as her climax struck, panting and clutching at his shoulders as if she were desperate for something to hold on to. Damian continued licking and sucking her with light flicks of his tongue until she eventually quieted.

When he finally slid back up her body, her face

was glistening with sweat. "Omigod!" she said as she looked into his eyes. "You were . . . That was—"

"Was as good for me as it was for you?" he offered as his lips curved into a smile. He had enjoyed lapping up her delicious juices.

"I'll have to return the favor," Jada said with a sly smile.

"Oh, most definitely. But that was just an appetizer. I'm ready for the entrée," Damian said and pulled her underneath him.

GENTLENESS WAS NO LONGER part of Damian's agenda. She heard the crackling of a foil packet, and then Damian was resetting himself between her thighs, gripping her hips, and surging inside her still damp, quivering body. Jada felt him deep inside her as he filled up every square inch. She wanted to close her eyes, but Damian was lacing his fingers through hers so he could pin them over her head. Then he drove into her. Harder. Faster. She tried to open her legs wider to give him more room, but she needn't have bothered, because in that moment, Damian owned her.

Nonsensical words erupted from her lips when he hit just the right spot, and she exploded. Ripples after ripples of pleasure coursed through her, and she clawed at his back and held on for the ride.

"Jada!" Damian was unleashed. He threw his head back as he thrust even deeper, ripping a cry from deep within her. Despite her second orgasm, Jada could feel herself cresting again and moving with him at a relentless pace. Their bodies were slick with sweat. She didn't care. It could go on forever, yet she wasn't sure she could withstand it.

Damian swore. "You feel so damn good." He had to feel as overwhelmed as she did by the intensity of their lovemaking because he gave one final thrust. Jada heard her own scream and the roar of Damian's groan as he found his own release and fell on top of her.

Slowly, he removed his weight and shifted onto his side. "I have to catch my breath," he whispered. "You wore me out."

"You made me come *three* times."

Damian grinned as he rolled onto his back. "Was that a record?"

"I think so." Jada had the soreness between her thighs to prove it. But it wasn't unwelcome. She'd wanted Damian just as badly.

"It's not been like this with other women."

"Have there been many?" They'd never talked about their past relationships, but she was curious and hoped he would answer.

Damian glanced down at her. "Not how you mean. I've had lovers, but they've all been temporary."

Jada scooted next to him and slid her fingers over his smooth chest. "Why do you think that is?"

"Are you trying to shrink me, Jada? If so, I've tried therapy before, and it didn't work."

She sat upright. "You have?"

He nodded. "I had a lot of pent-up anger at my mom's abandonment and the loss of power I felt being in those foster homes and then frustration at losing the Locketts right when I'd finally found my way."

"I can understand that. Do you think it's why you avoid relationships?"

"I don't avoid them. I've just chosen not to have any until now."

"You consider us a relationship?" If so, he had a lot to learn about male and female interactions.

"It's the closest thing to one I've ever had."

Jada pondered his statement. Damian could share his bed, but not his heart? It was the missing piece in their "relationship." He was willing to give her his body, but nothing else. What was he so afraid of? Of getting hurt? If so, Damian didn't have the monopoly on hurt. She'd been betrayed.

"We're a lot alike, Jada, you and me. You keep men at a distance. Have you ever even had a serious relationship?" Damian remembered what Duke had said about her once having her heart broken, but that's all he knew about Jada's romantic past.

Jada's eyes filled with tears because despite how much of a connection they had in bed, he didn't really know her. She turned away, onto her side. She didn't want him to see her cry, to see how deep the hurt went at not being wanted. "Yes, yes, I have, Damian. I was engaged once, and he canceled the wedding a week before we were to be married. So, I do know what it's like to commit to someone."

"Jada, you're crying." He reached across her and tried to turn her to face him, but Jada refused to budge. So Damian leapt over her until he could face her and lie down in front of her.

"Baby, I'm sorry. I had no idea." He swiped at the tears trickling down her face. "I'm sorry for being so callous and unfeeling." He scooped her in his arms and gently rubbed her back. "I didn't mean to hurt you. I'd never want to hurt you."

Jada sniffed and pulled away. She heard the regret in his tone. She knew he hadn't intentionally set out to drum up bad memories, but her failed engagement was a sore spot. "It's OK."

"Do you want to tell me about it?"

Jada shrugged. "Not really, but since I started the conversation, I might as well tell my story." She paused for several minutes, wondering just how much she should say. She settled for the unadulterated truth. "Joshua and I were childhood sweethearts. We grew up together. Our families knew each other and all that. It was a foregone conclusion we'd get married and I'd spit out a couple of kids. I was content with that, happy even, but a week before we were supposed to get married, Joshua turned the tables on me. Told me I had a pretty face but was a terrible lover, which is why he'd been dipping out the door for some time on me."

"That's awful, Jada."

"He was the only man I'd ever been with. I saved myself for him. Did he have to destroy me as he left? Anyway, I had to figure out what I was going to do with my life after it took a complete 360-degree turn. So I reinvented myself. Went to college and majored in journalism. Figured I'd be the next Katie Couric or Diane Sawyer. Then I set about learning a thing or two in the bedroom department." When she glanced at Damian, she didn't like the look of pity he was giving her. "Don't look at me like that. I'm no slut. I do discriminate who I take to my bed. But I vowed no man would ever tell me I was a lousy lay."

"Jada," Damian said her name softly. "You're the furthest thing from being bad in bed. I can tell you un-equivocally that you're the best lover I've ever had."

She shook her head and lowered her lashes. "You don't have to say that after I told you my sob story."

"Look at me." He stroked her cheek until she

glanced up at him. "I'm not lying. I think you're incredible. Why do you think you're the first woman I've asked to be in a monogamous relationship with me? So come here." He circled his arms around her again and pulled her downward. "Let's go to bed."

Jada chuckled inwardly. Damian didn't realize he'd left out the word *sexual*, and she wasn't about to tell him. Perhaps they'd both learn something about themselves from this experience.

18

———

Jada and Damian spent Sunday morning in bed before eventually emerging for food and drink. Jada was surprised when Damian managed to whip up some tasty scrambled eggs and bacon along with some orange juice.

"That was delicious."

"It was nothing but eggs and bacon."

"I know, but take it from someone who doesn't cook, that was impressive. I can't even boil an egg." Jada sipped on a cappuccino Damian had made. "Where did you learn to cook?"

"Well, when your mother can't be bothered to take you to school, you learn to be self-sufficient and make your own breakfast. It was trial and error."

"You had to deal with so much when you were young. It's incredible you survived."

Damian shrugged. "Let's not talk about my sad tale of woe. Let's talk about what we're going to do today. Any ideas?"

"How about going to Sausalito? It's a sleepy town that reminds me of the Mediterranean. There're lots of stores and souvenir shops, and they have some super-cool houseboats we can look at. We could take the ferry or drive across the Golden Gate Bridge, whichever you prefer."

"Sounds like a mighty fine idea. I'm game."

An hour later, they were on the bridge after making the half-hour toll-free drive into Sausalito in Damian's Tesla. There wasn't much street parking, but they found a paid lot just off the bridge.

"Is it warmer here?" Damian asked when he opened Jada's door. He removed his sweater and tossed it into the car. Now he was wearing only trousers and a button-down shirt, while Jada had opted for a simple shirtdress with a belt and some espadrilles.

"No, I just think it feels that way when you're away from the San Francisco smog. C'mon, let me show you the place."

Damian grasped her hand, and he and Jada meandered through boutiques and shops. Jada purchased a few odds and ends while Damian seemed to be content with just watching her, which was disconcerting. When they stopped at one of the many art galleries, he became more engaged and they had a lively discussion about the artist's vision. Eventually, they stopped at a side-street café and sat outside to eat, drink wine, and enjoy the sophisticated charm of the beautiful bayside community.

After their bellies were full, they found a houseboat community and walked the planks to tour it. There were a few battered survivors from the old era of improvised houseboats. But there were also some new, well-maintained floating homes with docks lined with flowers that some owners used as their front yard.

By the time the sun set, Damian and Jada were back in the car and on their way back into San Francisco. "I really enjoyed spending the day with you," Damian commented.

"You sound surprised."

He shook his head. "Not by your company, but the easy rapport we share. I feel like I can be myself with you. It's refreshing is all."

His honesty was immensely appealing, and Jada couldn't resist smiling. She just wished he could see that they could be more to each other than just bedmates. She was slowly starting to make her way around the wall he'd erected around himself. And she understood. She'd done the same. She hadn't had a close relationship with another man since Joshua, but the difference was that she was willing to take a risk again. It was scary. She could get hurt, but perhaps they both needed to stop playing it safe and venture out of their comfort zone.

Suddenly, her phone began to ring. It was Bree.

Jada's heart lurched, and she turned to look at Damian, whose mouth had pinched into a frown. "Bree? Is everything OK? Is it the baby?"

"Slow down, baby girl," Bree said on the other end of the phone. "We're both fine. I just called to see if you heard the news?"

"What news?"

"Mama and Daddy are getting remarried!"

"What?" Jada nearly dropped the phone at hearing the best family news in nearly two decades. "Are you sure? You're not punking me or something?"

"I would never do that on something as important and momentous as this. It's true. Our parents are getting hitched."

"Where? When? And why didn't they call me?" Jada could hardly contain her excitement. They'd been waiting for this day for so long. It hardly seemed real.

"They were going to tell you, but I think I beat them to the punch. Anyway, they're getting married in a month."

"A month?" Jada looked at Damian. He took his eyes off the road for a second and raised his brow. "How are we supposed to arrange a wedding in that time frame?"

"You know Mama. She doesn't want anything big. Just wants to get married at the ranch surrounded by family and friends."

Jada sighed. It was signature Abigail Hart not to want to make a fuss, but her daughters wouldn't let their parents slink away into the night. "I'm flying in next weekend to help."

"You have a job in San Fran. And you were just here for me. Take the time for the wedding, nothing more."

"I dunno."

"Trust your big sis. I've never led you wrong, have I?"

"Well, no, you haven't. But I'm still calling my planner, Deborah Kenney. She can help Mama plan something small, yet elegant."

"Alright, but don't go overboard. You know Mama."

"Will do." Jada ended the call just as Damian arrived to her condominium. "My place?"

"Didn't you say we needed to get to know each other? We can't spend all our time at my place, and I want to see how you live."

"But what about my things?"

"I had my maid pack them up and drop them off to your doorman."

Jada smiled. What was going on? First her parents'

sudden marriage and now Damian was acting like a real boyfriend by coming to her condo. "That sounds great."

As arranged, Jada's bag was indeed with the doorman. They grabbed it on the way up to her place. It was strange opening the door. She usually never had men over, choosing to stay at their place instead, but having Damian in her domain was significant.

"Here we are." Jada swept her arm around the room in a flourish after they entered the open-concept condo. Damian walked around, and she noticed he stopped in the living room and fingered the many family pictures on her mantel. Her parents. Her sisters Bree and London with their husbands. London's child. A group picture of the Arizona Harts. Uncle Isaac, Aunt Madelyn, and their kids with their spouses at their Golden Oaks dude ranch in Tucson. Noah and Chynna Hart. Rylee and Amar al' Mahmud. Caleb and Addison Hart along with Chynna's sister, Kenya, and her husband, Lucas Kingston, who'd been adopted into the family.

"You have a large family. I forgot that Chynna and Kenya Hart are part of your expansive group. What's it like having a wildly popular singer and Oscar-winning actress in the family?"

"Daunting. But I expect they'll all be at the wedding."

"It must be nice," he said wistfully before moving over to the kitchen. It wasn't spacious, but it suited Jada's needs and held the most important appliance: a coffeemaker.

"How long have you owned your place?" he asked.

"Several years," Jada said as she followed him. "When I first moved to San Fran, I lived it up in a hotel for months enjoying room service and never having to make my bed. But it got old not having a place to call my own, not being able to just unwind without having to worry about how I looked walking through the lobby."

"The kitchen is great." He'd noticed the Sub-Zero appliances. "But I doubt this gets used much."

"Ha-ha." Jada laughed. "I told you I don't cook, but . . ." Her sentence trailed off as she strolled over to a cabinet and pulled the lever on one of the drawers. She grabbed a fistful of flyers. She picked up where she left off. "I can order great takeout. So which would you like? I have Thai, Chinese, Korean, Italian, Indian. What floats your boat?"

"You," Damian said as he circled his arms around her hips and hauled her into a notch near him where she always seemed to fit properly.

"Maybe later," Jada said as she moved away. Besides jumping into bed, they also had to be able to hold a conversation—she was going to see to that. "So, which one?" She held up the menu.

He snatched her favorite Thai-spot menu out of her hand. "This one."

"Excellent choice." Within minutes, she made their delivery order and they retired to her couch. Jada's legs were slung over Damian's while he fiddled with the remote control to find something on TV. A thought occurred to Jada, and she decided to test just how into her Damian was. "So, I was thinking—"

"Yes?"

"If you're not doing anything at the end of the month . . .," she paused, "that you might like to come with me to the wedding."

Suddenly, Damian turned to her. She'd clearly stunned him with her offer because his dark eyes were searching her. But he was silent.

"Well?"

"You want me to come as your date to your parents' wedding, where your entire family will be in attendance?"

Jada's heart sunk. She didn't like the ominous tone that accompanied that statement. "It's OK." She shrugged. "It was a stupid idea."

He reached for her hand. "It wasn't stupid, Jada. It's just if I come as your date, it might give your family the wrong idea."

"And what idea might that be? That we might last and be more than a casual fling? Heaven forbid!" Jada rolled her eyes and pushed his hand away to sit upright. "I wouldn't want to push you into doing anything you don't want other than having me flat on my back."

"That's not fair, Jada. We spent a great day together—a day I immensely enjoyed because I spent it with you. I just don't want to confuse things between us or your folks that I'm capable of offering more than what is on the table."

Jada wanted to throw up. She swallowed back the bile rising in her throat even though his words destroyed the tiniest shred of hope she'd thought they'd gained by today's outing. All she could do was nod.

He must have seen how downcast she was, because he said, "But I can see how much this means to you, so I'll come if you still want me to."

She didn't want him to come because he'd been guilted into it. Jada wanted him to attend because he *wanted* to be with her. There was a difference. "It's fine. I'll go stag."

"Jada—"

"It's fine." The doorbell chimed. "It's our food. I'll get it." She needed to do something before she dissolved into a puddle at his feet. It was clear that she was starting to care more for him, but the feeling wasn't reciprocated.

After signing the receipt and tipping the driver, Jada returned with brown paper bags and brought them into the kitchen. Damian was quiet as he joined her. The mood had quickly shifted from fun to tense. Jada ignored him even though he was a few feet from her and busied herself with finding plates and cutlery. But eventually, she had to turn around to face him.

Damian was staring at her intently.

"Aren't you ready to eat?" she asked.

"I can't eat with this tension between us."

Jada turned around and began opening the bags and pulling out cartons of Thai food. When she reached her pan-seared dumplings, she couldn't resist snatching one and having a nibble. She had to do something to stop the tears that welled in her eyes.

Why did it matter to her one way or the other if he came with her or not? It's not like she hadn't been home alone before on her own. She just supposed that now that her cousins and siblings were coupled up, it was going to be incredibly difficult going stag. Maybe if she just focused on her parents' happiness she wouldn't notice how lonely she was.

"So, you're not even going to look at me?"

She heard him but didn't dare look his way.

Damian grasped her shoulders and swung her around. His eyes were cloudy and unreadable as he peered into hers. "Jada, I'm sorry. You asked me to attend something very personal and momentous with you, and like a new puppy, I kind of pissed all over it."

Tears slipped down her cheeks, and Jada felt silly for letting Damian see how he'd affected her; but she appreciated the analogy.

"I'm sorry," he apologized again. "You were so happy before about hearing of your parents' impending marriage. Please don't let me being a Neanderthal ruin that. I want to come with you to Texas, if you'll still have me."

"You don't have to—" She never got another word out because Damian lowered his head and planted a soft kiss on hers. It was his usual toe-curling-type kiss, but maybe that's what made it all the more potent. When he lifted his head, she said, "Alright, I'd like that."

Later that evening, after marathoning episodes of *Law and Order*, they adjourned to her bedroom, where after stripping each other of clothing, they tumbled onto the bed. Then they made love. Sometimes, it was hot and frenzied; other times, it was slow and sweet. Jada felt as if he were trying to pay penance for the embarrassing way he'd handled her request to come to Texas. To be honest, she didn't care because what their argument had shown Jada was that she wasn't falling for Damian. She was already there. She was in love with him.

19

Damian sat back in his executive chair at the McKnight Media offices and thought about the last several weeks that had passed. He and Jada had been spending a great deal of time together. His lust for her had no bounds. Sometimes, he would make up excuses to go to the station or to her apartment. When he did, he found Jada was more than willing to participate and it would have been a crime against nature not to take advantage. Just the other day, they'd found a storage closet at the station, where he'd backed her against the door.

Within minutes, he'd moved their clothes around just enough so his ravenous mouth could find hers in the dark before he entered her. He'd buried himself deep inside her, and Jada had loved every minute of it, riding the wave after their climaxes struck them long and hard. Somehow, they'd managed to exit the closet with no one being the wiser. And when they weren't together, they were texting each other throughout the day. Damian never thought he'd get excited to see the tiniest of sentences from Jada or wait with anticipation for her responses. It was the highlight of his day.

Last night, she'd even gotten him to dance even though he'd yet to have a drink. It had been a long day at the office, and she'd told him he needed to let loose and have some fun. Fun wasn't usually in his playbook, but when she'd turned on the sound system in his entertainment center that he hardly ever used, some old school Bell Biv DeVoe *Poison* had come blasting through the speakers. So, he'd gotten *turned up*. He believed that was the lingo young folks used today.

Jada had moved her amazing body and zigzagged her torso in time to the beat. Damian couldn't help but grin at her energy, exuberance, and carefreeness. Her hair was flying, and her hips were gyrating as if she didn't have a care in the world. When she dared him to join her, he had. Although his movements were more like someone suffering from an epileptic seizure rather than just simply dancing, he'd enjoyed stomping and moving his arms. Soon, his arms had encompassed her waist and he and Jada had begun a slow dance. Damian couldn't recall the last time he slow danced with anyone. Usually, he just went straight to the bedroom, but Jada brought out a romantic side of him that had previously gone untapped.

What's happening to me?

He supposed it started the night at Jada's place when he hurt her feelings by not agreeing to accompany her to her parents' wedding. He'd royally stuck his foot in his mouth on that one. He hadn't thought he'd be able to get out of the muck, but somehow she'd forgiven him and agreed to let him come. Damian knew he didn't deserve it. Underneath it all, Jada was a good girl—a Southern girl who'd once aspired to be a wife and mother before life had handled her a crummy deal.

But she had reinvented herself, and Damian respected that about her because he'd done the same. Poor, orphaned boy from a substance-addicted mother was a cliché if ever there was one, but he was determined not to be judged by his past. He wanted to be the man that the Locketts had seen in him. And he'd done that by achieving the highest levels of success in his media empire; but he'd done it without anyone to share his life with. And for the first time, he wasn't alone. He had Jada. To listen. To talk to. To make love to. And although the sex between them was off the charts, she was so much more to him than just her body, which is why going with her to Texas scared the living daylights out of him.

If he thought they'd been on display at the hospital and the ranch on the previous trip, it would be much worse with the entire Hart clan in attendance this time. He didn't know if he could handle that. What would it be like to feel like part of a family like Jada's for the weekend?

He would find out next week.

JADA COULDN'T BELIEVE how great life was going. She'd always known she had what it took to anchor the news, and every Friday she was doing just that . . . thanks to Damian. He'd recognized her talent even when he'd wanted to paddle her over his knee. She just wished it didn't come at Kyler's expense. Her dear friend had been down in the dumps for weeks now.

As a pick-me up, Jada was treating Kyler to an exclusive day spa on Saturday morning. Damian was working, so Jada had plenty of free time.

"Thank you so much for this," Kyler said as she leaned back on the plush reclining seat with her feet in the fragrant water. Kyler had arrived earlier that morning to pick Jada up from her condo. Jada had tried to say no, but Kyler had insisted, saying it was the least she could do since Jada was treating. "I need something like this since McKnight has essentially benched me."

"You're absolutely welcome," Jada responded, but thinking about Damian made her feel guilty. Although it wasn't Jada's fault, she felt partly responsible that maybe their relationship was clouding Damian's judgment in seeing Kyler's potential. She needed to change the subject. "I know I've been busy the last few weeks and we haven't had a chance to hang out. This is my apology."

Kyler gave her a suspicious look. "You have been rather secretive lately. Are you still seeing the same man you mentioned a few weeks ago?"

Jada stalled. "Um, yeah. I am."

"Well? Are you going to tell me more about him? What's he like? What does he do for a living? Knowing you, I'm sure he's absolutely gorgeous and has a hot body."

Jada smiled. "Yes. And yes." She thought about what details she could give without lying to her friend. "He's a business owner, and he's a very private person."

Kyler frowned as the nail technician lifted her leg to scrub her foot with a pumice stone. "Are you absolutely sure he's not married, Jada? The fact you're still not revealing very much about him is very telling. You're usually always so open."

"That's because he's not just one of my men. He's more than that, Kyler. We've been trying the monogamous relationship thing, or at least we are in the sex department."

"So, you're using each other for sex?" Kyler chuckled. "OK, that makes sense. I can't see you getting serious about anyone, not when your career has always been so important to you. You're finally sitting in the anchor chair. Or at least you are one day a week. I can't see you letting a man get in the way of that."

Jada stared back at Kyler. She was sure Kyler didn't mean to offend her. Kyler wouldn't hurt a fly, but she was right. Jada's usual MO was to not care about the men she was casually dating. *And* her career was important to her, but she wasn't just using Damian for sex. Somewhere along the line, their relationship had deepened, and they were more than just fuck buddies.

"You OK?" Kyler asked. When Jada remained silent, Kyler covered her mouth with her hands. "I'm sorry. Was I too forthright just now? It's just that it's what you've always said, Jada: That you don't need a man. I'm sorry if I got that wrong. I can see you've fallen for this guy."

"How can you tell?"

"Because this goofy faraway look came across your face. I'm sure you were thinking of him just now. Weren't you?"

A slow smile slid across Jada's lips. "Maybe."

"It's OK." Kyler dipped her feet back into the water to rinse them off. "If you can't admit it to me, your friend, who can you admit it to?"

Damian, Jada thought. She doubted he wanted to hear that despite her best efforts to keep their involvement strictly physical.

Yes, she was really in love with him.

DAMIAN WAS WAITING for Jada at her condo when she arrived later that evening. He watched her close the door and lean against it.

He came toward her with a glass of expensive red wine. "I take it you feel like putty after a day of non-stop pampering?"

"Yes." She accepted the glass and allowed him to walk her into the living room. She slid down onto her sofa, and he was right beside her, placing her legs over his lap. "It was heavenly."

"Glad you enjoyed it."

She sipped her wine and regarded him. "How was your day?"

"Productive." He loosened the straps on her sandals and released her delicate feet from those devices of torture. *How do women stand it?* "I've been very impressed with the numbers at the station as of late. They've shown some improvement."

"That's fantastic." Jada beamed at him and placed her wineglass on the cocktail table. Her smile had a way of tugging at his heartstrings. "Does this mean there might be room for more changes?" She scooted onto his lap and wrapped her arms around his neck.

"Possibly. Why?"

"Oh, I don't know." She shrugged.

He didn't believe that for one minute. Jada had something on her mind. "Just spit it out, Hart!"

"Well, I was hoping that you might find a place for Kyler on air."

Damian frowned. He didn't appreciate Jada telling him how to run his station no matter how well-intentioned her actions might be. He grabbed her by the hips and set her back on the sofa. Then he stood up.

"We should keep business at the office." He strode toward the kitchen to get more wine.

"Don't you think that's a little impossible since I work for you?" Jada said as she turned her head to look at him.

"Jada."

"Don't Jada me." She jumped to her feet and stalked over. "I'm merely stating that you might want to reconsider Kyler and that maybe you've overlooked her talents."

"I haven't overlooked a damn thing," Damian stated tightly. "I've evaluated Ms. Barnes, and I don't think she has what it takes to anchor the news. The ratings' numbers don't lie. Don't get me wrong. She's a beautiful woman, but I think she's more geared toward small-town America news than she is for a big market like San Francisco."

"You can't know that," Jada defended her friend. "You've only been here for all of a hot minute." She snapped her fingers. "Kyler's been there just like I've been, toiling and paying her dues. She deserves to at least be given a chance."

"She did have a chance, and her numbers were nowhere as good as yours. Everyone knows it. So, should I give her your slot?" He folded his arms across his chest.

"Well . . . no."

"Then what would you have me do, Jada? There is only so much room at the top. Quite frankly, she doesn't have star power."

Jada spun away from him and said underneath her breath, "That's because your judgment is clouded," but Damian heard her loud and clear. His hand reached out to spin her around. Then he swung her into his arms until they were pressed against each other.

"You think you've got me wrapped around your little finger, do you?"

"Don't I?"

Those big brown eyes of hers searched his, and Damian had to struggle to answer. Perhaps she had cast a spell on him so much so he couldn't think of anyone else. But again, the ratings were what they were. So no, no, no, he couldn't let her win. Damian released her. "I'm not that easy. I happen to know talent, and I watched each and every one of your tapes before I ever stepped foot in the studio."

"So, you always intended to give me a chance?" Surprise was evident in her voice.

"Yes."

"You little shit!" She punched his arm, but it was more like a love tap than anything else. When she attempted a second punch, he caught her hand. "Let me go!"

"Not until you calm down."

"I'm upset. You had me on pins and needles for weeks, so that what . . . you could get your jollies off?" She tried to wiggle out of his arms, but Damian wasn't letting her go. With all of her movements to get out his grasp, she'd twisted herself and her bottom was now against his fly. Every time she moved, his member swelled.

"No. I did it so I could see what you were made of. I needed to see if what I saw on that tape was real or just in my head because I was attracted to you. The former won out."

At his words, her lungs deflated and all fight left her body. Rather than stop moving, however, she began grinding her hips against his front. "Don't start something you can't stop," he murmured in her ear. He didn't know why she needed to argue with him. Perhaps she relished sparring because she anticipated the makeup sessions. He supposed it was the same for him.

"Who says I want to stop?"

"Don't say I didn't warn you." He reached around her to unbutton the front of her jeans, then he zipped them down as far as he could go. He slipped his hands inside her waistband and heard her sharp intake of breath when he pushed past the curls to go lower. His fingers slid across her seam, and then he slid one inside her. She was tight and damp and oh so *hot*. Damian couldn't wait to ravish her, and Jada was ready for it. She was rocking on his hand back and forth, urging him on. She spread her legs wider and threw her head back against his chest, moaning out her pleasure.

"That's it. Give it to me," he whispered, and seconds later her core throbbed against his fingers and she let out a cry that went straight to his shaft like Jane's jungle cry to Tarzan. She collapsed against his chest and he held her close, binding her to him while his other hand reached inside his jeans pocket for his wallet and the spare condom he kept. This woman made him *insane* with lust.

In seconds, he had his jeans unzipped and had yanked Jada's jeans and panty down to the floor in one fell swoop. He positioned himself between her legs and bent her over the counter. Then he pushed to the hilt inside her with one powerful thrust from behind. A spiral of heat and light flashed through his eyes, and Damian swore he saw colors just as Jada was coming alive again from her post-orgasmic high.

She grasped the edge of the counter and lifted her

hips to give him an even better angle so he could go deeper and faster inside her. His hands slid lower, and he fingered her clit, all while thrusting inside.

"Yes, yes, yes," she cried.

He pumped into her over and over until his passion pushed them both over the edge, and he groaned. Jada's muscles clenched rigidly around him seconds later, milking him of every last drop of energy he had left as she came again.

"God, that was incredible!" Damian said as he buried his face in her neck and breathed in her deliciously sweet yet salty scent.

"Yes, it was."

The doorbell rang and Jada popped up, glancing at the door. "Who could that be?"

"It's probably the takeout I ordered," Damian said.

"I'll get it." Before he knew it, Jada had pulled up her panty and jeans and was zipping up as she walked to the door.

Damian marveled at how beautiful she looked completely disshelved after he'd just made love to her.

All he could think of was the incredible moment they'd just shared.

~

JADA OPENED HER FRONT DOOR.

Kyler was on the other side.

Jada had no time to react. Kyler barged straight into her living room holding her Fendi wallet. "I was driving home when I saw your wallet on the car floor. It must have dropped out of your purse. I thought I'd bring it by—"

Her words instantly stopped when she caught sight of Damian standing behind the kitchen breakfast bar. Kyler turned to Jada, whose cheeks had turned a bold red at having been caught with Damian in her condo.

"Do either of you two want to tell me what the fuck is going on?" Kyler asked.

Jada was stunned. She'd never heard the Ohio woman use such foul language. "Kyler, I know how this must seem."

Kyler placed her hands on her hips and glared at Jada. "Really? You're going to go there?"

"Ms. Barnes," Damian started, but Kyler held up her hand.

"Don't you dare speak to me. This is between me and my *supposed* friend. The one who's been under-mining me behind my back the entire time. Sleeping with the boss? How cliché even for you, Jada."

"Kyler, please," Jada began.

"Please what? Don't feel hurt? Betrayed by someone I called my friend? Someone who I had as my confidante? Shared my struggles and upsets with over how this man," she said, pointing to Damian, "was treating me? Marginalizing me? And yet there you were, listening, being sympathetic, when you were the very person stabbing me in the back."

"It's not like that. You have it all wrong."

"Oh, I have it right. How long has this been going on?" Kyler looked at Jada and then at Damian and then back to Jada. "Omigod, *he's* the man you've been talking about. The man you've been sleeping with for weeks. Christ! What a fool I've been." She started toward the door, but Jada stood in her path.

"Kyler, please don't leave. Not like this. Let me explain."

"What's there to explain? For years, no one would give you a break to be anchor, but now that you've been using the casting couch suddenly you get ahead? You should be ashamed, Jada. Embarrassed even. I hope you both rot in hell!"

Seconds later, Kyler slammed the door and was gone.

20

"What the hell just happened?" Damian yelled. He moved quickly from the spot he'd been rooted in since Kyler's surprise appearance and walked toward Jada. Tears were streaming down her beautiful cheeks. "Are you OK?" He grasped her arms.

"Of course not! I'm not sure anything will ever be right again."

"Jada . . ." He tried to rub her arms, but she wrenched herself away.

"Did you just hear what Kyler said? What she accused me of? How could she think that I would do such a thing?" Jada volleyed the questions at him as she paced her living room floor.

"I don't know."

"I would never hurt her. I didn't set out to sabotage her career, but that's what she thinks. She thinks I'm using our relationship to get ahead."

"Well, she's wrong."

"Is she?" Jada asked.

Anger flared inside Damian. He hated that Kyler had undermined Jada's confidence. "Yes, she is. As I told you before, I recognized your potential well before we slept together and knew I was going to give you a shot. So don't do this. Don't second-guess yourself."

Jada shook her head. "How can I not? Kyler and I have been friends for four years. And I never kept anything from her until now. Until we began this, this—"

"This what?" He frowned. He didn't like the direction this conversation was going in. It could go down the rabbit hole quickly.

"Affair," she spit out. She leaned against her fireplace mantel and looked down as if she'd said a dirty four-letter word.

"I never asked you to lie," Damian said quietly. "If you recall, it was your decision to keep our relationship under wraps."

Slowly, Jada raised her head. Fire raged in her eyes as she spoke. "C'mon, Damian. Don't tell me you weren't happy when I made the suggestion. I doubted you wanted everyone to know you were banging the help."

"Christ, Jada! There's no need to hit below the belt."

"I, I'm sorry," she sniffed. "I just don't know what to do. What if she tells everyone at the studio? It could ruin my reputation."

Damian ran his hand over his head. "Do you really think she'd be that vindictive?"

"I don't know. She's hurt and confused. I can't much blame her. I lied to her."

"No, I believe you told her you were seeing someone. You just didn't to tell her who."

"Half truths. They are still lies of omission, and she has every right to be upset. I mean look at us." She glanced at him. "What the hell are we doing?" She moved away from the fireplace, dropped onto the sofa, and placed her head in her hands.

"Jada."

She glanced up at him with puffy eyes and wet cheeks that were stained red. "What are we doing here, Damian?"

"We're two consenting adults who've been enjoying each other," he said. "There's nothing wrong with that. Don't make what we've shared seem ugly and seedy."

Jada lowered her head, and she continued to cry. Damian didn't know what to do. He'd never stuck around in a relationship long enough to get to this part—the up and down part. He didn't know how to handle it or give Jada the comfort she needed. He wasn't cut out for the relationship thing. Did this mean they were in trouble?

~

How can *he not get it?* Jada thought. Kyler finding out about them changed everything. They were no longer in a bubble with no outside world. The world had slowly encroached upon the passion-induced fog they'd been under the last several weeks. Jada loved Kyler and valued her friendship. The fact that her good friend thought her capable of such horrific acts made Jada sick.

It also made her question what she was doing with Damian and where their relationship could go. Jada knew where she would like it to go. She wanted a commitment. She wanted him to say their relationship was more than just physical. But he'd put the sexual parameter there first. She was afraid to cross the line, but didn't she have to?

Kyler knew the truth. Soon, the entire station would too.

Jada had to know where she stood with Damian because if he wasn't in it for the long haul, she wasn't going to put herself out there and take the ridicule and abuse she knew was coming. People would think she was using the relationship to get ahead.

She walked over to her couch and sat down. "What we have isn't wrong, but . . . it isn't right either."

He regarded her for a long moment as if weighing his options, then he stepped to the adjacent chair and sat. "What do you mean?"

"I went into this with my eyes wide open. I accepted your terms for a monogamous sexual relationship."

"Why do I hear a 'but' in there?"

"Because there is one. Although we're extremely compatible in bed, I want more."

"More what?"

"I want a real relationship that I can share with the world, my friends, and family. I want someone who loves me and cares about me. Someone who wants a future with me."

"I thought you were happy with the status quo."

"I was. But when Kyler just barged in here, it knocked off my blinders that we can't continue on this way, not indefinitely at least."

"Why not? We were doing pretty well. No, we were doing darn good. Did you forget what happened before the doorbell rang?"

Jada blushed. How could she forget? She'd been completely abandoned with Damian, letting him take her doggy style. And it had been damn good, but it wasn't enough. If she stayed with him, she would resent him for not wanting a full commitment. She didn't want that to happen. "Of course not, but sex isn't everything."

"I know that, Jada. I like you a lot. You know that. I wouldn't spend time with you if I didn't."

"But you're happy with the ways things are, aren't you? You get to have all the benefits of a real relationship without giving up anything in return, without making yourself vulnerable, without letting anyone in."

"Are you saying I'm heartless?"

"No, but I'm saying you hold a lot inside, and it's not easy breaking through your walls."

"I never asked you to."

"No, you didn't, because you want nothing more from me than my body. Sure, you'll share a meal or spend the day with me as a prelude to sex. I thought that was OK because Joshua fucked up my head when he left me at the altar. He destroyed my self-confidence and belief in myself. But no more. I'm listening to my gut, and it's telling me to speak up, to say that I want to spend my life with someone. I want marriage and babies someday on top of having a career. Hell, if my sister Bree and cousins Rylee and Chynna can do it, surely I can. I want a family of my own."

Damian stared back at her. His eyes were dark as midnight and clouded. She couldn't read his expression because he'd turned stone cold.

"Did you hear what I just said?"

"Yes. I heard every word."

"And?"

"I love my life, and I've enjoyed our time together, but I'm not capable of giving you more than I already have."

Jada scooted forward on the couch until their knees touched. She reached for one of his large masculine hands and laced it with one of her own. Then she asked the question she was afraid to hear the answer to. "Won't you even try?" Jada heard the tremble in her voice. *Do I sound as desperate as I feel trying to hang on to him?*

"I'm sorry, Jada. I can't." His fingers slipped through hers, and he stood up. "I should go."

"You're going to leave? Just like that?"

"I think it's best." Damian glanced around the room. She didn't know what he was looking for because a haze of tears were covering her eyes. She saw him grab his phone and walk toward her bedroom. When he returned, he was carrying his overnight bag.

Jada refused to beg. She'd done that with Joshua—begged him to stay with her. They could have made it work. She would have done anything for him. Instead, he'd told her she wasn't good enough for him in or out of bed and had walked out. She wouldn't be that pitiful woman she'd been then. With Damian, she'd take this on the chin. Jada stood and followed him to the door.

He pulled out his keys and fumbled with the chain until he released her door key—the one she'd given him just a week ago so he could make himself comfortable without waiting for her to come home. Had it really only been that long since she'd trusted a man enough to give him her house keys?

She held out her hand, and Damian dropped the keys in her palm. "Thanks."

Damian looked pained as if he didn't want to leave, but he was still going to do it. "I'm sorry, Jada." He leaned forward, kissed her on the forehead, and walked out the door.

Jada closed it behind him. Only then did she let out the sob she'd been holding in.

Damian stared at Jada's door for several long minutes. She'd put up a brave front, but he could hear her cries after the door closed. He touched the door, then turned on his heel and headed down the corridor to the elevator lobby.

Dammit! Why am I so afraid? Why couldn't he grasp what Jada was offering and run with it? Hadn't he just been thinking how great it was to have someone to share his life with? Yet, when the moment of truth had come, he'd chickened out. Why, oh why did Kyler have to make an appearance tonight?

His and Jada's relationship had been solid. He was sure she liked him a lot. No, it was more. She cared for him. He could tell because he *felt* it. He hadn't had that feeling since the Locketts were alive. Jada made him feel cared for, wanted, *and loved*. Is that what was scaring him? Was he afraid to be loved and to allow himself to feel that emotion?

If he did, who could blame him?

His crack addict of a mother—he loved her once until she abandoned him. And the Locketts? He'd grown to love them too, but life had been cruel and snatched them away. No wonder he was afraid. To love again would make him vulnerable as Jada had said, and Damian couldn't bear the notion of losing another important person in his life. It would break him. So, he hadn't allowed himself to love Jada.

But wasn't it already too late? Hadn't he already lost his heart the first moment he'd laid eyes on her?

21

Jada was nervous when she walked into work on Monday morning. What was going to greet her? Would it be the scorn of all her peers for her perceived wrongs? Would they all want to hang the scarlet letter on her chest for having dared go after what she wanted? She wanted Damian. Of that she couldn't lie. So, if her penance was to deal with coworkers' hatred, then so be it.

But everyone treated her like normal.

There were no stares. Or whispers behind her back. Folks didn't congregate together and point fingers at her.

What gives? Had Kyler kept silent? And if she had, why?

Unfortunately, Jada wasn't going to have any answers until later because Kyler's desk was empty when she arrived. "Where's Kyler?" she asked another field reporter sitting in the next cubicle.

"She got an assignment. She should be back this afternoon."

"Thanks." Jada inclined her head and went back to her desk. So, Kyler hadn't told everyone her secret. Jada was appreciative and surprised. Although she knew Kyler didn't have a vindictive bone in her body, she had been upset last night. When Jada tried to call Kyler afterward, her phone had gone directly to voicemail. Kyler hadn't wanted to talk to anyone, or more specifically, to Jada.

Kyler wasn't the only person MIA today. So was Damian. Typically, he visited on Monday, but today he was conspicuously absent. Even Andrew commented about it during the morning meeting. No one knew that it might have to do with her. Or did it?

Just because they ended their sexual relationship could mean absolutely nothing to Damian. He certainly hadn't seemed brokenhearted. Not like Jada. She'd stayed up crying half the night. Eventually, she'd broken down and called Bree, who'd listened to her even though Jada hadn't given her very much to go on. She was sure she'd rambled nonsense for much of the call. When she finally fell asleep, it seemed as if the alarm went off an hour later when in fact she'd been sleeping for several hours.

She looked exhausted. She needed makeup in the worst way and had to cake it on to cover up the dark circles under her eyes from lack of sleep. Somehow, she would make it through the day until she could talk to Kyler.

That time came around six p.m., when they were both leaving for the day. Kyler had come in a few hours earlier, but had been busy in the editing room getting her piece ready for the five o'clock news.

"You have a minute?" Jada asked when she saw Kyler packing up to leave.

"No, I'm busy." Kyler didn't look in her direction.

"Kyler, please," Jada whispered, stepping toward her. "We need to talk."

Finally, Kyler's blue eyes connected with Jada's, but

instead of being the blue sky on a sunny day that they always were, they were stormy and gray. "The time to talk came and went weeks ago."

"This isn't you, Ky. You're a forgiving person."

"Not when someone stabs me in the back," she hissed. Kyler snatched her purse out of her desk drawer and began stalking down the hall.

Jada followed her and kept up because she'd ditched her stilettos in favor of some flats. She fell in step beside her friend. "Do you want to continue to hurl accusations at me? Or do you want to hear my side of the story?"

Kyler stopped walking and stared at Jada.

"Well?"

"Fine. Let's talk. We can go to the café around the corner."

"Sounds great."

Ten minutes later, with café lattes in hand, they sat outside at one of the wrought-iron patio tables. Kyler set her coffee cup on it and said to Jada, "The floor is yours."

"Thank you for agreeing to talk to me."

"Cut the crap, Jada. Get to the point."

Jada grinned. She liked Kyler's fiery, take no-bull-shit approach. She should use it more often and might be surprised at how far it would get her. "Alright. I'll do that. Initially, there was nothing going on between Damian and me. In my case, it was truly hate at first sight."

"Clearly something changed. When?" Reporter Kylie was in effect, and Jada was on the hot seat.

"The night of the media awards dinner. We were getting along well, but then Damian got upset that I was flirting with some sportscasters. Things got heated and before I knew it, he'd kissed me."

"Are you honestly going to sit there and tell me it was all him?"

"Of course not. I kissed him back."

"And?"

"That was the end of it." Jada would spare her the details of how much she'd liked the kiss and that she and Damian had stopped only because they'd heard people approaching. She continued, "We both tried to act like it didn't happen. It was an anomaly, you know? And then I did that Black Lives Matter segment. He asked me to dinner . . . and the chemistry between us wouldn't be denied, and we had sex."

Kyler's blue eyes flashed in anger. "This goes that far back?"

Jada nodded, but continued her story. "But then that very night I got the call about Bree. I instantly hopped on a plane to be with her. I never thought Damian and I would progress beyond that one night, but then he came to Dallas."

"He did what!"

"He followed me and came to the hospital. He met my family and stayed by my side until Bree was out of danger. I was in awe. I felt like I was in some alternate reality and when we came together again, the passion between us was off the charts. It was the best sex I'd ever had, and I think I started to catch feelings for him."

"Why couldn't you have told me that, Jada? I would have understood. Why did you continue carrying on this affair behind my back?"

Jada shrugged. "I don't know. When I got back, it all felt so complicated. In Dallas, we could be just a man and a woman in the throes of passion, but here in San Francisco, I felt like we had to keep our relationship under wraps. It wasn't Damian's request. It was mine. I didn't want anyone to judge me or think I was trying to sleep my way to the top. That couldn't be further from the truth, Kyler. I'm in love with Damian."

"I suspected as much."

Jada inclined her head. "But he doesn't love me. He only wanted the sex and to be sure no one else would have me while I was 'his.'" She made air quotes with her fingers.

"I don't think that's entirely true," Kyler said and took a sip of her latte. "He wouldn't have come to Dallas if he didn't care. He wouldn't have held your hand as you waited for word on Bree."

"Then why didn't he stay last night?" Jada asked. Because she'd thought the same thing before, but he'd left her, just as Joshua had.

"What are you talking about?"

"After you railed at me, it made me question what we were doing. I told Damian I wanted a real relationship out in the open, but more than that, I told him I wanted love, marriage, babies, the works. And he said, 'I can't.'"

"He can't? What the hell is that supposed to mean?"

"It means he doesn't want me." A hot tear trickled down Jada's cheek. "Same as Joshua. Why doesn't anyone want a future with me?"

Kyler shook her head. "You deserve a future, Jada. Truly you do. But you have to be a better friend too. I'm upset with you for keeping all of this from me. I could have been a sounding board for you. I could have steered you in the right direction before you got your heart crushed."

Jada frowned. "I know. I was wrong, and I freely admit that. I wasn't a good friend to you, Kyler. Maybe this is my just desserts, to be alone and miserable."

Kyler reached across the table. "You won't always be alone. You will find someone worthy of you, even if that person isn't Damian."

"But I want Damian."

"Well, sometimes we don't always get what we want. We both want the anchor chair, but only one of us could get there. And that's you."

"Kyler—"

"Damian had you in line for that promotion before you guys slept together. He saw something in you that I don't have and I'm going to have to accept it, even though I may not like it."

"You sound like you're giving up."

"I'm not giving up, Jada. I'm just considering whether WLB-TV or even San Francisco is where I belong."

"You would leave?"

"Maybe. I've been thinking about going home to Ohio. I could make a difference there instead of scrambling for crumbs in this rat race."

Jada reached for her hand. "I don't want you to leave, Kyler. There has to be a place for both of us here."

"You're a star, Jada. I've always known, and I'm glad that McKnight saw it. I just didn't like how it came about, but now that you've explained things, I believe you didn't set out to hurt me or have malice in your heart."

Tears welled in Jada's eyes. "Thank you, Kyler. That means a lot because if I didn't know that, how could I live with myself if you thought I was that kind of person?"

Kyler offered Jada the first smile Jada had seen since they'd sat down an hour ago. Had time really passed that fast? It had. And Damian had made no contact with her since he left the condo. His silence told Jada all she needed to know. Maybe Kyler was onto something. Perhaps Jada should consider going back home too, to Dallas, where *she* belonged. Hadn't she proven she had guts by leaving her family to come here? She'd shown them that the baby girl of the family had what it took to make it. She could go back with her head held high.

"So we're OK then?" Jada asked, looking at Kyler.

"Yes, we are." She leaned across the table and gave Jada a one-armed hug.

Jada didn't realize how much she needed that validation, but it felt good. Now, all she had to do was take the next step to take her life back and stop letting what happened in the past rule her future.

LATER THAT DAY, the sunset poured through Damian's office window. He swiveled his chair away from his laptop to look at the surrounding buildings, a mix of concrete, brick, and aluminum siding. It shouldn't be so difficult to concentrate, but this was usually around the time he called Jada to touch base. He couldn't go to the station today because he didn't want to make a fool of himself and beg her to resume their relationship. Why did it have to change? They had a good thing. If Kyler hadn't given Jada her two cents, she would have never looked at things through a different lens.

Jada genuinely liked him. And in bed, she was so expressive. The two of them seemed to anticipate the other's wants and needs on a physical as well as an *emotional* level. It was as if he'd come home. Damian had never felt that with other women. They had been a physical release, nothing more.

More.

That word had replayed in his mind since he'd left Jada's. Left her crying for him. That made him feel like such a heel, but he was so crippled by his fear and the possibility of loss that he was afraid to move forward and take what was being freely given.

Jada Hart was an incredible woman. She was smart and funny. Down to earth. A stunning beauty that he could never get tired of. Yet, he was willing to let her walk away and make the biggest mistake of his life? If he didn't conquer his irrational fear of being alone, it was going to become a self-fulfilling prophecy.

He realized he could lose Jada . . . forever.

~

KNOCK, knock.

Jada stood outside of Andrew's open door the following morning. She'd made a decision last night, and she didn't believe in waiting. If she did, she might chicken out and regret it.

"Jada, come on in."

"Thanks," Jada said as she walked inside the office. "Do you mind if I close the door?"

"No, of course not." Andrew peered at her. "Is everything OK?"

Jada nodded. "Actually, it is. I've come to a decision." She slid the envelope that was in her hand across the table.

Andrew reached for it, scanned the contents, and glanced up at her. "This is a resignation letter."

"I know." Jada smiled hesitantly. "It's time for me to move on."

"This is because you want the anchor slot, isn't it?" When Jada didn't respond, he continued. "You just have to be a little bit more patient, Jada. It'll come. You've already caught Mr. McKnight's eye. It's just a matter of time before you're in the anchor's chair every day of the week. Plus, I heard through the grapevine that Hilary is looking for bigger fish to fry."

"Really?"

"Yes. I'm not going to accept this." He pushed the letter back toward Jada. "Take some time and think about it. Didn't you say your parents were getting married this coming weekend?"

She nodded.

"Good. The long weekend will give you some time to reflect. When you get back, if you decide you still want to leave, I'll respect your decision. Sound fair?"

"It more than sounds fair, Andrew." She reached across the desk to shake his hand. "That's very generous of you."

"It's not generous. Like everyone else, I accepted the status quo, but the numbers don't lie. San Fran is liking the change of scene with you anchoring on Fridays. Perhaps we've all been a little shortsighted until now."

"Thanks, Andrew. Thanks a lot." Jada left his office feeling more confident about her place at the station than she'd felt in five years. But she also felt confused. She'd been pretty determined to leave San Francisco and head home. *What's holding me back?*

The answer to the question did not matter. By the end of the week, she'd be surrounded by the entire Hart clan and Damian McKnight would be the last thing on her mind.

~

"Jada!" Bree screamed when Jada got off the Hart jet at the private airfield on Friday afternoon. She'd worked half a day to ensure she left early and had plenty of time with her family.

"Bree." Jada grinned as she rushed toward her very pregnant sister and hugged her as best she could. The woman had blown up almost overnight. A month ago, she had a cute baby bump. Now, she was definitely in the final stretch. "What are you doing here?"

"I told Grayson I was picking you up, and he only agreed if Steve was driving."

Jada glanced over at Steve, who was standing next to Duke's Cadillac Town Car waving at her. "I don't care. I'm so happy you're here. Can you believe Mom and Dad? They are finally going to retie the knot."

"It's about time," Bree said. "I just think Mama had cold feet about jumping in again."

"It's understandable. It's hard to give yourself to someone knowing there's a possibility you could get hurt."

"Sounds like you're talking from personal experience. Speaking of which, have you heard from Damian?"

Jada shook her head. She hadn't heard or spoken to Damian all week, and he'd stayed away from the station too. He'd called in on the speakerphone the other day for a morning meeting, but that was it.

"Alright then." Bree slid her arm through Jada's. "Then we're going to leave him behind in San Francisco with all that drama, and we're going to focus instead on getting the parents hitched. How's that sound?"

"Sounds like the best medicine ever."

An hour later, they pulled into the ranch and the driveway was brimming with cars. Jada counted as least half a dozen of them. She couldn't wait to see her family from Arizona. She didn't have to wait long. The front door burst open, and her daddy and mama spilled out onto the front porch.

Duke ran down to greet her. "There's my baby girl." He spun Jada in his arms before she could take another step.

"Duke, put her down," Abigail said. "You're going to make her dizzy."

"Aww, woman, stop hovering. I've been doing this since Jada was a sprout." He grasped Jada around the shoulders and pulled her toward the steps, but then stopped for Bree. "You go on ahead with your mama. Bree needs me."

Jada walked ahead with Abigail, but turned behind her to hear Bree say, "I'm perfectly capable of walking, Daddy." But Duke wasn't hearing any of it and had taken her arm and was helping her up the steps.

Once inside the main house, Jada was overcome with Harts. Everywhere. Little kids were running down the hall. Other family members were sitting in the formal living room and milling throughout the house. Jada smiled. This is exactly what she needed to forget Damian.

"Someone's always fashionably late," Caleb said from the sofa he stood behind.

"Oh, let her be," Addison, Caleb's wife, said. "You know Jada has to make sure she looks good before making an appearance."

"I know the feeling," said Noah Hart, Jada's older cousin from Arizona. "This one," he said, smiling at his wife, Chynna, who was holding their second son, Aaron, "takes an hour to get ready."

"That's because I never know where the paparazzi are going to be," Chynna said. "You do recall what great lengths I went to to escape them, don't you?"

"What lengths?" asked Abigail. She and Duke had joined the fray in the now-crowded living room.

"Oh c'mon, you guys have all heard this story," Chynna's sister, Kenya, stated. "Chynna and I switched places because she'd stumbled on the Hart ranch in Arizona and met Noah." She glanced at her brother-in-law. "She fell madly in love and begged me to stay put for a while."

"Whereupon Kenya and I," said Kenya's husband, Lucas, "fell in love."

"Didn't you think she was Chynna?" Abigail asked.

Lucas shook his head. "I knew there was something different with Kenya because I'd never had sparks with Chynna before. And lo and behold, I was right. We've never looked back since."

"I just love a good old-fashioned love story," Abigail said. "Tell me more."

"Oh, I've got this one," Jada jumped in. "I love the story of the king and the veterinarian. What could be more romantic than Rylee falling in love with a king at the Kentucky Derby?"

"Prince," Amar clarified. "Nothing more. Nothing less."

"Don't be bashful among this clan, *Prince* Amar," Caleb emphasized his title. "We know we're in the presence of royalty. Anyway, where is my sister? You haven't impregnated her again, have you?"

His brother, Noah, glared at him.

"You know, Caleb," Amar said as he sidled up next to him, "it's a good thing you don't ride bulls anymore.

Otherwise, you might be run over by a very mean bull." He slammed his hand on Caleb's shoulder

"Ouch." Caleb stood up and headed for the wet bar to replenish his whiskey. "No reason to hit below the belt."

Amar's eyes darkened, and Jada could see he was embarrassed by such a *faux pas.* "Forgive me, Caleb. I meant it in jest."

Years ago, Caleb had had a hard time recovering from his bull-riding accident. It had cost him the ability to walk for nearly a year, and he'd broken up with Addison during that time. He'd clawed his way back during rehabilitation and thankfully won Addison back from her new fiancé. Jada had never been more proud of what he'd accomplished since then.

"Lighten up, Amar," Caleb said with a chuckle. "We're family. If I can't take a joke from you, who can I take it from?"

"You are too kind," Amar said, bowing his head.

"And you are too stiff, my friend," Duke said to Amar. "Let's have a drink." He clapped his arm on Amar's shoulder and led him to the wet bar.

"That was close," Bree whispered as she slid her arm through Jada's and pulled her aside.

"Yeah, but you know Caleb. He's always so easygoing and mild-mannered," Jada said.

"Thank God. That could have gone totally wrong," said Bree.

"You ain't lying." London had joined the conversation, and they moved to the far side of the room. "I thought Chase might have to jump in."

"Where is your gorgeous husband?" Jada asked.

"Putting Bella down for a nap. I don't know what it is, but he has the Midas touch when it comes to getting that girl to nap."

"I hope Grayson has the same," Bree said, "because I can't do it alone."

"And you don't have to," Jada said. "Grayson loves the ground you walk on. He can't wait for his baby girl to make her debut. By the way, it sucks that you won't tell us," she said, motioning to London, "our niece's name."

"Can't we keep something to ourselves?" Bree said with a smirk as she rubbed her belly. "Grayson and I didn't even want to know the sex, but someone," she said, glancing at Jada, "refused to let up."

"Hey, don't blame me because I can't wait to be an auntie again. I barely get to see Bella."

"That's because you're in San Francisco and you know with the restaurant it's hard for me to travel," London said.

"I know, I know," Jada apologized. "It's why I'm thinking about moving back home."

"To Dallas?" her sisters asked excitedly.

"Where else?"

"Well, you might want to rethink moving here," Bree said. "I stopped by the other day and found our parents *in flagrante delicto*, if you know what I mean."

Jada's eyes grew large with mirth. "Get out!"

"No, seriously. I think I was more embarrassed at having caught them about to have sex than they were. They're like two randy teenagers."

"Hey, at least they can get it up at their age," London said.

They all hooted with laughter.

"On that note, let's go get some lemonade," Bree suggested, and the girls all departed from the living room.

~

DAMIAN GLANCED down at his watch later that evening. He knew what time it was. He'd been watching the clock all day. It was the start of Jada's parents' weekend celebration. And he should be there with Jada.

Did it matter to her that he wasn't there? She'd be surrounded by her family. She wouldn't need him, want him even, would she? Damian knew he wanted her—with every fiber of his being. For days, he'd tried to convince himself that he could put Jada behind him and move forward with his life as it was before. But he couldn't. His mind would wander to what she might be doing, what she might be thinking, or how she might be feeling.

The last week, he'd taken to sleeping in the guest bedroom because he couldn't sleep in his own bed. Whenever he looked at it, he saw Jada. Felt her everywhere. Every time he walked into his bedroom, images of the two of them making love would flood his brain. She'd taken up permanent residence not only in his head but in his heart.

He was starting to realize what a mistake he'd made by letting her go. He'd given up on them without even trying to see if he could make it work. He'd hurt her terribly. Jada had been devastated to hear that despite all their time together, in and out of bed, he still wasn't ready to share his life with her.

But finally he'd admitted the truth to himself: He *did* want to be with her, but would she be willing to give him another chance? If he went to her now in Dallas and begged her to take him back, would she? Or would she slam the door in his face? Jada would have every right to, and no doubt the Hart family would back her up. Damian didn't relish having to stand in front of Duke with his hat in hand telling him he'd broken Jada's heart. If he did, there was sure to be a shotgun in his future.

But Damian didn't care. He wanted his woman back, and he would do anything, *confront* anyone to win her.

22

"Mama, you look so beautiful." Jada looked at the reflection of the two of them in a guest-bedroom mirror on Saturday afternoon.

She wrapped her arms around her mother's shoulders. She'd just helped Abigail don a beautiful taupe evening gown with beaded applique embellishments, see-through detail, and a scooped neckline. The sleeveless chiffon number had a straight floor-length skirt with a train that was perfect for walking down the aisle. Jada had done up Abigail's long, straight hair into an elegant chignon. Then she'd applied the lightest touch of makeup because her mama wanted to look natural.

"Thank you, honey," Abigail said. "You look beautiful too."

Jada had selected a simple halter neckline dress with a ruched bodice, deeply plunging V-neckline, and open back. Full length and flowing, the skirt was gathered up from the top and fell in a body skimming A-line silhouette. Her curled hair hung in waves down her back. "Thank you, Mama. But this day is about you and the happiness you deserve. You've shown me to never give up and that it's never too late to fall in love."

Abigail caressed her cheek. "Baby doll, what's wrong? Did something happen between you and Damian? I noticed he didn't come with you even though you RSVP'd for two."

Jada attempted a half smile. "No, it's just going to be me."

"Oh no." Abigail frowned. "Are you sure? I could have sworn that young man was in love with my baby girl."

"Love?" Jada shook her head. "Oh no, Mama. Damian doesn't love me. I don't think he's capable of loving anyone."

"And you? How do you feel about him?"

Jada shrugged. "It doesn't matter. Damian doesn't want me. So, whatever feelings I did or didn't have for him are irrelevant. It's over."

"Alright, honey." Her mother rubbed her arm. "You don't have to talk about it."

"I don't want to because today is about you, Mama—you and Daddy. You've finally figured out that you can't live without each other. I'm just glad you got tired of trying."

"Aren't we all," Bree said from the door. Her riotous shoulder-length curls were piled high atop her head with only a few tendrils allowed to be free. She was wearing a shift dress that hid her growing belly, but she was comfortable enough for the day.

"You look great, Bree."

"Oh, you lie to a pregnant woman," she said with a grin, "but that's OK. I'll take it. I know I look like a beached whale, but I've only got less than two months to go."

"Bree, you're not a whale," their mother said. "A woman expecting is one of God's greatest gifts."

"Thanks, Mama." Bree kissed her mother's cheek. "You look lovely."

"Has everyone arrived?" Jada asked. Although the ranch was quite large, they couldn't fit everyone on-site, so Bree, Grayson, Cameron, and Sonya, as well as London, Chase, her niece Bella, and her uncle Isaac, and aunt Madelyn had stayed in the guest bedrooms in the east, west, and south wings of the house.

Meanwhile, Noah, Chynna, their two boys, and Chynna's entire entourage, Kenya, Lucas, and their twin daughters, and Rylee and Amar and their son had stayed at the Ritz-Carlton in Dallas and were arriving later in the afternoon. Caleb and Addison and their two kids would be driving in from their estate about twenty miles away.

"Yep." Bree nodded. "Everyone is eating canapés and drinking champagne. The wedding planner you sent over to help Mama did an amazing job in such a short time. The backyard has been transformed into a romantic oasis instead of a pile of dirt."

Jada had touched base with Deborah earlier that morning. Deborah had everything under control. The staff she'd hired as well as the ranch hands had set up white folding chairs in a circle around a rose-covered archway in the backyard. The intent was to make the bride and groom feel like they were on center stage. Jada hoped her parents liked it.

"I can't wait to see it," Abigail said. "But more importantly, I can't wait to marry your father."

"Then let's get this party started," Jada said. She reached into the small box and pulled out bouquets, one for each of them. Jada's and Bree's were made of cream hydrangeas and roses wrapped in champagne ribbon, while their mother's was a simple arrangement of red roses and white calla lilies wrapped in a gold sparkly ribbon.

"Jada, you shouldn't have gone through all the trouble."

"I would do anything for you, Mama. Now c'mon, we've got to walk you down the aisle." She and Bree had determined they wanted to be part of the ceremony in some meaningful way. Walking their mother down the aisle was the best way to achieve that.

They started down the stairs and toward the backyard. "This is kind of surreal," Jada said. "It's hard to believe after all this time that you're finally going to marry Daddy."

"I've always loved your father, but I have to tell you I had to learn how to forgive. Your father wasn't perfect, but neither was I. I was so hurt over his past transgressions and angry at him for the betrayal that I didn't fight for us. So, if I had to give you both any advice in your relationships, it would be don't be too proud to forgive, especially when you love someone."

Jada nodded. She didn't know if her mother was speaking to her or to both of them, but she definitely heard her. Perhaps she was being too quick to judge Damian. He'd never been in love before. He'd freely admitted that. She, on the other hand, knew what it was like to give yourself to another person, to open yourself up to the possibility of getting hurt. Maybe he was afraid. Maybe it was up to her to show him what love looked like.

After they walked through the house and made it to the backyard deck, Jada stopped. She wanted her mother to see what she saw. Slowly, she stepped out of the way. Her mother gasped.

"Jada." Abigail turned to her. "It's beautiful."

Tears shone in Jada's eyes. "I'm so glad you like it."

"I love it, and I love that man." Her mother glanced through the circle to where their father Duke stood.

Everyone stood up as Bree and Jada each took one of their mother's arms and led her down the aisle to their father. He was wearing a black suit with a crisp white shirt and a bow tie. Jada wasn't used to her father looking so formal, but he looked very dapper. And happy. He was smiling from ear to ear as they approached. When they made it to him, Jada was surprised to find tears in his eyes.

Duke grasped Abigail's hand, and Jada and Bree stepped back and took a seat.

Seeing her parents' happiness made Jada realize just how much she loved Damian. She'd fooled herself into thinking it was just about fun sex. It was more than sex and had been for some time. She wanted *forever* with him just like her parents were going to vow at this very moment. Marriage no longer filled her with dread as it did after Joshua had left her at the altar. She was ready to love again.

Jada blinked back the tears and tried to stay in the moment. She was here with family who would support her and get her through another lost love. She turned to glance across the familiar faces of her cousins and other family members before stopping at a face that didn't belong here.

Damian.

He's here? He looked mouthwatering in a slim suit that appeared to be created for him. But why had he come here to her home, her refuge, where she felt safe from anything that could hurt her? So many questions filtered through her brain as his dark eyes remained fixed on her, but Jada couldn't think about him. Not now. This day had been a long time coming. She had to focus on her parents even though tears threatened to overtake her at the significance of his presence.

DAMIAN WAS NERVOUS. He'd barely arrived in time to make the wedding. He had called his pilot last night to make a flight plan for this morning. But at the private airstrip, a thick smog had grounded all flights. He'd waited two hours until it finally lifted and they could get off the ground. The flight to Dallas had seemed interminable. He'd been afraid he would miss the wedding. Miss being there for Jada. He'd freshened up in the small shower on the plane and dressed for the day in a slate gray suit with a purple tie.

A car had been waiting for him upon his arrival at a private airfield and had whisked him to the Hart ranch, an hour away. When he arrived, the family was already gathered in small circles chatting. Duke and Caleb had glanced up when they saw him, but neither had moved to welcome him. Had Jada told them what happened between them? It had been Grayson who'd seen his deer-in-the-headlights look and come over to rescue him.

"Damian," Grayson had said. "Didn't know you were coming."

Damian chuckled. "Neither did I."

Grayson smiled and patted him on the shoulder. "Trust me, I understand. It's something about those Hart women that makes it hard to stay away."

"You're not lying." Damian swallowed the lump in his throat.

"Bree didn't tell me much, but she mentioned that you and Jada were on the outs."

Damian nodded. "We are. I messed up, man. Real bad. It's why I'm here—to make things right."

"Good luck with that."

"Why?"

"Because Jada's father is coming over right now."

"Young man, what do you have to say for yourself?" Duke's tone told Damian that any favor he'd gained during his last visit was gone.

Damian turned around. "Mr. Hart."

"I told you to call me Duke."

"Duke—" he began, but was interrupted.

"What did you do to my daughter?" Duke asked harshly. "She came back to Dallas without you. Why is that?"

"Well, sir, I believe that is between Jada and me."

"You're on my land, son."

"I'm well aware. And no disrespect, Duke, but I need to discuss a few things with Jada first. Once I do, I'll come see you."

Duke's firm look loosened, and a small smile started to form. "Sounds like you've come to your senses."

"I have, sir. And if you'll allow me to stay, I'd love to see you remarry the love of your life."

"Alright, Damian." Duke's tone softened. "You can stay, but know this: If I get a whiff that my daughter is hurt or uncomfortable in any way, you'll have me and the rest of the Hart men," he said, motioning behind him to where several tall and able-bodied men stood, "to contend with."

"Duly noted."

Duke stepped away, and Grayson returned to his side. "My advice to you," Grayson whispered, "is don't mess up."

Damian didn't intend to. He was in love with Jada, and he was here to tell her so.

Jada heard her parents' vows to each other in the periphery of her brain. Her father declared, "I've never loved a woman like I've loved you, Abigail. You have and will always be the love of my life. I'm just sorry I screwed that up."

She saw her mother wipe away her father's tears with the back of her hand. Heard her mother's words: "You weren't the only one who screwed up. I made mistakes too. I was too proud to forgive even though I loved you. But I'm so happy that you never gave up on me, on us. I promise that from this day forth, I'll remember the good times no matter what life throws our way, to always have your back . . . and to catch you when you fall. I promise my heart will be your shelter . . . and my arms will be your home."

Jada wiped away an errant tear. She hadn't even known she was crying because she'd been looking at Damian the entire time her parents had said their vows. And when the preacher told Duke he could kiss the bride, Jada never felt so happy her entire life. Her parents were finally back together!

Jada stood as her parents accepted congratulations from the family and a few close friends who'd been invited.

"Looks like someone is here to see you," Bree whispered in her ear as Damian walked toward them. "Damian." Bree said and nodded at him, but Grayson immediately came forward to lead her away.

Abigail glanced behind her and winked at Jada. Then she and Duke departed to walk toward the house, where Deborah had laid out a feast of food and drinks. Jada caught some of her relatives looking at Damian with inquiring gazes, but she couldn't focus on any of them, not when her heart was beating at a rapid pace. She could barely hear herself think let alone breathe.

When it was just Jada and Damian alone outside, she finally asked, "What are you doing here?"

"I needed to see you."

"Why?"

"Will you sit with me?" Damian took another more tentative step toward her, and when she didn't move away, he took another until they were inches apart.

Jada could feel the invisible thread between them even though they weren't touching. "Very well." She walked beside him to sit in one of the white folding chairs facing the rose-covered wedding arch. As Damian took the seat next to her, his masculinity overwhelmed her as it always did when she smelled his clean male scent. "I'm listening."

Damian turned to her. "I've come to tell you what a fool I've been. I want to apologize for letting you go, for not telling you that I *want* to be with you . . . in a relationship for as long as you want me."

Jada wanted to be happy, but she was a bit stunned by his declaration. "Why now? What's changed?"

"Me. For years, I've always been alone, afraid to let anyone in because I was afraid of losing them. I loved my mother, but she left, abandoning me to the will of strangers. I loved my foster parents, but after they got pregnant, they chose to send me back into the system. When I'd finally hardened my heart enough to get through life, along came the Locketts. They took me in when no one else would. They gave me a home. They gave me love."

"Damian—"

"No." He held up his hand. "It's not easy for me to admit this, so please let me finish."

"Alright. Go on."

"The Locketts were kind, giving people, and they didn't deserve to die at the hands of some drunk driver. So, once again, after I'd finally found a place I could call home, people I could love, it was wrenched from me . . . at the morgue, when I had to identify their bodies."

"Oh." Jada clutched her hand to her mouth.

"That's when I vowed to never love anyone else because anything I valued was subject to be taken away. Then I met you. I told myself that it was just lust. We had such a strong physical connection that surely that's all it could be, but then slowly but surely you began creeping into my heart. You weren't like any of the other random women I'd been sleeping with. You truly understand me. You get me without me having to try to please you as I'd done with all those foster families in an attempt to get them to love me. You cared about me, *just me*. No, dare I say it?" He paused. "You *loved* me. So, I tried to divorce the emotion from the sex because it was making me wish for things that I knew were a fairytale and could never come true. I always felt like I could never be truly happy. But I was. I *am* with you, Jada. And it scared me. Made me push you away because the only way to beat fate to the punch was to let you go first."

Jada's stomach twisted into knots. She couldn't believe that Damian was being so open, so honest, so forthright about his feelings. "Wh-what are you saying?"

Damian reached for her hands and grasped them. Then he moved to kneel at her feet. "I'm saying that I love you, Jada. It may have taken me some time to get there, but I do. You challenge me and make me feel more alive than I've ever felt. I don't want to lose you.

Please tell me I haven't. Please tell me that you'll let me love you."

"Oh, Damian." The sentiment darted through whatever remaining barriers Jada might have had up. His feelings were something he'd just discovered because Damian had never looked at her with such fierce longing as he was doing right at this moment. She believed him and threw her arms around his neck. Damian clutched her to him as if she were his last breath.

"Thank God." He began kissing her neck, her cheeks, and then her lips. "Thank God I haven't lost you."

When they pulled apart, Jada peered at him through her tears. "You could never lose me, Damian, because I love you too."

He smiled. "You do?"

She nodded. "I think I fell in love with you here in Dallas when you came and stood by my side with Bree. I don't think I could admit it to myself then, but deep down I knew. I love you, Damian, for you." She grasped his face. "You never have to try to win my heart because you already have it."

He yanked her into his arms, and she fell on his knee. His mouth captured hers, and Jada melted into the kiss as her heart swelled and became whole again at hearing Damian's declaration of love.

A cough sounded from behind them and broke up their kiss. "If you two are done making out," said London, who was standing a few feet away, "we're going to toast the newlyweds."

Jada smiled and rose to her feet, holding out her hand to help Damian up. She didn't want to be too far away him. "Yes, we're coming."

Damian brought her hand to his lips. "Let's go celebrate with your parents."

23

———

When Jada and Damian arrived to the great room, the Hart clan was gathered and spread throughout it in small family clusters. Jada's parents were front and center. They were both holding the crystal champagne flutes Jada and her sisters had purchased for the occasion.

Jada and Damian grabbed a flute from a passing waiter. Jada caught Bree's large grin from where she sat, surrounded by Grayson, Cameron, and Sonya.

"As the oldest of the Hart children," London said as she held up her flute, "I'd like to make a toast."

Since Bree and Jada had walked their mother down the aisle, they'd all agreed that London would toast the happy couple. It hadn't always been easy for London to feel that she was part of the family, but she was.

"Daddy, Abigail," she said, glancing at her stepmother, "I can't tell you how excited your daughters are to see you both joined in marriage. You've taught us that it's never too late to forgive and to find happiness with your soul mate. To the Harts." She held her up her flute.

"To the Harts."

"To the Harts." Everyone clapped loudly for the happy couple.

Once the applause died down, Jada walked over to her parents with Damian in tow. "Daddy, Mama, you remember Damian." She smiled up at the man she loved.

"Of course," her mother said. She leaned over to kiss Damian's cheek. "Welcome to the family."

Damian's eyes grew large, and Jada could see how touched he was by the sentiment. "Thank you, ma'am."

"Glad to see you came to your senses," Duke said, "and got my daughter back."

"He never really lost me, Daddy."

"That's good to hear."

"Could I have a word with you, Duke?" Damian asked.

"You absolutely may." Duke grinned. "Excuse me for a second, Abby." He kissed her mother on the forehead. Damian let go of Jada's hand and walked off with her father.

"Do you know what that's about?" Abigail asked as she watched the men disappear around the corner.

Jada was bewildered. "No clue. But it doesn't matter. I'm just happy that he's here and that he loves me."

"Oh, Jada." Her mother clutched her pearls. "Did he really say that?"

Jada nodded, unable to hide her enthusiasm. "Yes, he did. And I told him I loved him too. Oh, Mama . . ." Her voice cracked. "I can hardly believe it."

"I told you it was never too late."

And Jada finally believed it. After everything she'd been through with Joshua, she was finally getting her happy ending.

~

DAMIAN WAS SO THANKFUL. Not only had Jada forgiven him and was willing to give him another chance, but she loved him too. He was so used to losing those he loved that he'd been afraid to hope for love. But it was true. Jada loved him.

Now he had to seal the deal, which is why he was nervous to stand with Duke in his study. His palms were clammy and his heart was thudding louder than a horse's on race day. He'd never asked anyone to marry him, but he wanted to spend the rest of his life with Jada. He saw no reason to wait. He wanted to ask her here with her family nearby, but first he had to ask her father for her hand in marriage.

He didn't fear Duke, but this occasion was different. He was usually so well-spoken, yet words were escaping him now.

"Alright, young man. You wanted to talk."

"Yes, I do."

"So, spit it out." Duke was watching him with an eagle eye, and Damian could feel beads of sweat forming on his forehead. "How about a whiskey first?"

"Would love one."

He watched Duke walk over to his wet bar, grab two glasses, and open the whiskey decanter. He poured them each two thumbs of whiskey and handed one to Damian. The younger man gulped it back in one swig.

"Easy, boy. That's twenty-year-old whiskey. It's meant to be savored."

Damian coughed. "I realize that now." He coughed again and placed his glass on the desk.

Duke chuckled. "Why don't I make this easy for you? You want to marry my daughter, am I right?"

How does he know? Am I that obvious? "Yes, I do. I love Jada very much."

"I know that." Duke grinned. "I knew it the moment you showed up at the hospital. I was just waiting for you to figure it out."

"You did?"

Duke sipped his whiskey. "A man doesn't fly to another city for a piece of ass, not unless he truly cares for the woman. I saw how you took care of Jada in the hospital and after. I was impressed. Therefore, you have my and Abigail's blessing."

"I do?"

"Don't sound so surprised, otherwise I'll have to rescind it."

Damian smiled. "Thank you, sir." He offered his hand. "You won't regret it."

Instead of shaking his hand, Duke pulled him into his embrace. "We're huggers in this family, so get used to it."

Damian patted his back. "I will. Now, if you'll excuse me, I have something very important to do."

He left Duke in his study and went in search of Jada. He found her in the living room holding one of her baby cousins. She had never looked lovelier, and Damian took a moment to envision Jada with a round belly and pregnant with their child. It was surprising because he'd never thought about children before, but with Jada anything was possible.

She looked up to find him watching her. She handed the baby back to Chynna. "Excuse me for a moment."

"I'm sorry to steal you away," Damian murmured softly in case anyone was listening, "but can I talk to you for a few minutes?"

"Of course."

He took her hand and led her outside to the front porch. Surprisingly, it was empty of occupants, which was perfect. He'd thought about proposing in front of her entire family, but this moment was theirs and theirs only.

Jada looked up at him questioningly. "Damian, what is it? You're scaring me."

"Out back, I didn't get to finish my speech."

"You didn't?" She laughed nervously. "I thought you did pretty good. What more is there to say?"

"I forgot one important thing." Damian dropped to his knees again. "I love you, Jada Hart. I want to spend the rest of my life making you happy. Would you do me the honor of being my wife?"

Wife! When they'd met, marriage had never crossed Jada's mind. She'd been so focused on her career, but Damian was everything she hadn't known she wanted and she couldn't be happier than to join her life with his.

"Yes, yes, yes!" Jada leaned down and kissed Damian hard on the lips. "I will marry you."

Damian reached inside his pocket and pulled out a blue Tiffany box. He'd been carrying around the five-carat diamond ring all day. Thank God he'd had the foresight to call in a favor last night. He'd placed an emergency call to a friend who owned a jewelry store and begged him to reopen. Damian had known he couldn't come to Dallas empty-handed. When Jada saw the ring, she gasped. "I hope you like it." He pulled it out of the box and slid it onto her left ring finger.

"I love it, Damian, and I love you. I can't wait to be Mrs. Damian McKnight, because you're the man I've waited for all my life."

EPILOGUE

O*ne year later*
"You look happy, baby doll," Abigail told Jada as she helped her mother set up the table for the barbeque at the Hart ranch. Her parents had invited her sisters, their respective spouses, and grandchildren to Dallas. Caleb and Addison had come with their two children as well because Caleb was like a son to Duke. He and Duke were in the stables watching a pony being born.

"I told her she was glowing, Mama," Bree said as she held her ten-month-old daughter on her lap.

"That's what everyone says to all mothers-to-be," Jada chimed in.

"But it's true," London said from her outdoor seat. "You look like you're at peace, Jada."

"That's because I understand what you were all saying about finding the person you were meant to be with. After that, everything seems to fall into place." And it had for her. After they'd returned from Dallas, newly engaged, she and Damian had come out of the dark about their relationship. Of course, there had been some sour faces at the station, but mostly everyone had wished them well, including Kyler, who eventually moved back to Ohio in favor of her small-town roots.

Within months, Hilary Reed, the morning anchor, got poached by a large station to anchor the evening news. This had left the position open for Jada. And she'd stepped right into it seamlessly because viewers were already used to seeing her on Fridays. It was like all of Jada's dreams had come true with a snap of a finger. She had her dream job and a man to come home to whom she loved every night.

"I told you." Addison smiled. "And look what happened. We're about to be aunties." She inclined her head toward Jada's growing belly.

"Yeah, well, this one," Jada said, rubbing her stomach, "was a bit unplanned. We were hoping to get the new house built before starting a family, but . . ." Her voice trailed off.

"You're newlyweds and couldn't keep your hands off each other?" London supplied. "It's OK, and it's to be expected. Enjoy the moment, because when my niece gets here you're going to need your energy."

Jada nodded. She couldn't believe she was going to be a mother. She'd always wanted this but never thought it was going to happen after her first failed attempt at getting married. She was excited and overwhelmed.

Jada glanced over at her husband, who stood around the grill with one of the ranch hands who was serving as pit master. Grayson and Chase were laughing and talking with him, and Damian was comfortable. Jada's heart filled with happiness and joy. She'd not only found her soul mate, but Damian was getting the family he'd always wanted and deserved. *What could be better than that?*

DAMIAN STOOD near the grill and watched Jada rush about with Bree and London in the backyard. Jada had never looked more radiant or lovelier with her belly swollen with his child. She wasn't quite six months pregnant, but that didn't stop him from lusting after her. It had been that way from the start with them, and Jada's pregnancy had done little to decrease the sexual hunger they had for each other.

Just this morning, she'd woken him up, sliding the shorts down he'd worn to bed and making him as naked as the day he was born. He'd glanced at the clock to see one a.m., then she slid up his body. She was warm and scrumptious, and she'd rolled herself into his arms, gluing herself to him. She didn't silently offer herself as she sometimes once did. Instead, Jada took what she wanted, covering his mouth with hers. His hands had skimmed her bottom to find she wasn't wearing any underwear. This had allowed him to slide his hand to all the places she craved.

When he did, he found her wet for him. Oh yes, instead of watching television, *this* was his favorite late-night show. Jada had eased her nightshirt over her head to reveal breasts that had grown rounder and fuller thanks to their child. He'd laved them with his tongue, taking his sweet time to pleasure her with his mouth and hands. But it wasn't his show. It was hers.

She'd straddled him and eased down onto his already burgeoning shaft. She'd taken him deep inside, and he'd relished every minute of the exquisite torment as she rocked herself against him. He'd cupped her ass and thrust upward to meet her, but she'd placed her hands on his chest, eager to set her own rhythm. So, he'd let her until she had him whispering nonsense in the dark of night and he'd lost himself in a world that no one else existed in but the two of them.

Afterward, they'd spooned and her eyes had glowed with something he'd never thought he'd ever have, let alone be able to hold on to: LOVE.

Yes, indeed. He'd finally found his home.

BOOKS BY YAHRAH ST. JOHN

<u>Connected Books</u>

One Magic Moment

Dare to Love

<u>Dirty Laundry Series</u>

Dirty Laundry

Can't Get Enough

<u>Stand Alone Novels</u>

Never Say Never

Risky Business of Love

<u>Hart Series</u>

Entangled Hearts

Entangled Hearts 2

Untamed Hearts

Restless Hearts

Unchained Hearts

Chasing Hearts Pub Date

Captivated Hearts

<u>Mitchell Brother Series</u>

Claimed by the Hero

Seducing the Seal

<u>Coming Soon in 2022</u>

Guarding His Princess

ABOUT THE AUTHOR

Yahrah St. John became a writer at the age of twelve when she wrote her first novella after secretly reading a Harlequin romance. Throughout her teens, she penned a total of twenty novellas. Her love of the craft continued into adulthood. She's the proud author of thirty-nine books with Harlequin Desire, Kimani Romance and Arabesque as well as her own indie works.

When she's not at home crafting one of her spicy romances with compelling heroes and feisty heroines with a dash of family drama, she is gourmet cooking or traveling the globe seeking out her next adventure. For more info: www.yahrahstjohn.com or find her on Facebook, Instagram, Twitter, Bookbub or Goodreads.